A MARIANNE MOORE READER

A MARIANNE MOORE
READER

NEW YORK / THE VIKING PRESS / 1961

Published in 1961 by The Viking Press, Inc.
625 Madison Avenue, New York 22, N.Y.
Published simultaneously in Canada by
The Macmillan Company of Canada Limited

Selections from *Collected Poems* reprinted by permission of The Macmillan
    Company (New York), copyright 1951 by Marianne Moore
Nine of the poems in this book were first published in *The New Yorker*
"The Ford Correspondence" (pages 215–24) copyright © 1957 by The New
    Yorker Magazine, Inc.
"Idiosyncrasy and Technique," copyright © 1958 by The Regents of the
    University of California

Designed by Sidney Feinberg

Library of Congress catalog card number: 61–17409

Printed in the U.S.A. by George McKibbin & Son

*Inscriptions, dedications—any printed personal acknowledg-
ment—may be inconsiderate, a dedication being implicit
in what is dedicated. . . . Generalities as attempting to
express complexities ignited by gratitude, I think miss
the mark. But imprudence is not considerate and, incon-
sistently, I am tempted to say that I associate much of what
is here, with friends; and as particular and very special friends,*

HILDEGARDE AND SIBLEY WATSON

The Ford letters should correct an impression persisting among inquirers that I succeeded in finding for the special new products division of an eminent manufacturer a name for the car I had been recruited to name; whereas I did not give the car the name it now has.

—MARIANNE MOORE

CONTENTS

O TO BE A DRAGON

OTHER POEMS

FOREWORD

Published: it is enough. The magazine was discontinued. The edition was small. One paragraph needs restating. Newspaper cuts on the fold or disintegrates. When was it published, and where? "The title was 'Words and . . .' something else. Could you say what it was?" I have forgotten. Happened upon years later, it seems to have been "Words and Modes of Expression." What became of "Tedium and Integrity," the unfinished manuscript of which there was no duplicate? A housekeeper is needed to assort the untidiness. For whom? A curioso or just for the author? In that case "as safe at the publisher's as if chained to the shelves of Bodley," Lamb said, smiling.

Verse: prose: a specimen or so of translation for those on whom completeness would weigh as a leg-iron. How would it seem to me if someone else had written it? Does it hold the attention? "Has it human value?" Or seem as if one had ever heard of "lucidity, force, and ease" or had any help from past thinkers? Is it subservient singsong or has it "muscles"?

La Fontaine's Fables. Professor Brower—if I am not inventing it—says a translator must have "depth of experience." The rhythm of a translation as motion, I think, should suggest the rhythm of the original, and the words be very nearly an equivalent of the author's meaning. After endless last choices, digressions, irrelevances, defiances, and futile imprudences, I am repaid for attempting to translate "The Grasshopper and the Ant" by hitting upon a substitute for an error, the most offensive and meaningless of a long list: "*an't* you please."

>—"I sang for those who might pass by chance—
>Night and day, an't you please"

for which I am substituting "Night and day. Please do not be repelled," with the ant's reply, "Sang? A delight when someone has excelled." In harmonizing notes or words, there is more room for originality than in moralizing, and "the point," prefixed or appended to a tale irresistibly told, seems redundant. Although La Fontaine's primary concern was the poetry; even so, for him and for us, indifference to being educated has been conquered, and certain lessons in these fables contrive to be indelible: *Greed:* The owner of the hen that laid the golden eggs, "cut the magic chain and she'd never lay again./ Think of this when covetous!" *Ingratitude:* The reanimated adder lunged at the farmer, "Its foster father who had been its rescuer./ . . . Two strokes made three snakes of the coil—/ A body, a tail, and a head./ The pestilent thirds writhed together to rear/ But of course could no longer adhere." "Ingrates," La Fontaine says, "will always die in agony." *Be content with your lot:* A shepherd "was lured to part with his one and only flock/ And invest all he'd earned, in a ship; but ah, the shock—/ Wrecked in return for all he'd paid."

Prose: mine will always be "essays" and verse of mine, observations. Of "Tedium and Integrity" the first few pages are missing— summarized sufficiently by: manner for matter; shadow for substance; ego for rapture. As antonym, integrity was suggested to me by a blossoming plum branch—a drawing by Hsieh Ho— reproduced above a *New York Times Book Review* notice of *The Mustard Seed Garden Manual of Painting* formulated about 500 A. D.— translated and edited by Miss Mai-mai Sze, published by the Bollingen Foundation in 1956 and as a Modern Library paperback in 1959. The plum branch led me to *The Tao of Painting,* of which "The Mustard Seed Garden" is a part, the (not *a*)Tao being a way of life, a "oneness" that is tireless; whereas egotism, synonymous with ignorance in Buddhist thinking, is tedious. And the Tao led me to the dragon in the classification of primary symbols, "symbol of the power of heaven"—changing at will to the size of a silkworm; or swelling to the totality of heaven and earth;* at will invisible, made personal by a friend at a party

* The dragon as lord of space makes relevant Miss Mai-mai Sze's emphasis on "space as China's chief contribution to painting; the essential part of the wheel being the inner space between its spokes; the space in a room, its usefulness" in keeping with the Manual: "a crowded ill-arranged composition is one of the Twelve Faults of Painting; as a man "if he had eyes all over his body, would be a monstrosity."

—an authority on gems, finance, painting, and music—who, exclaimed obligingly, as I concluded a digression on cranes, peaches, bats, and butterflies as symbols of long life and happiness, "O to be a dragon!" (The exclamation, lost sight of for a time, was appropriated as a title later.)

Verse: "Why the many quotation marks?" I am asked. Pardon my saying more than once, When a thing has been said so well that it could not be said better, why paraphrase it? Hence my writing is, if not a cabinet of fossils, a kind of collection of flies in amber.

More than once after a reading, I have been asked with circumspectly hesitant delicacy, "Your . . . poem, 'Marriage'; would you care to . . . make a statement about it?" Gladly. The thing (I would hardly call it a poem) is no philosophic precipitate; nor does it veil anything personal in the way of triumphs, entrapments, or dangerous colloquies. It is a little anthology of statements that took my fancy—phrasings that I liked.

Rhythm: The clue to it all (for me originally)—something built-in as in music.

> No man may him hyde
> From Deth holow-eyed.

I dislike the reversed order of words; don't like to be impeded by an unnecessary capital at the beginning of every line; I don't like, here, the meaning; the cadence coming close to being the sole reason for all that follows, the accent on "holow" rather than on "eyed," so firmly placed that the most willful reader cannot misplace it. "A fig for thee, O Death!"—meaning the opposite—has for me the same fascination. Appoggiaturas—a charmed subject. A study of trills can be absorbing to the exclusion of everything else—"the open, over-lapping, regular.". . . A London *Times Literary Supplement* reviewer (perforce anonymous), reviewing *The Interpretation of Bach's Keyboard Works* by Erwin Bodky (Oxford University Press) on April 7, 1961, says, "phrasing is rarely marked by Bach . . . except as a warning that something abnormal is intended"—a remark which has a bearing, for prose and verse, on the matter of "ease" alluded to earlier. I like straight writing, end-stopped lines, an effect of flowing continuity, and after 1929—perhaps earlier—wrote no verse that did not (in my opinion) rhyme. *However,* when a friendly, businesslike, shrewd, valiant government official in a broadcast summarizes me in handsome style—a man who feels that in writing as in conduct I distinguish between liberty and license, agrees with me that punctuation and syntax have a bearing on meaning, and looks at human weakness to determine possibilities of strength—when he says in conclusion, "She writes in free verse," I am not irascible.

Why an inordinate interest in animals and athletes? They are subjects for art and exemplars of it, are they not? minding their own business. Pangolins, hornbills, pitchers, catchers, do not pry or prey—or prolong the conversation; do not make us self-conscious; look their best when caring least; although in a Frank Buck documentary I saw a leopard insult a crocodile (basking on a river bank—head only visible on the bank)—bat the animal on the nose and continue on its way without so much as a look back. Perhaps I really don't know. I do know that I don't know how to account for a person who could be indifferent to miracles of dexterity, a certain feat by Don Zimmer—a Dodger at the time—making a backhand catch, of a ball coming hard from behind on the left, fast enough to take his hand off. "The fabric of existence weaves itself whole," as Charles Ives said (*Time,* August 22, 1960). "You cannot set art off in a corner and hope for it to have vitality, reality and substance. My work in music helped my business [insurance] and my work in business helped my music."

I am deplored "for extolling President Eisenhower for the very reasons for which I should reprehend him." Attacked for vetoing the Farm Bill—April 1956—he said, "To produce more crops when we need less, squandering resources on what we cannot eat or sell . . . would it solve the problem? Is it in the best interests of all?" Anything reprehensible in that? While visiting Mr. Macmillan—London, May 6, 1959—he said, "Our strength is in dedication to freedom; . . . if we are sufficiently dedicated, we will discipline ourselves to make the sacrifices to do what needs to be done." He was not speaking to political aesthetes but to those who do not wish to join theorists in Suzanne Labin's *The Anthill:* those who farmed and were starved; the worker who was "overworked and underpaid"; thinkers who were "forced to lie"—a confederation in which "all were terrified" (*New York Herald Tribune,* December 25, 1960). "I think I might call you a moralist," the inquirer began, "or do you object?" "No," I said. "I think perhaps I am. I do not thrust promises and deeds of mercy right and left to write a lyric—if what I write ever is one"—a qualification received with smiles by a specialist (or proseur turned poseur)—(leopard and crocodile).

"Poetry must not be drawn by the ears," Sidney says; in either the writing or the reading. T. S. Eliot is convinced that the work of contemporary poets should be read by students for enjoyment, not for credits; not taught formally but out of enthusiasm—with the classics as criterion (*New York Times,* December 30, 1960—printed a year earlier in Chicago). He is right about it, I think.

Prosody is a tool; poetry is "a maze, a trap, a web"—Professor Richards' epitome—and the quarry is captured in his own lines, "Not No" (in *Goodbye Earth*).

> *Not mine this life that must be lived in me.*
>
> Inside as out Another's: let it be.
> Ha, Skater on the Brink!
> Come whence,
> Where go?
>
> Anywhere
> Elsewhere
> Where I would not know
> *Not mine, not mine, all this lived through in me.*
>
> Who asks? Who answers? What ventriloquy!

My favorite poem? asked not too aggressively—perhaps recalling that Henry James could not name his "favorite letter of the alphabet or wave of the sea." The Book of Job, I have sometimes thought—for the verity of its agony and a fidelity that contrives glory for ashes. I do not deplore it that Sir Francis Bacon was often scathing, since he said, "By far the greatest obstacle . . . to advancement of anything is despair." Prizing Henry James, I take his worries for the most part with detachment; those of William James to myself when he says, "man's chief difference from the brutes lies in the exuberant excess of his subjective propensities. Prune his extravagance, sober him, and you undo him."

From COLLECTED POEMS (1951)

THE STEEPLE-JACK

(*Revised,* 1961)

Dürer would have seen a reason for living
  in a town like this, with eight stranded whales
to look at; with the sweet air coming into your house
on a fine day, from water etched
  with waves as formal as the scales
on a fish.

One by one in two's and three's, the seagulls keep
  flying back and forth over the town clock,
or sailing around the lighthouse without moving their wings—
rising steadily with a slight
  quiver of the body—or flock
mewing where

a sea the purple of the peacock's neck is
  paled to greenish azure as Dürer changed
the pine green of the Tyrol to peacock blue and guinea
gray. You can see a twenty-five-
  pound lobster; and fishnets arranged
to dry. The

whirlwind fife-and-drum of the storm bends the salt
  marsh grass, disturbs stars in the sky and the
star on the steeple; it is a privilege to see so
much confusion. Disguised by what
  might seem the opposite, the seaside flowers and

trees are favored by the fog so that you have
  the tropics at first hand: the trumpet-vine,
fox-glove, giant snap-dragon, a salpiglossis that has

spots and stripes; morning-glories, gourds,
    or moon-vines trained on fishing-twine
at the back

door; cat-tails, flags, blueberries and spiderwort,
    stripped grass, lichens, sunflowers, asters, daisies—
yellow and crab-claw ragged sailors with green bracts—toad-
                                                        plant,
petunias, ferns; pink lilies, blue
    ones, tigers; poppies; black sweet-peas.
The climate

is not right for the banyan, frangipani, or
    jack-fruit trees; or an exotic serpent
life. Ring lizard and snake-skin for the foot, if you see fit;
but here they've cats, not cobras, to
    keep down the rats. The diffident
little newt

with white pin-dots on black horizontal spaced
    out bands lives here; yet there is nothing that
ambition can buy or take away. The college student
named Ambrose sits on the hillside
    with his not-native books and hat
and sees boats

at sea progress white and rigid as if in
    a groove. Liking an elegance of which
the source is not bravado, he knows by heart the antique
sugar-bowl shaped summer-house of
    interlacing slats, and the pitch
of the church

spire, not true, from which a man in scarlet lets
    down a rope as a spider spins a thread;
he might be part of a novel, but on the sidewalk a

sign says C. J. Poole, Steeple Jack,
     in black and white; and one in red
and white says

Danger. The church portico has four fluted
     columns, each a single piece of stone, made
modester by white-wash. This would be a fit haven for
waifs, children, animals, prisoners,
     and presidents who have repaid
sin-driven

senators by not thinking about them. The
     place has a school-house, a post-office in a
store, fish-houses, hen-houses, a three-masted
     schooner on
the stocks. The hero, the student,
     the steeple-jack, each in his way,
is at home.

It could not be dangerous to be living
     in a town like this, of simple people,
who have a steeple-jack placing danger-signs by the church
while he is gilding the solid-
     pointed star, which on a steeple
stands for hope.

THE BUFFALO

     Black in blazonry means
prudence; and niger, unpropitious. Might
hematite-
     black, compactly incurved horns on bison
          have significance? The

soot-brown tail-tuft on
a kind of lion-

tail; what would that express?
And John Steuart Curry's Ajax pulling
grass—no ring
in his nose—two birds standing on the back?

.   .   .   .   .   .

The modern
ox does not look like the Augsburg ox's
portrait. Yes,
the great extinct wild Aurochs was a beast
to paint, with stripe and six-
foot horn-spread—decreased
to Siamese-cat-

Brown Swiss size or zebu-
shape, with white plush dewlap and warm-blooded
hump; to red-
skinned Hereford or to piebald Holstein. Yet
some would say the sparse-haired
buffalo has met
human notions best—

unlike the elephant,
both jewel and jeweller in the hairs
that he wears—
no white-nosed Vermont ox yoked with its twin
to haul the maple-sap,
up to their knees in
snow; no freakishly

Over-Drove Ox drawn by
Rowlandson, but the Indian buffalo,
albino-

footed, standing in a mud-lake with a
    day's work to do. No white
Christian heathen, way-
      laid by the Buddha,

    serves him so well as the
buffalo—as mettlesome as if check-
reined—free neck
    stretching out, and snake tail in a half-twist
      on the flank; nor will so
cheerfully assist
      the Sage sitting with

    feet at the same side, to
dismount at the shrine; nor are there any
ivory
    tusks like those two horns which when a tiger
      coughs, are lowered fiercely
and convert the fur
      to harmless rubbish.

    The Indian buffalo,
led by bare-leggèd herd-boys to a hay
hut where they
stable it, need not fear comparison
    with bison, with the twins,
    indeed with any
      of ox ancestry.

NINE NECTARINES AND
OTHER PORCELAIN

Arranged by two's as peaches are,
at intervals that all may live—
   eight and a single one, on twigs that
   grew the year before—they look like
a derivative;
   although not uncommonly
the opposite is seen—
nine peaches on a nectarine.
   Fuzzless through slender crescent leaves
      of green or blue or
      both, in the Chinese style, the four

   pairs' half-moon leaf-mosaic turns
out to the sun the sprinkled blush
   of puce-American-Beauty pink
   applied to bees-wax gray by the
uninquiring brush
   of mercantile bookbinding.
Like the peach Yu, the red-
cheeked peach which cannot aid the dead,
   but eaten in time prevents death,
      the Italian
      peach-nut, Persian plum, Ispahan

   secluded wall-grown nectarine,
as wild spontaneous fruit was
   found in China first. But was it wild?
   Prudent de Candolle would not say.
One perceives no flaws
   in this emblematic group
of nine, with leaf window

unquilted by *curculio*
   which fancy once depicted on
      this much-mended plate
      or in the also accurate

   unantlered moose or Iceland horse
or ass asleep against the old
    thick, low-leaning nectarine that is the
    colour of the shrub-tree's brownish
flower.

     .   .   .   .   .   .

   A Chinese "understands
the spirit of the wilderness"
   and the nectarine-loving kylin
   of pony appearance—the long-
tailed or the tailless
   small cinnamon-brown, common
camel-haired unicorn
with antelope feet and no horn,
   here enameled on porcelain.
     It was a Chinese
     who imagined this masterpiece.

THE FISH

wade
through black jade.
   Of the crow-blue mussel-shells, one keeps
   adjusting the ash-heaps;
     opening and shutting itself like

an
injured fan.
    The barnacles which encrust the side
    of the wave, cannot hide
        there for the submerged shafts of the

sun,
split like spun
    glass, move themselves with spotlight swiftness
    into the crevices—
        in and out, illuminating

the
turquoise sea
    of bodies. The water drives a wedge
    of iron through the iron edge
        of the cliff; whereupon the stars,

pink
rice-grains, ink-
    bespattered jelly-fish, crabs like green
    lilies, and submarine
        toadstools, slide each on the other.

All
external
    marks of abuse are present on this
    defiant edifice—
        all the physical features of

ac-
cident—lack
    of cornice, dynamite grooves, burns, and
    hatchet strokes, these things stand
        out on it; the chasm-side is

dead.
Repeated
    evidence has proved that it can live
    on what can not revive
       its youth. The sea grows old in it.

A GRAVE

Man looking into the sea,
taking the view from those who have as much right to it as you
                           have to yourself,
it is human nature to stand in the middle of a thing,
but you cannot stand in the middle of this;
the sea has nothing to give but a well excavated grave.
The firs stand in a procession, each with an emerald turkey-foot at
                                the top,
reserved as their contours, saying nothing;
repression, however, is not the most obvious characteristic of
                                the sea;
the sea is a collector, quick to return a rapacious look.
There are others besides you who have worn that look—
whose expression is no longer a protest; the fish no longer
                          investigate them
for their bones have not lasted:
men lower nets, unconscious of the fact that they are desecrating
                            a grave,
and row quickly away—the blades of the oars
moving together like the feet of water-spiders as if there were no
                        such thing as death.
The wrinkles progress among themselves in a phalanx—beautiful
                    under networks of foam,
and fade breathlessly while the sea rustles in and out of the
                            seaweed;

the birds swim through the air at top speed, emitting catcalls as
heretofore—
the tortoise-shell scourges about the feet of the cliffs, in motion
beneath them;
and the ocean, under the pulsation of lighthouses and noise of
bell-buoys,
advances as usual, looking as if it were not that ocean in which
dropped things are bound to sink—
in which if they turn and twist, it is neither with volition nor
consciousness.

NEW YORK

the savage's romance,
accreted where we need the space for commerce—
the center of the wholesale fur trade,
starred with tepees of ermine and peopled with foxes,
the long guard-hairs waving two inches beyond the body of
the pelt;
the ground dotted with deer-skins—white with white spots,
"as satin needlework in a single color may carry a varied pattern,"
and wilting eagle's-down compacted by the wind;
and picardels of beaver-skin; white ones alert with snow.
It is a far cry from the "queen full of jewels"
and the beau with the muff,
from the gilt coach shaped like a perfume-bottle,
to the conjunction of the Monongahela and the Allegheny,
and the scholastic philosophy of the wilderness
to combat which one must stand outside and laugh
since to go in is to be lost.
It is not the dime-novel exterior,
Niagara Falls, the calico horses and the war-canoe;
it is not that "if the fur is not finer than such as one sees others
wear,

one would rather be without it"—
that estimated in raw meat and berries, we could feed the universe;
it is not the atmosphere of ingenuity,
the otter, the beaver, the puma skins
without shooting-irons or dogs;
it is not the plunder,
but "accessibility to experience."

MARRIAGE

This institution,
perhaps one should say enterprise
out of respect for which
one says one need not change one's mind
about a thing one has believed in,
requiring public promises
of one's intention
to fulfil a private obligation:
I wonder what Adam and Eve
think of it by this time,
this fire-gilt steel
alive with goldenness;
how bright it shows—
"of circular traditions and impostures,
committing many spoils,"
requiring all one's criminal ingenuity
to avoid!
Psychology which explains everything
explains nothing,
and we are still in doubt.
Eve: beautiful woman—
I have seen her
when she was so handsome

she gave me a start,
able to write simultaneously
in three languages—
English, German, and French—
and talk in the meantime;
equally positive in demanding a commotion
and in stipulating quiet:
"I should like to be alone";
to which the visitor replies,
"I should like to be alone;
why not be alone together?"
Below the incandescent stars
below the incandescent fruit,
the strange experience of beauty;
its existence is too much;
it tears one to pieces
and each fresh wave of consciousness
is poison.
"See her, see her in this common world,"
the central flaw
in that first crystal-fine experiment,
this amalgamation which can never be more
than an interesting impossibility,
describing it
as "that strange paradise
unlike flesh, stones,
gold or stately buildings,
the choicest piece of my life:
the heart rising
in its estate of peace
as a boat rises
with the rising of the water";
constrained in speaking of the serpent—
shed snakeskin in the history of politeness
not to be returned to again—
that invaluable accident

exonerating Adam.
And he has beauty also;
it's distressing—the O thou
to whom from whom,
without whom nothing—Adam;
"something feline,
something colubrine"—how true!
a crouching mythological monster
in that Persian miniature of emerald mines,
raw silk—ivory white, snow white,
oyster white and six others—
that paddock full of leopards and giraffes—
long lemon-yellow bodies
sown with trapezoids of blue.
Alive with words,
vibrating like a cymbal
touched before it has been struck,
he has prophesied correctly—
the industrious waterfall,
"the speedy stream
which violently bears all before it,
at one time silent as the air
and now as powerful as the wind."
"Treading chasms
on the uncertain footing of a spear,"
forgetting that there is in woman
a quality of mind
which as an instinctive manifestation
is unsafe,
he goes on speaking
in a formal customary strain,
of "past states, the present state,
seals, promises,
the evil one suffered,
the good one enjoys,
hell, heaven,

everything convenient
to promote one's joy."
In him a state of mind
perceives what it was not
intended that he should;
"he experiences a solemn joy
in seeing that he has become an idol."
Plagued by the nightingale
in the new leaves,
with its silence—
not its silence but its silences,
he says of it:
"It clothes me with a shirt of fire."
"He dares not clap his hands
to make it go on
lest it fly off;
if he does nothing, it will sleep;
if he cries out, it will not understand."
Unnerved by the nightingale
and dazzled by the apple,
impelled by "the illusion of a fire
effectual to extinguish fire,"
compared with which
the shining of the earth
is but deformity—a fire
"as high as deep
as bright as broad
as long as life itself,"
he stumbles over marriage,
"a very trivial object indeed"
to have destroyed the attitude
in which he stood—
the ease of the philosopher
unfathered by a woman.
Unhelpful Hymen!
a kind of overgrown cupid

reduced to insignificance
by the mechanical advertising
parading as involuntary comment,
by that experiment of Adam's
with ways out but no way in—
the ritual of marriage,
augmenting all its lavishness;
its fiddle-head ferns,
lotus flowers, opuntias, white dromedaries,
its hippopotamus—
nose and mouth combined
in one magnificent hopper—
its snake and the potent apple.
He tells us
that "for love that will
gaze an eagle blind,
that is with Hercules
climbing the trees
in the garden of the Hesperides,
from forty-five to seventy
is the best age,"
commending it
as a fine art, as an experiment,
a duty or as merely recreation.
One must not call him ruffian
nor friction a calamity—
the fight to be affectionate:
"no truth can be fully known
until it has been tried
by the tooth of disputation."
The blue panther with black eyes,
the basalt panther with blue eyes,
entirely graceful—
one must give them the path—
the black obsidian Diana
who "darkeneth her countenance

as a bear doth,"
the spiked hand
that has an affection for one
and proves it to the bone,
impatient to assure you
that impatience is the mark of independence,
not of bondage.
"Married people often look that way"—
"seldom and cold, up and down,
mixed and malarial
with a good day and a bad."
"When do we feed?"
We occidentals are so unemotional,
we quarrel as we feed;
self lost, the irony preserved
in "the Ahasuerus *tête-à-tête* banquet"
with its small orchids like snakes' tongues,
with its "good monster, lead the way,"
with little laughter
and munificence of humor
in that quixotic atmosphere of frankness
in which, "four o'clock does not exist,
but at five o'clock
the ladies in their imperious humility
are ready to receive you";
in which experience attests
that men have power
and sometimes one is made to feel it.
He says, " 'What monarch would not blush
to have a wife
with hair like a shaving-brush?'
The fact of woman
is 'not the sound of the flute
but very poison.' "
She says, "Men are monopolists
of 'stars, garters, buttons

and other shining baubles'—
unfit to be the guardians
of another person's happiness."
He says, "These mummies
must be handled carefully—
'the crumbs from a lion's meal,
a couple of shins and the bit of an ear';
turn to the letter M
and you will find
that a 'wife is a coffin,'
that severe object
with the pleasing geometry
stipulating space not people,
refusing to be buried
and uniquely disappointing,
revengefully wrought in the attitude
of an adoring child
to a distinguished parent."
She says, "This butterfly,
this waterfly, this nomad
that has 'proposed
to settle on my hand for life.'—
What can one do with it?
There must have been more time
in Shakespeare's day
to sit and watch a play.
You know so many artists who are fools."
He says, "You know so many fools
who are not artists."
The fact forgot
that 'some have merely rights
while some have obligations,'
he loves himself so much,
he can permit himself
no rival in that love.
She loves herself so much,

she cannot see herself enough—
a statuette of ivory on ivory,
the logical last touch
to an expansive splendor
earned as wages for work done:
one is not rich but poor
when one can always seem so right.
What can one do for them—
these savages
condemned to disaffect
all those who are not visionaries
alert to undertake the silly task
of making people noble?
This model of petrine fidelity
who "leaves her peaceful husband
only because she has seen enough of him"—
that orator reminding you,
"I am yours to command."
"Everything to do with love is mystery;
it is more than a day's work
to investigate this science."
One sees that it is rare—
that striking grasp of opposites
opposed each to the other, not to unity,
which in cycloid inclusiveness
has dwarfed the demonstration
of Columbus with the egg—
a triumph of simplicity—
that charitive Euroclydon
of frightening disinterestedness
which the world hates,
admitting:

> "I am such a cow,
>   if I had a sorrow
>   I should feel it a long time;

I am not one of those
who have a great sorrow
in the morning
and a great joy at noon;"

which says: "I have encountered it
among those unpretentious
protégés of wisdom,
where seeming to parade
as the debater and the Roman,
the statesmanship
of an archaic Daniel Webster
persists to their simplicity of temper
as the essence of the matter:

'Liberty and union
now and forever';

the Book on the writing-table;
the hand in the breast-pocket."

AN EGYPTIAN PULLED GLASS BOTTLE IN THE SHAPE OF A FISH

Here we have thirst
And patience, from the first,
   And art, as in a wave held up for us to see
   In its essential perpendicularity;

Not brittle but
Intense—the spectrum, that
   Spectacular and nimble animal the fish,
   Whose scales turn aside the sun's sword with their polish.

SILENCE

My father used to say,
"Superior people never make long visits,"
have to be shown Longfellow's grave
or the glass flowers at Harvard.
Self-reliant like the cat—
that takes its prey to privacy,
the mouse's limp tail hanging like a shoelace from its mouth—
they sometimes enjoy solitude,
and can be robbed of speech
by speech which has delighted them.
The deepest feeling always shows itself in silence;
not in silence, but restraint.
Nor was he insincere in saying, "Make my house your inn."
Inns are not residences.

WHAT ARE YEARS?

What is our innocence,
what is our guilt? All are
naked, none is safe. And whence
is courage: the unanswered question,
the resolute doubt,—
dumbly calling, deafly listening—that
in misfortune, even death,
encourages others
and in its defeat, stirs

the soul to be strong? He
sees deep and is glad, who
accedes to mortality

and in his imprisonment rises
upon himself as
the sea in a chasm, struggling to be
free and unable to be,
 in its surrendering
 finds its continuing.

 So he who strongly feels,
behaves. The very bird,
 grown taller as he sings, steels
his form straight up. Though he is captive,
his mighty singing
says, satisfaction is a lowly
thing, how pure a thing is joy.
 This is mortality,
 this is eternity.

RIGORISTS

 "We saw reindeer
browsing," a friend who'd been in Lapland, said:
"finding their own food; they are adapted

 to scant *reino*
or pasture, yet they can run eleven
miles in fifty minutes; the feet spread when

 the snow is soft,
and act as snow-shoes. They are rigorists,
however handsomely cutwork artists

 of Lapland and
Siberia elaborate the trace
or saddle-girth with saw-tooth leather lace.

One looked at us
with its firm face part brown, part white,—a queen
of alpine flowers. Santa Claus' reindeer, seen

at last, had gray-
brown fur, with a neck like edelweiss or
lion's foot,—*leontopodium* more

exactly." And
this candelabrum-headed ornament
for a place where ornaments are scarce, sent

to Alaska,
was a gift preventing the extinction
of the Eskimo. The battle was won

by a quiet man,
Sheldon Jackson, evangel to that race
whose reprieve he read in the reindeer's face.

HE "DIGESTETH HARDE YRON"

Although the aepyornis
  or roc that lived in Madagascar, and
the moa are extinct,
the camel-sparrow, linked
  with them in size—the large sparrow
Xenophon saw walking by a stream—was and is
a symbol of justice.

This bird watches his chicks with
  a maternal concentration—and he's
been mothering the eggs
at night six weeks—his legs
  their only weapon of defense.

He is swifter than a horse; he has a foot hard
as a hoof; the leopard

   is not more suspicious. How
   could he, prized for plumes and eggs and young, used
even as a riding-
beast, respect men hiding
   actor-like in ostrich-skins, with
the right hand making the neck move as if alive and
from a bag the left hand

   strewing grain, that ostriches
   might be decoyed and killed! Yes this is he
whose plume was anciently
the plume of justice; he
   whose comic duckling head on its
great neck revolves with compass-needle nervousness
when he stands guard, in S-

   like foragings as he is
   preening the down on his leaden-skinned back.
The egg piously shown
as Leda's very own
   from which Castor and Pollux hatched,
was an ostrich-egg. And what could have been more fit
for the Chinese lawn it

   grazed on, as a gift to an
   emperor who admired strange birds, than this
one who builds his mud-made
nest in dust yet will wade
   in lake or sea till only the head shows.

      ·   ·   ·   ·   ·   ·

   Six hundred ostrich-brains served
   at one banquet, the ostrich-plume-tipped tent

and desert spear, jewel-
gorgeous ugly egg-shell
   goblets, eight pairs of ostriches
in harness, dramatize a meaning always missed
by the externalist.

   The power of the visible
   is the invisible; as even where
no tree of freedom grows,
so-called brute courage knows.
   Heroism is exhausting, yet
it contradicts a greed that did not wisely spare
the harmless solitaire

   or great auk in its grandeur;
   unsolicitude having swallowed up
all giant birds but an
alert gargantuan
   little-winged, magnificently speedy running-bird. This one
remaining rebel
is the sparrow-camel.

BIRD-WITTED

With innocent wide penguin eyes, three
   large fledgling mocking-birds below
the pussy-willow tree,
   stand in a row,
wings touching, feebly solemn,
till they see
      their no longer larger
      mother bringing
something which will partially
feed one of them.

Toward the high-keyed intermittent squeak
   of broken carriage-springs, made by
the three similar, meek-
   coated bird's-eye
freckled forms she comes; and when
from the beak
      of one, the still living
      beetle has dropped
out, she picks it up and puts
it in again.

Standing in the shade till they have dressed
   their thickly-filamented, pale
pussy-willow-surfaced
   coats, they spread tail
and wings, showing one by one,
the modest
      white stripe lengthwise on the
      tail and crosswise
underneath the wing, and the
accordion

is closed again. What delightful note
   with rapid unexpected flute-
sounds leaping from the throat
   of the astute
grown bird, comes back to one from
the remote
      unenergetic sun-
      lit air before
the brood was here? How harsh
the bird's voice has become.

A piebald cat observing them,
   is slowly creeping toward the trim
trio on the tree-stem.
   Unused to him

the three make room—uneasy
new problem.
    A dangling foot that missed
    its grasp, is raised
and finds the twig on which it
planned to perch. The

parent darting down, nerved by what chills
   the blood, and by hope rewarded—
of toil—since nothing fills
   squeaking unfed
mouths, wages deadly combat,
and half kills
    with bayonet beak and
    cruel wings, the
intellectual cautious-
ly creeping cat.

VIRGINIA BRITANNIA

   Pale sand edges England's Old
   Dominion. The air is soft, warm, hot
above the cedar-dotted emerald shore
    known to the red-bird, the red-coated musketeer,
    the trumpet-flower, the cavalier,
    the parson, and the wild parishioner. A deer-
track in a church-floor
   brick, and a fine pavement tomb with engraved top, remain.
   The now tremendous vine-encompassed hackberry
    starred with the ivy-flower,
    shades the church tower;
And a great sinner lyeth here under the sycamore.

A fritillary zigzags
   toward the chancel-shaded resting-place
of this unusual man and sinner who
      waits for a joyful resurrection. We-re-wo-
      co-mo-co's fur crown could be no
      odder than we were, with ostrich, Latin motto,
and small gold horse-shoe
   as arms for an able sting-ray-hampered pioneer—
   painted as a Turk, it seems—continuously
         exciting Captain Smith
         who, patient with
his inferiors, was a pugnacious equal, and to

   Powhatan as unflattering
   as grateful. Rare Indian, crowned by
Christopher Newport! The Old Dominion has
      all-green box-sculptured grounds.
      An almost English green surrounds
      them. Care has formed among unEnglish insect sounds,
the white wall-rose. As
   thick as Daniel Boone's grape-vine, the stem has wide-spaced
                                             great

   blunt alternating ostrich-skin warts that were thorns.
      Care has formed walls of yew
      since Indians knew
the Fort Old Field and narrow tongue of land that Jamestown was.

   Observe the terse Virginian,
   the mettlesome gray one that drives the
owl from tree to tree and imitates the call
      of whippoorwill or lark or katydid—the lead-
      gray lead-legged mocking-bird with head
      held half away, and meditative eye as dead
as sculptured marble
   eye, alighting noiseless, musing in the semi-sun,

standing on tall thin legs as if he did not see,
    conspicuous, alone,
    on the stone-
topped table with lead cupids grouped to form the pedestal.

    Narrow herring-bone-laid bricks,
    a dusty pink beside the dwarf box-
bordered pansies, share the ivy-arbor shade
        with cemetery lace settees, one at each side,
        and with the bird: box-bordered tide-
        water gigantic jet black pansies—splendor; pride—
not for a decade
        dressed, but for a day, in over-powering velvet; and
        gray-blue-Andalusian-cock-feather pale ones,
            ink-lined on the edge, fur-
            eyed, with ocher
on the cheek. The at first slow, saddle-horse quick cavalcade

    of buckeye-burnished jumpers
    and five-gaited mounts, the work-mule and
show-mule and witch-cross door and "strong sweet prison"
        are a part of what has come about—in the Black
        idiom—from "advancin' back-
        wards in a circle"; from taking the Potomac
cowbirdlike, and on
        The Chickahominy establishing the Negro,
        inadvertent ally and best enemy of tyranny. Rare
            unscent-
            ed, provident-
ly hot, too sweet, inconsistent flower-bed! Old Dominion

    flowers are curious. Some wilt
    in daytime and some close at night. Some
have perfume; some have not. The scarlet much-quilled
        fruiting pomegranate, the African violet,
        fuchsia and camellia, none; yet
        the house-high glistening green magnolia's velvet-

textured flower is filled
   with anaesthetic scent as inconsiderate as
   the gardenia's. Even the gardenia-sprig's
      dark vein on greener
      leaf when seen
against the light, has not near it, more small bees than the frilled

   silk substanceless faint flower of
   the crape-myrtle has. Odd Pamunkey
princess, birdclaw-ear-ringed; with a pet racoon
     from the Mattaponi (what a bear!) Feminine
     odd Indian young lady! Odd thin-
     gauze-and-taffeta-dressed English one! Terrapin
meat and crested spoon
   feed the mistress of French plum-and-turquoise-piped chaise-
                             longue
   of brass-knobbed slat front door, and everywhere open
     shaded house on Indian-
     named Virginian
streams in counties named for English lords. The rattlesnake soon

   said from our once dashingly
   undiffident first flag, "Don't tread on
me"—tactless symbol of a new republic.
     Priorities were cradled in this region not
     noted for humility; spot
     that has high-singing frogs, cotton-mouthed snakes and cot-
ton-fields; a unique
   Lawrence pottery with loping wolf design; and too
   unvenomous terrapin in tepid greenness,
     idling near the sea-top;
     tobacco-crop
records on church walls; a Devil's Woodyard; and the one-brick-

   thick serpentine wall built by
   Jefferson. Like strangler figs choking

a banyan, not an explorer, no imperialist,
    not one of us, in taking what we
    pleased—in colonizing as the
    saying is—has been a synonym for mercy.
The redskin with the deer-
    fur crown, famous for his cruelty, is not all brawn
    and animality. The outdoor tea-table,
        the mandolin-shaped big
        and little fig,
the silkworm-mulberry, the French mull dress with the Madeira-

    vine-accompanied edge are,
    when compared with what the colonists
found here in Tidewater Virginia, stark
    luxuries. The mere brown hedge-sparrow, with reckless
    ardor, unable to suppress
    his satisfaction in man's trustworthy nearness,
even in the dark
    flutes his ecstatic burst of joy—the caraway seed-
    spotted sparrow perched in the dew-drenched juniper
        beside the window-ledge;
        this little hedge-
sparrow that wakes up seven minutes sooner than the lark.

    The live oak's darkening filigree
    of undulating boughs, the etched
solidity of a cypress indivisible
    from the now agèd English hackberry,
    become with lost identity,
    part of the ground, as sunset flames increasingly
against the leaf-chiseled
    blackening ridge of green; while clouds, expanding above
    the town's assertiveness, dwarf it, dwarf arrogance
        that can misunderstand
        importance; and
are to the child an intimation of what glory is.

SPENSER'S IRELAND

has not altered;—
    a place as kind as it is green,
    the greenest place I've never seen.
Every name is a tune.
Denunciations do not affect
      the culprit; nor blows, but it
is torture to him to not be spoken to.
They're natural—
        the coat, like Venus'
mantle lined with stars,
buttoned close at the neck—the sleeves new from disuse.

If in Ireland
    they play the harp backward at need,
    and gather at midday the seed
of the fern, eluding
their "giants all covered with iron," might
      there be fern seed for unlearn-
ing obduracy and for reinstating
the enchantment?
      Hindered characters
seldom have mothers
in Irish stories, but they all have grandmothers.

It was Irish;
    a match not a marriage was made
    when my great great grandmother'd said
with native genius for
disunion, "although your suitor be
      perfection, one objection
is enough; he is not
Irish." Outwitting
      the fairies, befriending the furies,

whoever again
and again says, "I'll never give in," never sees

that you're not free
   until you've been made captive by
   supreme belief—credulity
you say? When large dainty
fingers tremblingly divide the wings
     of the fly for mid-July
with a needle and wrap it with peacock-tail,
or tie wool and
        buzzard's wing, their pride,
like the enchanter's
is in care, not madness. Concurring hands divide

flax for damask
   that when bleached by Irish weather
   has the silvered chamois-leather
water-tightness of a
skin. Twisted torcs and gold new-moon-shaped
     lunulae aren't jewelry
like the purple-coral fuchsia-tree's. Eire—
the guillemot
      so neat and the hen
of the heath and the
linnet spinet-sweet—bespeak relentlessness? Then

they are to me
   like enchanted Earl Gerald who
   changed himself into a stag, to
a great green-eyed cat of
the mountain. Discommodity makes
     them invisible; they've dis-
appeared. The Irish say your trouble is their
trouble and your
     joy their joy? I wish

I could believe it;
I am troubled, I'm dissatisfied, I'm Irish.

FOUR QUARTZ CRYSTAL CLOCKS

There are four vibrators, the world's exactest clocks;
   and these quartz time-pieces that tell
time intervals to other clocks,
   these worksless clocks work well;
independently the same, kept in
     the 41° Bell
       Laboratory time

vault. Checked by a comparator with Arlington,
   they punctualize the "radio,
cinema," and "presse"—a group the
   Giraudoux truth-bureau
of hoped-for accuracy has termed
     "instruments of truth." We know—
       as Jean Giraudoux says

certain Arabs have not heard—that Napoleon
   is dead; that a quartz prism when
the temperature changes, feels
   the change and that the then
electrified alternate edges
     oppositely charged, threaten
       careful timing; so that

this water-clear crystal as the Greeks used to say,
   this "clear ice" must be kept at the
same coolness. Repetition, with
   the scientist, should be
synonymous with accuracy.

The lemur-student can see
        that an aye-aye is not

an angwan-tíbo, potto, or loris. The sea-
        side burden should not embarrass
the bell-boy with the buoy-ball
        endeavoring to pass
hotel patronesses; nor could a
        practiced ear confuse the glass
                eyes for taxidermists

with eye-glasses from the optometrist. And as
        MEridian-7 one-two
one-two gives, each fifteenth second
        in the same voice, the new
data—"The time will be" so and so—
        you realize that "when you
                hear the signal," you'll be

hearing Jupiter or jour pater, the day god—
        the salvaged son of Father Time—
telling the cannibal Chronos
        (eater of his proxime
newborn progeny) that punctuality
        is not a crime.

THE PANGOLIN

Another armored animal—scale
        lapping scale with spruce-cone regularity until they
form the uninterrupted central
        tail-row! This near artichoke with head and legs and grit-
                                        equipped giz-
        zard, the night miniature artist engineer is
                Leonardo—da Vinci's replica—

impressive animal and toiler of whom we seldom hear.
Armor seems extra. But for him,
    the closing ear-ridge—
        or bare ear lacking even this small
        eminence and similarly safe

contracting nose and eye apertures
    impenetrably closable, are not. A true ant-eater,
not cockroach-eater, he endures
    exhausting solitary trips through unfamiliar ground at night,
    returning before sunrise; stepping in the moonlight,
        on the moonlight peculiarly, that the outside
            edges of his hands may bear the weight and save the claws
    for digging. Serpentined about
        the tree, he draws
            away from danger unpugnaciously,
            with no sound but a harmless hiss. Keeping

the fragile grace of the Thomas-
    of-Leighton Buzzard Westminster Abbey wrought-iron vine, he
rolls himself into a ball that has
    power to defy all effort to unroll it; strongly intailed, neat
    head for core, on neck not breaking off, with curled-in feet.
        Nevertheless he has sting-proof scales; and nest
            of rocks closed with earth from inside, which he can
                                            thus darken.
        Sun and moon and day and night and man and beast
            each with a splendor
                which man in all his vileness cannot
                set aside; each with an excellence!

"Fearful yet to be feared," the armored
    ant-eater met by the driver-ant does not turn back, but
engulfs what he can, the flattened sword-
    edged leafpoints on the tail and artichoke set leg- and body-
                                            plates

quivering violently when it retaliates
and swarms on him. Compact like the furled fringed frill
on the hat-brim of Gargallo's hollow iron head of a
matador, he will drop and will
then walk away
unhurt, although if unintruded on,
he cautiously works down the tree, helped

by his tail. The giant-pangolin-
tail, graceful tool, as prop or hand or broom or ax, tipped like
the elephant's trunk with special skin,
is not lost on this ant- and stone-swallowing uninjurable
artichoke which simpletons thought a living fable
whom the stones had nourished, whereas ants had done
so. Pangolins are not aggressive animals; between
dusk and day they have the measured
tread of the machine—
the slow frictionless creep of a thing
made graceful by adversities, con-

versities. To explain grace requires
a curious hand. If that which is at all were not forever,
why would those who graced the spires
with animals and gathered there to rest, on cold luxurious
low stone seats—a monk and monk and monk—between the thus
ingenious roof-supports, have slaved to confuse
grace with a kindly manner, time in which to pay a debt,
the cure for sins, a graceful use
of what are yet
approved stone mullions branching out across
the perpendiculars? A sailboat

was the first machine. Pangolins, made
for moving quietly also, are models of exactness,
on four legs; or hind feet plantigrade,

with certain postures of a man. Beneath sun and moon, man
                                                        slaving
to make his life more sweet, leaves half the flowers worth having,
      needing to choose wisely how to use his strength;
         a paper-maker like the wasp; a tractor of food-stuffs,
      like the ant; spidering a length
         of web from bluffs
            above a stream; in fighting, mechanicked
            like the pangolin; capsizing in

disheartenment. Bedizened or stark
      naked, man, the self, the being we call human, writing-
master to this world, griffons a dark
      "Like does not like like that is obnoxious"; and writes error
                                                        with four
r's. Among animals, one has a sense of humor.
         Humor saves a few steps, it saves years. Unignorant,
            modest and unemotional, and all emotion,
         he has everlasting vigor,
            power to grow,
               although there are few creatures who can make one
               breathe faster and make one erecter.

Not afraid of anything is he,
      and then goes cowering forth, tread paced to meet an obstacle
at every step. Consistent with the
      formula—warm blood, no gills, two pairs of hands and a few
                                                        hairs—that
is a mammal; there he sits in his own habitat,
         serge-clad, strong-shod. The prey of fear, he, always
            curtailed, extinguished, thwarted by the dusk, work
                                                        partly done,
      says to the alternating blaze,
         "Again the sun!
            anew each day; and new and new and new,
            that comes into and steadies my soul."

THE PAPER NAUTILUS

For authorities whose hopes
are shaped by mercenaries?
   Writers entrapped by
   teatime fame and by
commuters' comforts? Not for these
   the paper nautilus
   constructs her thin glass shell.

Giving her perishable
souvenir of hope, a dull
   white outside and smooth-
   edged inner surface
glossy as the sea, the watchful
   maker of it guards it
   day and night; she scarcely

   eats until the eggs are hatched.
Buried eight-fold in her eight
   arms, for she is in
   a sense a devil-
fish, her glass ramshorn-cradled freight
   is hid but is not crushed.
   As Hercules, bitten

by a crab loyal to the hydra,
was hindered to succeed,
   the intensively
   watched eggs coming from
the shell free it when they are freed—
   leaving its wasp-nest flaws
   of white on white, and close-

   laid Ionic chiton-folds
like the lines in the mane of

a Parthenon horse,
    round which the arms had
wound themselves as if they knew love
    is the only fortress
    strong enough to trust to.

NEVERTHELESS

you've seen a strawberry
        that's had a struggle; yet
        was, where the segments met,

a hedgehog or a star-
        fish for the multitude
        of seeds. What better food

than apple-seeds—the fruit
        within the fruit—locked in
        like counter-curved twin

hazel-nuts? Frost that kills
        the little rubber-plant-
        leaves of *kok-saghyz*-stalks, can't

harm the roots; they still grow
        in frozen ground. Once where
        there was a prickly-pear-

leaf clinging to barbed wire,
        a root shot down to grow
        in earth two feet below;

as carrots form mandrakes
        or a ram's-horn root some-
        times. Victory won't come

to me unless I go
  to it; a grape-tendril
  ties a knot in knots till

knotted thirty times,—so
  the bound twig that's under-
  gone and over-gone, can't stir.

The weak overcomes its
  menace, the strong overcomes itself. What is there

like fortitude! What sap
  went through that little thread
  to make the cherry red!

THE MIND IS AN ENCHANTING THING

is an enchanted thing
    like the glaze on a
katydid-wing
        subdivided by sun
        till the nettings are legion.
Like Gieseking playing Scarlatti;

like the apteryx-awl
    as a beak, or the
kiwi's rain-shawl
        of haired feathers, the mind
        feeling its way as though blind,
walks along with its eyes on the ground.

It has memory's ear
    that can hear without

having to hear.
      Like the gyroscope's fall,
      truly unequivocal
because trued by regnant certainty,

it is a power of
      strong enchantment. It
is like the dove-
      neck animated by
      sun; it is memory's eye;
it's conscientious inconsistency.

It tears off the veil; tears
      the temptation, the
mist the heart wears,
      from its eyes—if the heart
      has a face; it takes apart
dejection. It's fire in the dove-neck's

iridescence; in the
      inconsistencies
of Scarlatti.
      Unconfusion submits
      its confusion to proof; it's
not a Herod's oath that cannot change.

IN DISTRUST OF MERITS

Strengthened to live, strengthened to die for
      medals and positioned victories?
They're fighting, fighting, fighting the blind
      man who thinks he sees—
who cannot see that the enslaver is

enslaved; the hater, harmed. O shining O
firm star, O tumultuous
ocean lashed till small things go
as they will, the mountainous
wave makes us who look, know

depth. Lost at sea before they fought! O
star of David, star of Bethlehem,
O black imperial lion
of the Lord—emblem
of a risen world—be joined at last, be
joined. There is hate's crown beneath which all is
death; there's love's without which none
is king; the blessed deeds bless
the halo. As contagion
of sickness makes sickness,

contagion of trust can make trust. They're
fighting in deserts and caves, one by
one, in battalions and squadrons;
they're fighting that I
may yet recover from the disease, My
Self; some have it lightly; some will die. "Man
wolf to man"; yes. We devour
ourselves. The enemy could not
have made a greater breach in our
defenses. One pilot-

ing a blind man can escape him, but
Job disheartened by false comfort knew
that nothing can be so defeating
as a blind man who
can see. O alive who are dead, who are
proud not to see, O small dust of the earth
that walks so arrogantly,
trust begets power and faith is
an affectionate thing. We
vow, we make this promise

to the fighting—it's a promise—"We'll
        never hate black, white, red, yellow, Jew,
Gentile, Untouchable." We are
        not competent to
make our vows. With set jaw they are fighting,
fighting, fighting—some we love whom we know,
        some we love but know not—that
                hearts may feel and not be numb.
        It cures me; or am I what
                I can't believe in? Some

in snow, some on crags, some in quicksands,
        little by little, much by much, they
are fighting fighting fighting that where
        there was death there may
be life. "When a man is prey to anger,
he is moved by outside things; when he holds
        his ground in patience patience
                patience, that is action or
        beauty," the soldier's defense
                and hardest armor for

the fight. The world's an orphans' home. Shall
        we never have peace without sorrow?
without pleas of the dying for
        help that won't come? O
quiet form upon the dust, I cannot
look and yet I must. If these great patient
        dyings—all these agonies
                and woundbearings and bloodshed—
        can teach us how to live, these
                dyings were not wasted.

Hate-hardened heart, O heart of iron,
        iron is iron till it is rust.
There never was a war that was
        not inward; I must

fight till I have conquered in myself what
causes war, but I would not believe it.
   I inwardly did nothing.
    O Iscariotlike crime!
   Beauty is everlasting
    and dust is for a time.

A FACE

"I am not treacherous, callous, jealous, superstitious,
supercilious, venomous, or absolutely hideous":
   studying and studying its expression,
   exasperated desperation
    though at no real impasse,
    would gladly break the glass;

when love of order, ardor, uncircuitous simplicity,
with an expression of inquiry, are all one needs to be!
   Certain faces, a few, one or two—or one
   face photographed by recollection—
    to my mind, to my sight,
    must remain a delight.

PROPRIETY

   is some such word
   as the chord
    Brahms had heard
    from a bird,
sung down near the root of the throat;

it's the little downy woodpecker
        spiraling a tree—
        up up up like mercury:

a not long
sparrow-song
      of hayseed
      magnitude—
a tuned reticence with rigor
from strength at the source. Propriety is
      Bach's Solfegietto—
      harmonica and basso.

The fish-spine
on firs, on
      somber trees
      by the sea's
walls of wave-worn rock—have it; and
a moonbow and Bach's cheerful firmness
      in a minor key.
      It's an owl-and-a-pussy-

both-content
agreement.
      Come, come. It's
      mixed with wits;
it's not a graceful sadness. It's
resistance with bent head, like foxtail
      millet's. Brahms and Bach,
      no; Bach and Brahms. To thank Bach

for his song
first, is wrong.
      Pardon me;
      both are the
unintentional pansy-face
uncursed by self-inspection; blackened
      because born that way.

LIKE A BULWARK

LIKE A BULWARK

Affirmed. Pent by power that holds it fast—
a paradox. Pent. Hard pressed,
    you take the blame and are inviolate.
        Abased at last?
        Not the tempest-tossed.
Compressed; firmed by the thrust of the blast
    till compact, like a bulwark against fate;
        lead-saluted,
        saluted by lead?
As though flying Old Glory full mast.

APPARITION OF SPLENDOR

Partaking of the miraculous
    since never known literally,
Dürer's rhinoceros
    might have startled us equally
    if black-and-white-spined elaborately.

Like another porcupine, or fern,
    the mouth in an arching egret
was too black to discern
    till exposed as a silhouette;
    but the double-embattled thistle of jet—

disadvantageous supposedly—
    has never shot a quill. Was it
some joyous fantasy,
    plain eider-eared exhibit
    of spines rooted in the sooty moss,

or "train supported by porcupines—
    a fairy's eleven yards long"? . . .
as when the lightning shines
    on thistlefine spears, among
      prongs in lanes above lanes of a shorter prong,

"with the forest for nurse," also dark
    at the base—where needle-debris
springs and shows no footmark;
    the setting for a symmetry
      you must not touch unless you are a fairy.

Maine should be pleased that its animal
    is not a waverer, and rather
than fight, lets the primed quill fall.
    Shallow oppressor, intruder,
      insister, you have found a resister.

THEN THE ERMINE:

"rather dead than spotted"; and believe **it**
    despite reason to think not,
I saw a bat by daylight;
hard to credit

but I knew that I was right. It charmed me—
    wavering like a jack-in-
the-green, weaving about me
insecurely.

Instead of hammer-handed bravado
    adopting force for fashion,
momentum with a motto:
Mutare sperno

vel timere—I don't change, am not craven;
    although on what ground could I
say that I am hard to frighten?
Nothing's certain.

Fail, and Lavater's physiography
    has another admirer
of skill in obscurity—
now a novelty.

So let the *palisandre* settee express
    change—"ebony violet,"
Master Corbo in full dress,
and shepherdess,

at once; exhilarating hoarse crow-note
    and dignity with intimacy.
Foiled explosivenes is yet
a kind of prophet,

a perfecter, and so a concealer—
    with the power of implosion;
like violets by Dürer;
even darker.

TOM FOOL AT JAMAICA

    Look at Jonah embarking from Joppa, deterred by
the whale; hard going for a statesman whom nothing could detain,
    although one who would not rather die than repent.
      Be infallible at your peril, for your system will fail,
and select as a model the schoolboy in Spain
    who at the age of six, portrayed a mule and jockey
      who had pulled up for a snail.

"There is submerged magnificence, as Victor Hugo
said." *Sentir avec ardeur*; that's it; magnetized by feeling.
   Tom Fool "makes an effort and makes it oftener
      than the rest"—out on April first, a day of some significance
in the ambiguous sense—the smiling
   Master Atkinson's choice, with that mark of a champion, the
                                                                extra

      spurt when needed. Yes, yes. "Chance

   is a regrettable impurity"; like Tom Fool's
left white hind foot—an unconformity; though judging by
   results, a kind of cottontail to give him confidence.
      Up in the cupola comparing speeds, Signor Capossela keeps
                                                         his head.
"It's tough," he said; "but I get 'em; and why shouldn't I?
   I'm relaxed, I'm confident, and I don't bet." Sensational. He
                                                            does not

      bet on his animated

   valentines—his pink and black-striped, sashed or dotted silks.
Tom Fool is "a handy horse," with a chiseled foot. You've the beat
   of a dancer to a measure or harmonious rush
      of a porpoise at the prow where the racers all win easily—
like centaurs' legs in tune, as when kettledrums compete;
   nose rigid and suede nostrils spread, a light left hand on the rein,
                                                                till

      well—this is a rhapsody.

   Of course, speaking of champions, there was Fats Waller
with the feather touch, giraffe eyes, and that hand alighting in
   Ain't Misbehavin'! Ozzie Smith and Eubie Blake
      ennoble the atmosphere; you recall the Lippizan school;
the time Ted Atkinson charged by on Tiger Skin—
   no pursuers in sight—cat-loping along. And you may have seen a
                                                            monkey

      on a greyhound. "But Tom Fool . . .

THE WEB ONE WEAVES OF ITALY

grows till it is not what but which,
blurred by too much. The very blasé alone could
    choose the contest or fair to which to go.
    The crossbow tournament at Gubbio?

For quiet excitement, canoe-ers
or peach fairs? or near Perugia, the mule-show;
    if not the Palio, slaying the Saracen.
    One salutes—on reviewing again

this modern *mythologica*
esopica—its nonchalances of the mind,
    that "fount by which enchanting gems are spilt."
    Are we not charmed by the result?—

quite different from what goes on
at the Sorbonne; but not entirely, since flowering
    in more than mere talent for spectacle.
    Because the heart is in it all is well.

The greater part of stanzas 1 and 2 above is quoted from an article by Mitchell Goodman, "Festivals and Fairs for the Tourist in Italy," New York Times, April 18, 1954.

THE STAFF OF AESCULAPIUS

A symbol from the first, of mastery,
    experiments such as Hippocrates made
        and substituted for vague
    speculation, stayed
        the ravages of a plague.

A "going on"; yes, *anastasis* is the word
for research a virus has defied,
and for the virologist
with variables still untried—
too impassioned to desist.

Suppose that research has hit on the right one
and a killed vaccine is effective
say temporarily—
for even a year—although a live
one could give lifelong immunity,

knowledge has been gained for another attack.
Selective injury to cancer
cells without injury to
normal ones—another
gain—looks like prophecy come true.

Now, after lung resection, the surgeon fills space.
To sponge implanted, cells following
fluid, adhere and what
was inert becomes living—
that was framework. Is it not

like the master-physician's Sumerian rod?—
staff and effigy of the animal
which by shedding its skin
is a sign of renewal—
the symbol of medicine.

THE SYCAMORE

Against a gun-metal sky
I saw an albino giraffe. Without
leaves to modify,

chamois-white as
said, although partly pied near the base,
    it towered where a chain of
        stepping-stones lay in a stream nearby;
        glamour to stir the envy

    of anything in motley—
    Hampshire pig, the living lucky-stone; or
        all-white butterfly.
A commonplace:
there's more than just one kind of grace.
    We don't like flowers that do
        not wilt; they must die, and nine
        she-camel-hairs aid memory.

    Worthy of Imami,
    the Persian—clinging to a stiffer stalk
        was a little dry
thing from the grass,
in the shape of a Maltese cross,
    retiringly formal
        as if to say: "And there was I
        like a field-mouse at Versailles."

ROSEMARY

Beauty and Beauty's son and rosemary—
Venus and Love, her son, to speak plainly—
born of the sea supposedly,
at Christmas each, in company,
braids a garland of festivity.
    Not always rosemary—

since the flight to Egypt, blooming differently.
With lancelike leaf, green but silver underneath,
its flowers—white originally—
turned blue. The herb of memory,
imitating the blue robe of Mary,
      is not too legendary

to flower both as symbol and as pungency.
Springing from stones beside the sea,
the height of Christ when thirty-three—
not higher—it feeds on dew and to the bee
"hath a dumb language"; is in reality
      a kind of Christmas-tree.

STYLE

      revives in Escudero's constant of the plumbline,
axis of the hairfine moon—his counter-camber of the skater.
No more fanatical adjuster
          of the tilted hat
    than Escudero; of tempos others can't combine.
         And we—besides evolving
        the classic silhouette, Dick Button whittled slender—

have an Iberian-American champion yet,
the deadly Etchebaster. Entranced, were you not, by Soledad?
black-clad solitude that is not sad;
        like a letter from
    Casals; or perhaps say literal alphabet-
        S soundholes in a 'cello
        set contradictorily; or should we call her

la lagarta? or bamboos with fireflies a-glitter;
or glassy lake and the whorls which a vertical stroke brought about,
of the paddle half-turned coming out.
        As if bisecting
a viper, she can dart down three times and recover
        without a disaster, having
     been a bull-fighter. Well; she has a forgiver.

   Etchebaster's art, his catlike ease, his mousing pose,
his genius for anticipatory tactics, preclude envy
as the traditional unwavy
        Sandeman sailor
Is Escudero's; the guitar, Rosario's—
        wrist-rest for a dangling hand
    that's suddenly set humming fast fast fast and faster.

   There is no suitable simile. It is as though
the equidistant three tiny arcs of seeds in a banana
had been conjoined by Palestrina;
        it is like the eyes,
   or say the face, of Palestrina by El Greco.
      O Escudero, Soledad,
     Rosario Escudero, Etchebaster!

LOGIC AND "THE MAGIC FLUTE"

   Up winding stair,
here, where, in what theater lost?
was I seeing a ghost—
a reminder at least
    of a sunbeam or moonbeam

that has not a waist?
    By hasty hop
    or accomplished mishap,
the magic flute and harp
somehow confused themselves
        with China's precious wentletrap.

    Near Life and Time
in their peculiar catacomb,
abalonean gloom
and an intrusive hum
        pervaded the mammoth cast's
small audience-room.
    Then out of doors,
        where interlacing pairs
of skaters raced from rink
to ramp, a demon roared
        as if down flights of marble stairs:

    " 'What is love and
shall I ever have it?' " The truth
is simple. Banish sloth,
fetter-feigning uncouth
        fraud. Trapper Love with noble
noise, the magic sleuth,
        as bird-notes prove—
        first telecolor-trove—
illogically wove
what logic can't unweave:
        one need not shoulder, need not shove.

BLESSED IS THE MAN

who does not sit in the seat of the scoffer—
　　the man who does not denigrate, depreciate, denunciate;
　　　who is not "characteristically intemperate,"
who does not "excuse, retreat, equivocate; and will be heard."

(Ah, Giorgione! there are those who mongrelize
　　and those who heighten anything they touch; although it may
　　　　　　　　　　　　　　　　　　　　　　well be
　　that if Giorgione's self-portrait were not said to be he,
it might not take my fancy. Blessed the geniuses who know

that egomania is not a duty.)
　　"Diversity, controversy; tolerance"—in that "citadel
　　of learning" we have a fort that ought to armor us well.
Blessed is the man who "takes the risk of a decision"—asks

himself the question: "Would it solve the problem?
　　Is it right as I see it? Is it in the best interests of all?"
　　　Alas. Ulysses' companions are now political—
living self-indulgently until the moral sense is drowned,

having lost all power of comparison,
　　thinking license emancipates one, "slaves whom they themselves
　　　　　　　　　　　　　　　　　　　　　have bound."
　　　Brazen authors, downright soiled and downright spoiled, as if
　　　　　　　　　　　　　　　　　　　　　sound
and exceptional, are the old quasi-modish counterfeit,

mitin-proofing conscience against character.
　　Affronted by "private lies and public shame," blessed is the
　　　　　　　　　　　　　　　　　　　　　author
　　Who favors what the supercilious do not favor—
who will not comply. Blessed, the unaccommodating man.

Blessed the man whose faith is different
    from possessiveness—of a kind not framed by "things which do
                            appear"—
    who will not visualize defeat, too intent to cower;
whose illumined eye has seen the shaft that gilds the sultan's
                             tower.

O TO BE A DRAGON

O TO BE A DRAGON

> If I, like Solomon, . . .
> could have my wish—
>
> my wish . . . O to be a dragon,
> a symbol of the power of Heaven—of silkworm
> size or immense; at times invisible.
>   Felicitous phenomenon!

I MAY, I MIGHT, I MUST

If you will tell me why the fen
appears impassable, I then
will tell you why I think that I
can get across it if I try.

TO A CHAMELEON

Hid by the august foliage and fruit
    of the grape-vine
    twine
        your anatomy
            round the pruned and polished stem,
                Chameleon.
                Fire laid upon
            an emerald as long as
        the Dark King's massy
    one,
could not snap the spectrum up for food
    as you have done.

A JELLYFISH

Visible, invisible,
   a fluctuating charm
an amber-tinctured amethyst
   inhabits it, your arm
approaches and it opens
   and it closes; you had meant
to catch it and it quivers;
   you abandon your intent.

VALUES IN USE

I attended school and I liked the place—
grass and little locust-leaf shadows like lace.

Writing was discussed. They said, "We create
values in the process of living, daren't await

their historic progress." Be abstract
and you'll wish you'd been specific; it's a fact.

What was I studying? Values in use,
"judged on their own ground." Am I still abstruse?

Walking along, a student said offhand,
" 'Relevant' and 'plausible' were words I understand."

A pleasing statement, anonymous friend.
Certainly the means must not defeat the end.

HOMETOWN PIECE FOR MESSRS. ALSTON AND REESE

To the tune:
"Li'l baby, don't say a word: Mama goin' to buy you a mocking-
*   bird.*
Bird don't sing: Mama goin' to sell it and buy a brass ring."

"Millennium," yes; "pandemonium"!
Roy Campanella leaps high. Dodgerdom

crowned, had Johnny Podres on the mound.
Buzzie Bavasi and the Press gave ground;

the team slapped, mauled, and asked the Yankees' match,
"How did you feel when Sandy Amoros made the catch?"

"I said to myself"—pitcher for all innings—
"as I walked back to the mound I said, 'Everything's

getting better and better.' " (Zest: they've zest.
" 'Hope springs eternal in the Brooklyn breast.' "

And would the Dodger Band in 8, row 1, relax
if they saw the collector of income tax?

Ready with a tune if that should occur:
"Why Not Take All of Me—All of Me, Sir?")

Another series. Round-tripper Duke at bat,
"Four hundred feet from home-plate"; more like that.

A neat bunt, please; a cloud-breaker, a drive
like Jim Gilliam's great big one. Hope's alive.

Homered, flied out, fouled? Our "stylish stout"
so nimble Campanella will have him out.

A-squat in double-headers four hundred times a day,
he says that in a measure the pleasure is the pay:

catcher to pitcher, a nice easy throw
almost as if he'd just told it to go.

Willie Mays should be a Dodger. He should—
a lad for Roger Craig and Clem Labine to elude;

but you have an omen, pennant-winning Peewee,
on which we are looking superstitiously.

Ralph Branca has Preacher Roe's number; recall?
and there's Don Bessent; he can really fire the ball.

As for Gil Hodges, in custody of first—
"He'll do it by himself." Now a specialist—versed

in an extension reach far into the box seats—
he lengthens up, leans and gloves the ball. He defeats

expectation by a whisker. The modest star,
irked by one misplay, is no hero by a hair;

in a strikeout slaughter when what could matter more,
he lines a homer to the signboard and has changed the score.

Then for his nineteenth season, a home run—
with four of six runs batted in—Carl Furillo's the big gun;

almost dehorned the foe—has fans dancing in delight.
Jake Pitler and his Playground "get a Night"—

Jake, that hearty man, made heartier by a harrier
who can bat as well as field—Don Demeter.

Shutting them out for nine innings—hitter too—
Carl Erskine leaves Cimoli nothing to do.

Take off the goat-horns, Dodgers, that egret
which two very fine base-stealers can offset.

You've got plenty: Jackie Robinson
and Campy and big Newk, and Dodgerdom again
watching everything you do. You won last year. Come on.

ENOUGH

Jamestown, 1607–1957

Some in the Godspeed, the Susan C.,
others in the Discovery,

found their too earthly paradise.
Dazzled, the band with grateful cries,

clutched the soil; then worked upstream,
safer if landlocked, it would seem;

to pests and pestilence instead—
the living outnumbered by the dead.

Their namesake ships traverse the sky
as jets to Jamestown verify.

The same reward for best and worst
doomed communism, tried at first.

Three acres each, initiative,
six bushels paid back, they could live.

Captain Dale became kidnaper—
the master—lawless when the spur

was desperation, even though
his victim had let her victim go—

Captain John Smith. Poor Powhatan
had to make peace, embittered man.

Then teaching—insidious recourse—
enhancing Pocahontas, flowered of course

in marriage. John Rolfe fell in love
with her and she—in rank above

what she became—renounced her name
yet found her status not too tame.

The crested moss-rose casts a spell;
and bud of solid green as well;

the Old Pink Moss—with fragrant wings
imparting balsam scent that clings

where redbrown tanbark holds the sun,
resilient beyond comparison.

Not to begin with. No select
artlessly perfect French effect

mattered at first. (Small point to rhymes
for maddened men in starving-times.)

Tested until unnatural,
one became a cannibal.

Marriage, tobacco, and slavery,
initiated liberty

when the Deliverance brought seed
of that now controversial weed—

a blameless plant Red-Ridinghood.
Who, after all, knows what is good!

A museum of the mind "presents";
one can be stronger than events.

The victims of a search for gold
cast yellow soil into the hold.

With nothing but the feeble tower
to mark the site that did not flower,

could the most ardent have been sure
that they had done what would endure?

It was enough; it is enough
if present faith mend partial proof.

MELCHIOR VULPIUS
c. 1560–1615

a contrapuntalist—
             composer of chorales
and wedding-hymns to Latin words
but best of all an anthem:
    "God be praised for conquering faith
        which feareth neither pain nor death."

We have to trust this art—
                              this mastery which none
can understand. Yet someone has
acquired it and is able to
    direct it. Mouse-skin-bellows'-breath
    expanding into rapture saith

"Hallelujah." Almost
                        utmost absolutist
and fugue-ist, Amen; slowly building
from miniature thunder,
    crescendos antidoting death—
    love's signature cementing faith.

NO BETTER THAN
A "WITHERED DAFFODIL"

Ben Jonson said he was? "O I could still
Like melting snow upon some craggy hill,
        Drop, drop, drop, drop."

I too until I saw that French brocade
blaze green as though some lizard in the shade
        became exact—

set off by replicas of violet—
like Sidney, leaning in his striped jacket
        against a lime—

a work of art. And I too seemed to be
an insouciant rester by a tree—
        no daffodil.

IN THE PUBLIC GARDEN

Boston has a festival—
compositely for all—
and nearby, cupolas of learning
(crimson, blue, and gold) that
    have made education individual.

My first—an exceptional,
an almost scriptural—
taxi-driver to Cambridge from Back Bay
said, as we went along, "They
    make some fine young men at Harvard." I recall

the summer when Faneuil Hall
had its weathervane with gold ball
and grasshopper, gilded again by
a -leafer and -jack
    till it glittered. Spring can be a miracle

there—a more than usual
bouquet of what is vernal—
"pear blossoms whiter than the clouds," pin-
oak leaves that barely show
    when other trees are making shade, besides small

fairy iris suitable
for Dulcinea del
Toboso; O yes, and snowdrops
in the snow, that smell like
    violets. Despite secular bustle,

let me enter King's Chapel
   to hear them sing: "My work be praise while
others go and come. No more a stranger
or a guest but like a child
   at home." A chapel or a festival

   means giving what is mutual,
      even if irrational:
black sturgeon-eggs—a camel
from Hamadan, Iran;
   a jewel, or, what is more unusual,

   silence—after a word-waterfall of the banal—
      as unattainable
as freedom. And what is freedom for?
For "self-discipline," as our
   hardest-working citizen has said—a school;

   it is for "freedom to toil"
      with a feel for the tool.
Those in the trans-shipment camp must have
a skill. With hope of freedom hanging
   by a thread—some gather medicinal

   herbs which they can sell.
   Ineligible if they ail.
            Well?

There are those who will talk for an hour
without telling you why they have
   come. And I? This is no madrigal—
   no medieval gradual.
      It is a grateful tale—
without that radiance which poets

are supposed to have—
   unofficial, unprofessional. Still one need not fail

   to wish poetry well
   where intellect is habitual—
glad that the Muses have a home and swans—
that legend can be factual;
   happy that Art, admired in general,
   is always actually personal.

THE ARCTIC OX (OR GOAT)

*Derived from "Golden Fleece of the Arctic," by John J. Teal, Jr.,
who rears musk oxen on his farm in Vermont, as set forth
by him in the March 1958 issue of the* Atlantic Monthly.

To wear the arctic fox
you have to kill it. Wear
   qiviut—the underwool of the arctic ox—
pulled off it like a sweater;
your coat is warm; your conscience, better.

I would like a suit of
qiviut, so light I did not
   know I had it on; and in the
course of time, another
since I had not had to murder

the "goat" that grew the fleece
that made the first. The musk ox
   has no musk and it is not an ox—
illiterate epithet.
Bury your nose in one when wet.

It smells of water, nothing else,
and browses goatlike on

hind legs. Its great distinction
is not egocentric scent
but that it is intelligent.

Chinchillas, otters, water rats,
and beavers, keep us warm
    but think! a "musk ox" grows six pounds
of *qiviut*; the cashmere ram,
three ounces—that is all—of pashm.

Lying in an exposed spot,
basking in the blizzard,
    these ponderosos could dominate
the rare-hairs market in Kashan and yet
you could not have a choicer pet.

They join you as you work;
love jumping in and out of holes,
    play in water with the children,
learn fast, know their names,
will open gates and invent games.

While not incapable
of courtship, they may find its
    servitude and flutter, too much
like Procrustes' bed;
so some decide to stay unwed.

Camels are snobbish
and sheep, unintelligent;
    water buffaloes, neurasthenic—
even murderous.
Reindeer seem over-serious,

whereas these scarce *qivies*,
with golden fleece and winning ways,

outstripping every fur-bearer—
there in Vermont quiet—
could demand Bold Ruler's diet:

Mountain Valley water,
dandelions, carrots, oats—
   encouraged as well—by bed
made fresh three times a day,
to roll and revel in the hay.

Insatiable for willow
leaves alone, our goatlike
   qivi-curvi-capricornus
sheds down ideal for a nest.
Song-birds find *qiviut* best.

Suppose you had a bag
of it; you could spin a pound
   into a twenty-four-or-five-
mile thread—one, forty-ply—
that will not shrink in any dye.

If you fear that you are
reading an advertisement,
   you are. If we can't be cordial
to these creatures' fleece,
I think that we deserve to freeze.

SAINT NICHOLAS,

   might I, if you can find it, be given
a chameleon with tail
that curls like a watch spring; and vertical
on the body—including the face—pale

tiger-stripes, about seven;
   (the melanin in the skin
  having been shaded from the sun by thin
    bars; the spinal dome
     beaded along the ridge
    as if it were platinum).

If you can find no striped chameleon,
might I have a dress or suit—
I guess you have heard of it—of *qiviut?*
and to wear with it, a taslon shirt, the drip-dry fruit
  of research second to none;
    sewn, I hope, by Excello;
     as for buttons to keep down the collar-points, no.
      The shirt could be white—
       and be "worn before six,"
      either in daylight or at night.

But don't give me, if I can't have the dress,
a trip to Greenland, or grim
trip to the moon. The moon should come here. Let him
make the trip down, spread on my dark floor some dim
  marvel, and if a success
    that I stoop to pick up and wear,
     I could ask nothing more. A thing yet more rare,
      though, and different,
       would be this: Hans von Marées'
      St. Hubert, kneeling with head bent,

  form erect—in velvet, tense with restraint—
hand hanging down: the horse, free.
Not the original, of course. Give me
a postcard of the scene—huntsman and divinity—
  hunt-mad Hubert startled into a saint

by a stag with a Figure entined
But why tell you what you must have divined?
   Saint Nicholas, O Santa Claus,
      would it not be the most
   prized gift that ever was!

FOR FEBRUARY 14TH

      Saint Valentine,
although late, would "some interested law
impelled to plod in the poem's cause"
         be unwelcome with a line?

      Might you have liked a stone
from a De Beers Consolidated Mine?
or badger-neat saber-thronged thistle
         of Palestine—the leaves alone

      down'd underneath,
worth a touch? or that mimosa-leafed vine
called an "alexander's armillary
         sphere" fanning out in a wreath?

      Or did the ark
preserve paradise-birds with jet-black plumes,
whose descendants might serve as presents?
      But questioning is the mark
      of a pest! Why think
only of animals in connection
with the ark or the wine Noah drank?
      but that the ark did not sink.

COMBAT CULTURAL

One likes to see a laggard rook's high
speed at sunset to outfly the dark,
    or a mount well schooled for a medal—
front legs tucked under for the barrier,
    or team of leapers turned aerial.

I recall a documentary
of Cossacks: a visual fugue, a mist
    of swords that seemed to sever
heads from bodies—feet stepping as through
    harp-strings in a scherzo. However,

the quadrille of Old Russia for me:
with aimlessly drooping handkerchief
    snapped like the crack of a whip;
a deliriously spun-out-level
    frock-coat skirt, unswirled and a-droop

in remote promenade. Let me see . . .
Old Russia, did I say? Cold Russia
    this time: the prize bunnyhug
and platform-piece of experts in the
    trip-and-slug of wrestlers in a rug.

"Sacked" and ready for bed apparently—
with a jab, a kick, pinned to the wall,
    they work toward the edge and stick;
stagger off, and one is victim of a
    flipflop—leg having circled leg as thick.

"Some art, because of high quality,
is unlikely to command high sales";
    yes, no doubt; but here, oh no;

not with the frozen North's Nan-ai-ans
    of the sack in their tight touch-and-go.

  These battlers, dressed identically—
just one person—may, by seeming twins,
    point a moral, should I confess;
we must cement the parts of any
    objective symbolic of *sagesse*.

LEONARDO DA VINCI'S

    Saint Jerome and his lion
      in that hermitage
  of walls half gone,
      share sanctuary for a sage—
joint-frame for impassioned ingenious
      Jerome versed in language—
and for a lion like one on the skin of which
      Hercules' club made no impression.

    The beast, received as a guest,
      although some monks fled—
  with its paw dressed
      that a desert thorn had made red—
stayed as guard of the monastery ass . . .
      which vanished, having fed
its guard, Jerome assumed. The guest then, like an ass,
      was made carry wood and did not resist,

    but before long, recognized
      the ass and consigned
  its terrorized
      thieves' whole camel-train to chagrined

Saint Jerome. The vindicated beast and
　　　saint somehow became twinned;
and now, since they behaved and also looked alike,
　　　their lionship seems officialized.

　　　Pacific yet passionate—
　　　　for if not both, how
　　　could he be great?
　　　　Jerome—reduced by what he'd been through—
with tapering waist no matter what he ate,
　　　　left us the Vulgate. That in *Leo*,
the Nile's rise grew food checking famine,
　　　　made lion's-mouth fountains appropriate,

　　　if not universally,
　　　　at least not obscure.
　　　And here, though hardly a summary, astronomy—
　　　　or pale paint—makes the golden pair
in Leonardo da Vinci's sketch, seem
　　　　sun-dyed. Blaze on, picture,
saint, beast; and Lion Haile Selassie, with household
　　　　lions as symbol of sovereignty.

OTHER POEMS

TELL ME, TELL ME

where might there be a refuge for me
from egocentricity
and its propensity to bisect,
mis-state, misunderstand
and obliterate continuity?
Why, oh why, one ventures to ask, set
flatness on some cindery pinnacle
as if on Lord Nelson's revolving diamond rosette?

It appeared: gem, burnished rarety
and peak of delicacy—
in contrast with grievance touched off on
any ground—the absorbing
geometry of a fantasy:
a James, Miss Potter, Chinese
"passion for the particular," of a
tired man who yet, at dusk,
cut a masterpiece of cerise—

for no tailor-and-cutter jury—
only a few mice to see,
who "breathed inconsistency and drank
contradiction," dazzled
not by the sun but by "shadowy
possibility." (I'm referring
to Henry James and Beatrix Potter's Tailor.)
I vow, rescued tailor
of Gloucester, I am going

to flee; by engineering strategy—
the viper's traffic-knot—flee
to metaphysical newmown hay,
honeysuckle, or woods fragrance.

Might one say or imply T.S.V.P.—
     Taisez-vous? "Please" does not make sense
to a refugee from verbal ferocity; I am
perplexed. Even so, "deference";
     yes, deference may be my defense.

A *précis?*
    In this told-backward biography
    of how the cat's mice when set free
by the tailor of Gloucester, finished
the Lord Mayor's cerise coat—
    the tailor's tale ended captivity
     in two senses. Besides having told
of a coat which made the tailor's fortune,
it rescued a reader
     from being driven mad by a scold.

CARNEGIE HALL: RESCUED

"It spreads," the campaign—carried on
by long-distance telephone,
    with "Saint Diogenes
     supreme commander."
    At the fifty-ninth minute
     of the eleventh hour, a rescuer

makes room for Mr. Carnegie's
music hall, which by degrees
    became (becomes)
     our music stronghold
    (accented on the "né," as
     perhaps you don't have to be told).

Paderewski's "palladian
majesty" made it a fane;
    Tschaikovsky, of course,
        on the opening
night, 1891;
        and Gilels, a master, playing.

With Andrew C. and Mr. R.,
"our spearhead, Mr. Star"—
    in music, Stern—
        has grown forensic,
    and by civic piety
        has saved our city panic;

rescuer of a music hall
menaced by the "cannibal
    of real estate"—bulldozing potentate,
        land-grabber, the human crab
    left cowering like a neonate.

As Venice "in defense of children"
has forbidden for the citizen,
    by "a tradition of
        noble behavior,
    dress too strangely shaped or scant,"
        posterity may impute error

to our demolishers of glory. Cocteau's "Preface
to the Past" contains the phrase
    "When very young my dream
        was of pure glory."
    Must he say "was" of his "light
        dream," which confirms our glittering story?

They need their old brown home. Cellist,
violinist, pianist—

used to unmusical
  impenetralia's
massive masonry—have found
  reasons to return. Fantasias
of praise and rushings to the front
dog the performer. We hunt
  you down, Saint Diogenes—
    are thanking you for glittering,
  for rushing to the rescue
    as if you'd heard yourself performing.

"SUN"

Hope and Fear accost him

  "No man may him hyde
  From Deth holow-eyed";
    For us, this inconvenient truth does not suffice.
  You are not male or female, but a plan
  deep-set within the heart of man.
Splendid with splendor hid you come, from your Arab abode,
a fiery topaz smothered in the hand of a great prince who rode
  before you, Sun—whom you outran,
  piercing his caravan.

  O Sun, you shall stay
  with us. Holiday
    and day of wrath shall be one, wound in a device
  of Moorish gorgeousness, round glasses spun
  to flame as hemispheres of one
great hour-glass dwindling to a stem. Consume hostility;
employ your weapon in this meeting-place of surging enmity!
  Insurgent feet shall not outrun
  multiplied flames, O Sun.

RESCUE WITH YUL BRYNNER

(Appointed special consultant to the United Nations High Commissioner for Refugees, 1959–1960)

"Recital? 'Concert' is the word,"
and stunning, by the Budapest Symphony—
   displaced but not deterred—
listened to by me,
     though with detachment then,
       like a grasshopper that did not
     know it missed the mower, a pygmy citizen;
       a case, I'd say, of too slow a grower.
There were thirty million; there are thirteen still—
healthy to begin with, kept waiting till they're ill.
History judges. It will
salute Winnipeg's incredible
conditions: "Ill; no sponsor; and no kind of skill."
   Odd—a reporter with guitar—a puzzle.
   Mysterious Yul did not come to dazzle.

Magic bird with multiple tongue—
five tongues—equipped for a crazy twelve-month tramp
   (a plod), he flew among
the damned, found each camp
     where hope had slowly died
       (some had never seen a plane).
     Instead of feathering himself, he exemplified
       the rule that, self-applied, omits the gold.
He said, "You may feel strange; nothing matters less.
Nobody notices; you'll find some happiness.
No new 'big fear'; no distress."
Yul can sing—twin of an enchantress—
elephant-borne dancer in silver-spangled dress,
   swirled aloft by trunk, with star-tipped wand, Tamara,
   as true to the beat as *Symphonia Hungarica*.

Head bent down over the guitar,
he barely seemed to hum; ended "all come home";
   did not smile; came by air;
did not have to come.
      The guitar's an event.
         Guests of honor can't dance; don't smile.
      "Have a home?" a boy asks. "Shall we live in a tent?"
         "In a house," Yul answers. His neat cloth hat
has nothing like the glitter reflected on the face
of milkweed-witch seed-brown dominating a palace
that was nothing like the place
where he is now. His deliberate pace
is a king's, however. "You'll have plenty of space."
   Yule—Yul log for the Christmas-fire tale-spinner—
   of fairy tales that can come true: Yul Brynner.

TO VICTOR HUGO OF MY CROW PLUTO

"Even when the bird is walking we know that it has wings"
                                        —*Victor Hugo.*

Of:

   my crow   Victor Hugo,
   Pluto,   it is true

   the true   we know
   Plato,   that the crow

   azzurro-   "has wings," how-
   negro   ever pigeon-toe-

   green-blue   inturned on grass. We do.
   rainbow—   (adagio)

Vivo-
rosso

"corvo,"
although

con dizio-
nario

io parlo
Italiano—

this pseudo
Esperanto

which, savio
ucello

you speak too—
my vow and motto

(boto e totto)
io giuro

è questo
credo:

lucro
è peso morto.

And so
dear crow—

gioièllo
mio—

I have to
let you go;

a bel bosco
generoso,

tuttuto
vagabondo,

serafino
uvaceo.

Sunto,
oltremarino

verecondo
Plato, addio.

Impromptu equivalents for *esperanto madinusa* (made in U.S.A.) for those who might not resent them.

azzurro-negro: blue-black
vivorosso: lively
con dizionario: with dictionary
savio ucello: knowing bird
boto e totto: vow and motto
io giuro: I swear
è questo credo: is this credo
lucro è peso morto: profit is a
   dead weight

gioièllo mio: my jewel
a bel bosco: to lovely woods
tuttuto vagabondo: complete
   gypsy
serafino uvaceo: grape-black
   seraph
sunto: in short
verecondo: modest

From THE FABLES OF LA FONTAINE

I sing when Aesop's wand animates my lyre.
Make-believe is here in its antique attire—
Insight confirmed by direct observation;
Even fish speak. As each finds expression,
Animals enact my universal theme,
Educating man, fantasist though I seem.
Dazzling child of a prince whom the gods have made their care,
All eyes converge upon what you may be and are.
With the noblest minds acknowledging your sway,
You'll count your days by conquests in glittering array.
Resonance deeper than mine must sing
What it was and is to have been born a king.
These verses sketch on unassuming textures,
The byplay of inconsequential creatures;
And if I have failed to give you real delight,
My reward must be that I had hoped I might.

From BOOK ONE

1. THE GRASSHOPPER AND THE ANT

Until fall, a grasshopper
Chose to chirr;
With starvation as foe
When northeasters would blow,
And not even a gnat's residue
Or caterpillar's to chew,
She chirred a recurrent chant
Of want beside an ant,
Begging it to rescue her
With some seeds it could spare
Till the following year's fell.

"By August you shall have them all,
Interest and principal."
Share one's seeds? Now what is worse
For any ant to do?
Ours asked, "When fair, what brought you through?"
—"I sang for those who might pass by chance—
Night and day. Please do not be repelled."
—"Sang? A delight when someone has excelled.
A singer! Excellent. Now dance."

2. THE FOX AND THE CROW

On his airy perch among the branches
    Master Crow was holding cheese in his beak.
Master Fox, whose pose suggested fragrances,
    Said in language which of course I cannot speak,
        "Aha, superb Sir Ebony, well met.
How black! who else boasts your metallic jet!
        If your warbling were unique,
        Rest assured, as you are sleek,
One would say that our wood had hatched nightingales."
All aglow, Master Crow tried to run a few scales,
        Risking trills and intervals,
Dropping the prize as his huge beak sang false.
The fox pounced on the cheese and remarked, "My dear sir,
        Learn that every flatterer
    Lives at the flattered listener's cost:
A lesson worth more than the cheese that you lost."
        The tardy learner, smarting under ridicule,
Swore he'd learned his last lesson as somebody's fool.

22. THE OAK AND THE REED

The oak said to the reed, "You grow
Too unprotectedly. Nature has been unfair;
A tiny wren alights, and you are bending low;
    If a fitful breath of air
    Should freshen till ripples show,
    You heed her and lower your head;
My form not only makes shade where the sun would play
But like the Caucasus it does not sway.
    However it is buffeted.
Your so-called hurricanes are too faint to fear.
Would that you'd been born beneath this towering tent I've made,
    Which could afford you ample shade;
    Your hazards would not be severe:
    I'd shield you when the lightning played;
    But grow you will, time and again,
On the misty fringe of the wind's domain.
I perceive that you are grievously oppressed."
The rush said, "Bless you for fearing that I might be distressed;
    It is you alone whom the winds should alarm.
I bend and do not break. You've seemed consistently
    Impervious to harm—
    Erect when blasts rushed to and fro;
As for the end, who can foresee how things will go?"
Relentless wind was on them instantly—
    A fury of destruction
Which the North had nursed in some haunt known to none.
    The bulrush bent, but not the tree.
    Confusion rose to a roar,
    Until the hurricane threw prone
That thing of kingly height whose head had all but touched God's
                              throne—
Who had shot his root to the threshold of Death's door.

From B O O K   T W O

7. *BITCH AND FRIEND*

      A bitch who approached each hutch with a frown,
Since a-shiver to shelter an imminent litter,
Crouched perplexed till she'd coaxed from a vexed benefactor
A lean-to as a loan and in it lay down.
The benefactor returned but the barefaced borrower
Begged a fortnight's extension and still she lingered—
Must stay till her puppies no longer lumbered.
      Well, least said the better.
When that term had lapsed too, the friend made a plea
      For her house, her room, and bed;
The coaxer bared her teeth and said,
"I'm prepared to depart and with my family
      If you will turn us out of doors."
      The puppies were by then tall curs.

One certainly rues aid to the malevolent.
      If you'd recover what you lent,
      A physical blow is all they feel.
      You have to beg and then to beat.
      Yield but a foot to their appeal
      And find they have usurped four feet.

From B O O K   T H R E E

1. *THE MILLER, HIS SON, AND THE ASS*

To Monsieur de Maucrois

An aptitude for art, birthright of ancient Greece,
Made fables possible, and we have some of these;

Even so, irrespective of what we have read,
A few gleanings may still be harvested.
Given the wilderness of fancy anywhere,
Every author finds himself a discoverer.
Now here is a tale ingeniously constructed
For young Racan whom Malherbe as it were adopted—
Both heirs as well as rivals of Horace's lyre,
Apollo's sons, each a master whom we admire.
Exchanging inmost thoughts and queries when alone,
Since sure they would not be disturbed by anyone,
Racan began, "Might I ask if not a liberty,
That you tell me, for you have seen life thoroughly
And by now have come to know its every turning
As well as all I shall eventually be learning,
What course to pursue, now that I must choose at once.
You have known me well and my every circumstance.
Shall I live in the country, perhaps become a squire?
Try the army? Might court life be what I require?
Life has its bitterness and its beatitudes:
Marriage can drive you mad; war has its interludes.
If I did as I please, I'd know how to proceed.
But to friends, court, and the public, one must concede."
"You would please them all!" said Malherbe. "Quite unsound.
Consider this story in which my answer is found.
In what book I can't say—I was reading casually—
A miller and his son just short of maturity,
Not more than fifteen if I'm trustworthy there,
Had a donkey to sell and were going to the fair.
That the beast might seem fresh and show agility,
They cat-cradled his legs to a limb from a tree
And carried him suspended as though a chandelier:
Pathos personified, the poor pair were so queer!
The first person met, laughed until his sides ached
And asked, 'What is the farce they are going to act?
It's not the ass this time, who really is the dunce.'
The miller saw the point of the insult at once,

Set longears on his feet and bade the beast proceed.
It complained in its dialect. Contented on that score,
The miller, with son riding, was plodding as before,
Passed by three rich merchants they seemed to annoy.
The oldest called back in his loudest voice to the boy,
'My, oh my, get down, my fine youth, it is not just
That your old gray lackey follow in the dust!
Ride and have him walking? This must be corrected.'
The miller said, 'Good sirs, I'll do as you've directed.'
The younger bade the elder mount to meet the plaint,
Till three girls came along. One said, ' 'Twould try a saint;
A monster of injustice up there if you ask me—
Grizzled Bishop Bones with an air of majesty
At ease while his son walks! You'd think he'd have some pride.'
—'At ease,' said the miller. 'And why should years not ride?
The back's the best part of a goose. Be off. You heard.'
After more cross-firing and flinging back of a word,
Old age took heed and had the younger riding too—
Scarcely thirty steps till a third three came in view,
Who taunted the pair thus: 'Uneducated boors!
Beating an ass to death however much he endures:
Thin him down till he's merely a starved drudge's skin,
Goading an old friend who has served year out, year in;
Perhaps sell his drubbed hide at the fair when he drops.'
—'Bless me,' said the miller, 'there's a point at which one stops
Exhausting one's self trying to do as folk desire;
Accommodate one's self to the world and his sire?
Even patience gives out.' For fear the ass collapse,
The two then dismounted and walked some yards perhaps
When someone else they met, inquired, 'Is it the mode
For the ass to take his ease and master tramp the road?
Ought it to be the ass or man whom toil abases?
Asses, since such rarities, merit crystal cases;
Conserving donkey bones although their shoes wear thin.
Not Nicholas riding to Jeanne, whom he was hoping to win,
On his donkey as in the song, handed down from antiquity.

A trio of donkeys.' The miller said, 'I agree.
For once you are right; on my soul, I say so:
Hereafter accord me a blessing or a blow,
Be content or be rasped, till your patience is gone;
I shall do as I please,' and he did from then on.

"As for you, go to war; court kings' or Love's bans;
Live agog and a-flutter; be a squire who will not dance;
Politician, functionary; monk; have wife or none;
The world will be carping, no matter what you've done."

9. THE WOLF AND THE STORK

Wolves can outeat anyone;
Indeed at a festivity,
Such gluttony second to none
Almost ended fatally
When a bone choked a wolf as he gulped what he ate;
But happily since he was inarticulate,
A stork chanced to hear him groan,
Was besought by frowns to run and peer,
And ah, had soon relieved the beast of the bone;
Then, having done him a service, had no fear,
So asked him how compensate her.
"Compensate?" he inquired with bared teeth,
"A humorist, I infer!
You should be glad that you draw breath.
Thrust your beak down my throat and you somehow escaped
death?

Be off. You are unappreciative;
Shun my paws if you care to live."

11. THE FOX AND THE GRAPES

A fox of Gascon, though some say of Norman descent,
When starved till faint gazed up at a trellis to which grapes
were tied—
    Matured till they glowed with a purplish tint
    As though there were gems inside.
Now grapes were what our adventurer on strained haunches
chanced to crave,
    But because he could not reach the vine
He said, "These grapes are sour; I'll leave them for some knave."

Better, I think, than an embittered whine.

From BOOK FOUR

1. THE LION IN LOVE

To Mademoiselle de Sévigné

Mademoiselle—goddess instead—
In whom the Graces find a school
Although you are more beautiful,
Even if with averted head,
Might you not be entertained
By a tale that is unadorned—
Hearing with no more than a quiver
Of a lion whom Love knew how to conquer.
Love is a curious mastery,
In name alone a felicity.
Better know of than know the thing.
If too personal and thus trespassing,
I'm saying what may seem to you an offense,
A fable could not offend your ear.

This one, assured of your lenience,
Attests its devotion embodied here,
And kneels in sworn obedience.

Before their speech was obstructed,
Lions or such as were attracted
To young girls, sought an alliance.
Why not? since as paragons of puissance,
They were at that time knightly fellows
Of mettle and intelligence
Adorned by manes like haloes.
The point of the preamble follows.
A lion—one in a multitude—
Met in a meadow as he fared,
A shepherdess for whom he cared.
He sought to win her if he could,
Though the father would have preferred
A less ferocious son-in-law.
To consent undoubtedly was hard;
Fear meant that the alternate was barred.
Moreover, refuse and he foresaw
That some fine day the two might explain
Clandestine marriage as the chain
That fettered the lass, bewitched beyond cure,
By fashions conducive to hauteur,
And a fancy that shaggy shoulder fur
Made her willful lover handsomer.
The father with despair choked down,
Said though at heart constrained to frown,
"The child is a dainty one; better wait;
You might let your claw points scratch her
When your heavy forepaws touch her.
You could if not too importunate,
Have your claws clipped. And there in front,
See that your teeth are filed blunt,
Because a kiss might be enjoyed

By you the more, I should think,
If my daughter were not forced to shrink
Because improvidently annoyed."
The enthralled animal mellowed,
His mind's eyes having been shuttered.
Without teeth or claws it followed
That the fortress was shattered.
Dogs were loosed; defenses were gone:
The consequence was slight resistance.

Love, ah Love, when your slipknot's drawn,
We can but say, "Farewell, good sense."

2. THE SHEPHERD AND THE SEA

As carefree as his flock, it seems there was a man
Who lived by the sea and life was a delight.
    At shearing time his gains were slight
    But at least there would be gain.
Then, sad; he saw a trader's gorgeousness displayed,
Was thus lured to part with his one and only flock
And invest what he'd earned in a ship; but ah, the shock—
    Wrecked in return for all he'd paid.
He was hired to tend sheep that had been his property—
As merely a herd of course with no authority,
Since he had financed the sea with his cavalcade.
Thyrsis or Corydon as he had been formerly,
    Was now Hodge whom none but sheep obeyed.
But he had saved money presently,
    Bought back a few sheep of his own,
And then one morning when the wind had died down
And boats crept in so gently they did not even rock,
He said, "Ladies of the sea, find someone else to mock,
Might I suggest? since it's money you expect.
Bless me! no more ships of mine shall be wrecked!"

Not just a whimsy it has amused me to expand.

> This should help us to understand
> What one learns by experience—
> That you've more with a single sou in hand
> Than with promise of five some days hence.

That we be content with our situation has been shown:
To temptations which ambition and the sea intone,

> We must be deaf—our ears, citadels.

For one who gains from the sea she makes ten thousand groan—

> Promising mountains and miracles,

Providing storms and piracy. Stand stiff if you'd not be undone.

20. *THE MISER WHO LOST HIS HOARD*

Only use gives possession. Let me ask one question then
Of misers, since the obsession which dominates such men
Is to add and add more till they have a surplus,
What have they, after all, more than the rest of us?
Dead Diogenes has as much in his grave
As penurious persons have who save and save.
Here, Aesop's miser's hoard, which had been of no use,

> Should certainly warn all of us.

>   To profit by what he had,
He would have needed earthly immortality.
He did not own but was owned by the gold he coveted
When he buried it out of doors secretly—

>   His heart as well—having no other delight
>   Than to brood on it day and night.

His obsession with money soon became so bad,
Whether he ate or drank, if he came or went away,
There was scarcely a moment when his thoughts did not stray
To the spot in which the hoard had been interred.
A ditchdigger saw him there intermittently,
So suspected a hoard and stole it without a word.

Then, as before, our miser went and found vacuity;
Shed tears of despair, groaned and sighed till all could hear,
        Tore his hair and trembled with fear.
A person passing paused to ask why such misery;
        The man said, "Someone took my hoard from me."
—"Your hoard? Where should it be?"—"By that stone heretofore."
        —"But why? We are not at war.
Why so far away? Could you not have been satisfied
To hide it in your wall cupboard there at your side,
        Instead of take it quite so far?
Your trips to it might then have been regular."
—"Regular? Heavens, man! Use some of it every day?
        Spend more than might ever again come my way?
I would not have touched it."—"Tell me, sir, if you please,"
Asked Good Sense, "why you should feel such piercing pain,
Since the money was a thing from which you must refrain?
        Bury a stone in the place,
        And be just as well off again."

From BOOK FIVE

2. THE POT OF CLAY AND THE POT OF IRON

        A pot of iron's proposal
        That a clay pot fare afield,
        Met with a prompt refusal:
        "Any joy that journeys yield
        Is afforded by our warm hearth;
        Brittle pots of breakable earth
        Are inured to sacrifice,
        Since jostles are far from wise:
        I might be crushed by a blow;
        But don't feel that you should not go.

Since iron is accustomed to strain,
No reason why you should remain."
Then the other turned arguer
And said, "As for shocks you'd incur,
Or objects you saw to fear,
If you felt that you'd come too near,
I'd expose myself instead
And you'd not be buffeted."
The clay pot was satisfied
So they fared forth side by side—
The iron, and the clay one protected,
Each on three legs as pots are constructed.
Clipper-clap-clip they tried their luck
And then at each jolt conflicted
If even pebbles were struck.
The clay pot suffered, in less than fifty paces, the worst that could
befall—
Left by the iron pot in fragments so minute you could not count
them all
And with only himself to blame.

Take as an equal a person who is not,
And your fate may be the same
As that of the earthen pot.

13. *THE HEN THAT LAID THE GOLDEN EGGS*

Take all that is there and forfeit increment,
Is a truth too clear for argument
In the old fairy tale in which golden eggs were laid,
One a day. The poor owner would stare
At the hen, till sure there was gold in her to share,
Then killed, spread out the bird, and of course was repaid
By no more than would be found in an ordinary hen.

He had cut the magic chain and she'd never lay again.
　　　　Think of this when covetous!
How many we have seen in our own century
Reduced to poverty by striving hard to be
　　　　Prematurely prosperous.

16. *THE SERPENT AND THE FILE*

A snake, so they say, lived near a watchmaker
(Rather unfortunate for a man with just that work);
The serpent glided in for something to stay hunger.
　　　　However, his flickering fork
Could find nothing but a file to endanger.
Kindly, with anything but an injured air,
　　The file said, "Poor worm, aren't you courting despair?
　　　　A great fool, little snake, although small.
　　　　By the time my filings could yield
　　　　The fourth of an obol in all,
　　　　You would break your two teeth in.
　　　　Only Time's tooth wears me thin."

Now this is meant for you, vapid second-rate minds,
Good-for-nothings who try to harm worth of all kinds.
　　　　Your gnashed teeth imply nothing profound.
Do you think that you could leave a toothmark
　　　　On any masterwork?
Bite steel or burnished brass or dent the diamond?

From BOOK SIX

13. *THE FARMER AND THE ADDER*

　　　　Aesop tells how a countryman,
　　　　As imprudent as he was benevolent,

Had an estate he'd gone out to scan
One winter day, and observed as he went
A snake on the snow in a plight that was serious,
Mummied from head to tail till no longer dangerous.
He dared not delay; it would die if left there;
So the man picked it up, took it home, gave it care,
And failed to foresee the result of an action
In which compassion had been complete;
He stirred circulation by friction
And laid the maimed form near heat,
Which no sooner had tempered the torpid blood
Than animus stirred and grew livelier.
The adder hissed, raised its head as best it could,
Coiled, and made a long lunge toward where the farmer stood—
Its foster father who had been its rescuer.
The farmer said, "Ingrate! You'd be my murderer?
You shall die!" With indignation which nothing could foil,
He picked up his ax and the dastard was dead.
Two strokes made three snakes of the coil—
A body, a tail, and a head.
The pestilent thirds writhed together to rear
But of course could no longer adhere.

All should practice charity
Toward all? I've thrown some light on this.
Ingrates, I say with emphasis,
Will always die in agony.

17. *THE DOG WHO DROPPED SUBSTANCE FOR SHADOW*

Everyone is self-deceived:
Of all the fooled, agog to catch a phantom,
The number if you knew it would never be believed;
It is a permanent conundrum.

We ought to be reminded of Aesop's dog, who set out
With a bone, but, on seeing what he had in his mouth doubled
By water, dropped it for the shadow and just about
Drowned. The brook was instantly troubled;
      And having worn himself out, he'd neither substance nor
                                     shadow to thank
       Himself for on regaining the bank.

EPILOGUE TO BOOK SIX

       Our peregrination must end there.
       One's skin creeps when poets persevere.
       Don't press pith from core to perimeter;
       Take the flower of the subject, the thing that is rare.
       Besides, I'd best conserve my pen
       And energies to write again
       And sound another kind of praise.
       Love, who inspires my fantasies,
       Is restive and craves a change, he says—
       The tyrant whom I have to please.
Let Psyche be my theme again; Damon, you ask that I express
Her mourning and her joyousness.
       I shall try; I kindle when
       She bids me tune and touch my lute,
So long as Love does not torment me again,
       Setting similar tasks to execute!

From BOOK EIGHT

10. THE BEAR AND THE GARDEN-LOVER

A bear with fur that appeared to have been licked backward
Wandered a forest once where he alone had a lair.

This new Bellerophon, hid by thorns which pointed outward.
Had become deranged. Minds suffer disrepair
When every thought for years has been turned inward.
We prize witty byplay and reserve is still better,
But too much of either and health has soon suffered.
            No animal sought out the bear
            In coverts at all times sequestered,
            Until he had grown embittered
And, wearying of mere fatuity,
By now was submerged in gloom continually.
            He had a neighbor rather near,
            Whose own existence had seemed drear;
Who loved a parterre of which flowers were the core,
            And the care of fruit even more.
But horticulturalists need, besides work that is pleasant,
            Some shrewd choice spirit present.
When flowers speak, it is as poetry gives leave
            Here in this book; and bound to grieve,
Since hedged by silent greenery to tend,
The gardener thought one sunny day he'd seek a friend.
            Nursing some thought of the kind,
            The bear sought a similar end
            And the pair just missed collision
            Where their paths came in conjunction.
Numb with fear, how ever get away or stay there?
Better be a Gascon and disguise despair
In such a plight, so the man did not hang back or cower.
            Lures are beyond a mere bear's power
And this one said, "Visit my lair." The man said, 'Yonder bower,
Most noble one, is mine; what could be friendlier
Than sit on tender grass, sharing such plain refreshment
As native products laced with milk? Since it's an embarrassment
To lack what lordly bears would have as daily fare,
Accept what is here." The bear appeared flattered.
Each found, as he went, a friend was what most mattered;
Before they'd neared the door, they were inseparable.

As confidant, a beast seems dull.
Best live alone if wit can't flow,
And the gardener found the bear's reserve a blow,
But conducive to work, without sounds to distract.
Having game to be dressed, the bear, as it puttered,
Diligently chased or slaughtered
Pests that filled the air, and swarmed, to be exact,
Round his all too weary friend who lay down sleepy—
Pests—well, flies, speaking unscientifically.
One time as the gardener had forgot himself in dream
And a single fly had his nose at its mercy,
The poor indignant bear who had fought it vainly
Growled, "I'll crush that trespasser; I have evolved a scheme."
Killing flies was his chore, so as good as his word,
The bear hurled a cobble and made sure it was hurled hard,
Crushing a friend's head to rid him of a pest.
With bad logic, fair aim disgraces us the more;
He'd murdered someone dear, to guarantee his friend rest.

Intimates should be feared who lack perspicacity;
Choose wisdom, even in an enemy.

15. THE RAT AND THE ELEPHANT

I fear that appearances are worshiped throughout France:
Whereas pre-eminence perchance
Merely means a pushing person.
An extremely French folly—
A weakness of which we have more than our share—
Whereas false pride, I'd say, has been the Spaniard's snare.
To be epigrammatical,
They're foolish folk; we're comical.
Well, I've put us in this tale
Which came to mind as usable.

A mite of a rat was mocking an elephant
As it moved slowly by, majestically aslant,
>   Valued from antiquity,
>   Towering in draped solemnity
>   While bearing along in majesty
>   A queen of the Levant—
>   With her dog, her cat, and sycophant,
Her parakeet, monkey, anything she might want—
>   On their way to relics they wished to see.
>   But the rat was not one whom weight could daunt
And asked why observers should praise mere size.
"Who cares how much space something occupies?"
He said. "Size does not make a thing significant!
All crowding near an elephant? Why must I worship him?
Servile to brute force at which mere tots might faint?
Should persons such as I admire his heavy limb?
>   I pander to an elephant!"
>   About to prolong his soliloquy
>   When the cat broke from captivity
>   And instantly proved what her victim would grant:
>   That a rat is not an elephant.

From BOOK NINE

7. *THE MOUSE METAMORPHOSED INTO A MAID*

A mouse fell from a screech-owl's beak—a thing I can not pretend
>   To be Hindoo enough to have cared
To pick up. But a Brahmin, as I can well believe, straightened
>   The fur which the beak had marred.
>   Each country's code is what is preferred.
>   We are not much concerned about pain

Which a mouse endures, yet a Brahmin would as soon disdain
         A relative's; feeling that we submit to a fate
         That transforms us at death, to a worm
Or beast, and lends even kings a transition state—
A tenet Pythogoras chose to affirm,
Deduced from that system, of which he was a ponderer.
Based on the same belief, the Brahmin sought a sorcerer,
Eager to right what had been unfair and procure a key
To restore to the mouse her true identity.
         Well, there she was, a girl and real,
Of about fifteen, who was so irresistible
Priam's son would have toiled harder still to reward her
Than for Helen who threw the whole world in disorder.
The Brahmin said to her, marveling at the miracle—
         At charm so great that it scarcely seemed true,
"You have but to choose. Any suitor I know
         Contends for the honor of marrying you."
         —"In that case," she said, "the most powerful;
         I would choose the strongest I knew."
Kneeling, the Brahmin pled, "Sun, it shall be you.
         Be my heir; share my inheritance."
         —"No, a cloud intervening," it said,
"Would be stronger than I and I be discredited.
         Choose the cloud for her defense."
—"Very well," said the Brahmin to the cloud, sailing on,
"Were you meant for her?"—"Alas," it answered, "not the one.
The wind drives me from place to place; I'm whirled through the
                                                  void:
I must not anger Boreas; I might be destroyed."
         The distraught Brahmin cried
         To the wind that blew: "O Wind, abide.
         Be embraced by my child in whom graces dwell."
Boreas complied with a rush, but met a mountainside.
         Deterred lest interests coincide,
The ground demurred and said: "I might incur trouble—
         Would be unwise—since a rat who was incommoded

114 / FABLES OF LA FONTAINE

Might weaken me by some tunnel he needed."
        Rat! at the word, Love cast his spell
        On an ear attuned. Wed? at last she knew.
        A rat! a rat! Can names not do
        Love service? Ah, you follow well:
        Silence here between us two.

We retain the traits of the place from which we came. This tale
Bears me out; but a nearer view would seem good
Of what sophism never had quite understood:
We all love sun; yet more, what has a heart and will.
But affirm the premise? queer supposition
That when devoured by fleas, giants are outdone!
The rat would have had to transfer the maid in his care
        And call a cat; the cat, a wolf-hound;
        The hound, a wolf. Carried around
        By a force that was circular,
Pilpay would bear the maid to the sun's infinitude
Where the sun would blaze in endless beatitude.
Well, return if we can, to metamorphosis;
The Brahmin's sorcerer, as bearing upon this,
Had not proved anything but man's foolhardihood,
In fact had shown that the Brahmin had been wrong
        In supposing, and far too long,
That man and worms and mice have in unison
Sister souls of identical origin—
        By birth equally exempt
        From change, whose diverse physiques, you'll own,
        Have gradually won
        Reverence or contempt.
Explain how a lass so fair, incomparably made,
        Could not earn for herself redress
And have married the sun. Fur tempted her caress.

        Now mouse and girl—both have been well weighed
And we've found them, as we have compared their souls,
        As far apart as opposite poles.

We are what we were at birth, and each trait has remained
In conformity with earth's and with heaven's logic:
      Be the devil's tool, resort to black magic,
None can diverge from the ends which Heaven foreordained.

From BOOK TWELVE

4. *TO HIS GRACE THE DUKE OF BURGUNDY*

Who requested of Monsieur de La Fontaine a Fable to be called

THE CAT AND THE MOUSE

Desiring to show a young prince her esteem
      And bow here literarily,
Fame asks that Cat and Mouse be my theme.
      Cat and Mouse—let me see.

Ought I to portray someone beautiful
And charming, but so sportive and unmerciful
That she tortures the person in captivity
      As cats tease mice they will not free?

Or should I take as my theme the whims of Fate?
Nothing more to the point than demonstrate
How smiling Fortune treats folk contradictorily,
      As cats treat mice they will not free.

Or should some king, a great one, be my simile,
At whose word even Fortune's wheel stands still,
Undeterred by all sorts of hostility,
Who makes sport of the mightiest if he will,
      As cats toss mice they will not free.

But the windings of my thought have imperceptibly
Brought me out where each step I take will be a loss
If I let myself drone on suicidally
And make my Muse a mouse for the young prince to toss,
   Like one the cat pretends to free.

10. CRAYFISH AND DAUGHTER

The almost backward walk of crayfishes,
Rear end first, recalls a philosopher;
And oarsmen face the stern; sound strategists no less
Will concentrate their power while making noise elsewhere,
At another point from the one where they are,
To magnetize an adversary here or there.
My metaphor, though slight, portrays a heroic man;
Or should I say one who has done what few have done—
Who alone dispersed a hundred-headed pact
And conceals what he'll do or not, from everyone,
Preserving his secret till an accomplished fact.
Don't probe for plans he makes and does not care to give away;
When Fate ordains results we might as well obey:
As combined rains descend in a roaring waterfall,
A hundred gods are powerless when matched with Jupiter.
Together, destiny and our King concur
To rule the universe. Now for our tale, lest I pall:

A crayfish's mother said to her one day,
"My, my, you are grotesque! Why must you lurch awry?"
—"Much like yourself!" rejoined her progeny.
"Since shaped like my mother, how should I walk differently?
When you advance backward, should I walk forward?"
   And logically the standard
   Has a far-reaching effect
   Upon all able to reflect.
For good or ill, it can make wits lag or glow
Though for the most part lag. But a moment ago

I spoke of how crayfish walk. It is how most wars are won;
      Yet a method we had better shun
      Unless precisely apropos.

16. *THE WOODS AND THE WOODMAN*

A woodcutter had split or perhaps had mislaid
The ax-handle to which he had fitted the blade.
Replacing it meant that the man was delayed
And the forest was spared from which wood was conveyed.
      A suppliant then, as his manner made plain,
      The man asked the woods to afford him again
      A branch, just one which he would take
      For one more haft which he would make
And he would fell trees in a place farther on,
Permitting oaks and pines to flourish where they'd grown,
Since everyone admired their vast height and fair form.
This was a service the woods did without alarm,
Followed by deep regret, since with his ax helved as before,
      The hard wretch slashed to the core,
      The very trees that had staunched his grief,
      Felling trunks he could barely span
      Although they groaned as their sap ran—
      Martyred to benefit a thief.

Ingrates are typical of our world everywhere—
Downright turncoats against him who made them his care.
I tire of laboring the point. Show me the kindly wood
      That has not known ingratitude
      And could not tell what I'm telling you.
Irony, alas, for one to argue long and hard.
      Ingratitude and violence too,
      Are evils nothing can retard.

18. THE FOX AND THE TURKEYS

       Baiting a fox who'd spring in air,
Some turkeys had perched in a tree, their citadel.
The furred foe was trotting up near and circling far,
       Scanning each feathered sentinel;
Then snarled, "How now! I, set at naught by turkeycocks!
Shallow gobblers defy an experienced fox!
Never, by all the gods, no"; and caught them as will appear.
The moon glared so white that his every move was clear;
The birds could see as plainly as if it were noon,
Yet he was used to vigils despite a brilliant moon,
With tricks in his bag to offset any plight.
His forepaws trod air as he made his body light;
He'd feign that death had cut him short, then in a flash would rise;
       Harlequin in each new disguise
       Was not so varied a multitude.
He'd willow out his tail like flame that sinks and flies;
       His effort knew no interlude;
He did so well not a turkey could close its eyes.
As he trotted to and fro, each overweary bird
       Would stare till its scared eyes blurred.
The poor things held to the perch so dizzily
That one by one the flock fell; each was borne from the tree
To Master Fox's lair; he took nearly half of them home,
Indeed, had endless turkeys for his use.

Defeat is a thing which constant fear can induce.
       Beg for trouble and it will come.

20. THE SCYTHIAN PHILOSOPHER

Once a philosopher famed for austerity,
Left Scythia that he might taste luxury
And sailed to Greece where he met in his wanderings

A sage like the one Vergil has made memorable—
Who seemed a king or god, remote from mundane things,
Since like the gods he was at peace and all seemed well.
Now a garden enabled his life to expand
And the Scythian found him pruning hook in hand
Lopping here and there what looked unprofitable.
He sundered and slendered, curtailing this and that,
      Careful that not a dead twig be spared;
Then for care to excess, Nature paid a sure reward.
      "But are you not inconsiderate?"
The Scythian inquired. He said, "Is it good
To denude a tree of twigs and leave it scarcely one?
Lay down your pruning hook; your onslaught is too rude.
      Permit Time to do what needs to be done:
Dead wood will soon be adrift on the Styx' dark flood."
The sage said, "Remove sere boughs and when they are gone,
      One has benefited what remain."
The Scythian returned to his bleak shore,
Seized his own pruning hook, was at work hour on hour,
Enjoining upon any in the vicinity
      That they work—the whole community.
He sheared off whatever was beautiful,
Indiscriminately trimmed and cut down,
      Persevering in reduction
      Beneath new moons and full
Till none of his trees could bear.

      In this Scythian
      We have the injudicious man
      Or so-called Stoic, who would restrain
His best emotions along with the depraved—
      Renouncing each innocent thing that he craved.
As for me, such perverted logic is my bane.
Don't smother the fire in my heart which makes life dear;
Do not snuff me out yet. I'm not laid on my bier.

From PREDILECTIONS

HUMILITY, CONCENTRATION, AND GUSTO

In times like these we are tempted to disregard anything that has not a direct bearing on freedom; or should I say, an obvious bearing, for what is more persuasive than poetry, though, as Robert Frost says, it works obliquely and delicately. Commander King-Hall, in his book *Total Victory*, is really saying that the pen is the sword when he says the object of war is to persuade the enemy to change his mind.

Three foremost aids to persuasion which occur to me are humility, concentration, and gusto. Our lack of humility, together with anxiety, has perhaps stood in the way of initial liking for Caesar's *Commentaries*, which now seem to me masterpieces. I was originally like the Hill School boy to whom I referred in one of my pieces of verse, who translated *summa diligentia* (with all speed): Caesar crossed the Alps on the top of a diligence.

In Caxton, humility seems to be a judicious modesty, which is rather different from humility. Nevertheless, could anything be more persuasive than the preface to his *Aeneid*, where he says, "Some desired me to use olde and homely termes . . . and some the most curyous termes that I could fynde. And thus between playn, rude and curyous, I stande abasshed"? Daniel Berkeley Updike has always seemed to me a phenomenon of eloquence because of the quiet objectiveness of his writing. And what he says of printing applies equally to poetry. It is true, is it not, that "style does not depend on decoration but on simplicity and proportion"? Nor can we dignify confusion by calling it baroque. Here, I may say, I am preaching to myself, since, when I am as complete as I like to be, I seem unable to get an effect plain enough.

We don't want war, but it does conduce to humility; as someone said in the foreword to an exhibition catalogue of his work, "With what shall the artist arm himself save with his humility?" Humility, indeed, is armor, for it realizes that it is impossible to be original, in the sense of doing something that has never been thought of before. Originality is in any case a by-product of sincerity; that is to say, of feeling that is honest and accordingly rejects anything that might cloud the impression, such as unnecessary commas, modifying clauses, or delayed predicates.

Concentration avoids adverbial intensives such as "definitely," "positively," or "absolutely." As for commas, nothing can be more stultifying than needlessly overaccented pauses. Defoe, speaking in so low a key that there is a fascinatioin about the mere understatement, is for me one of the most persuasive of writers. For instance, in the passage about the pickpocket in *The Life of Colonel Jacque*, he has the Colonel say to the pickpocket, "Must we have it all? Must a man have none of it again, that lost it?" But persuasiveness has not died with Defoe; E. E. Cummings' "little man in a hurry" (254, *No Thanks*) has not a comma in it, but by the careful ordering of the words there is not an equivocal emphasis:

> little man
> (in a hurry
> full of an
> important worry)
> halt stop forget relax
>
> wait

And James Laughlin, the author of *Some Natural Things*, is eminent in this respect, his "Above the City" being an instance of inherent emphasis:

> You know our office on the 18th
> floor of the Salmon Tower looks
> right out on the
>
> Empire State & it just happened
> we were finishing up some
> late invoices on

a new book that Saturday morning
when a bomber roared through the
    mist and crashed

flames poured from the windows
into the drifting clouds & sirens
    screamed down in

the streets below it was unearthly
but you know the strangest thing
    we realized that

none of us were much surprised because we'd always known that those
    two Paragons of

progress sooner or later would per-
form before our eyes this demon-
    stration of their
    true relationship

Concentration—indispensable to persuasion—may feel to itself crystal clear, yet be through its very compression the opposite, and William Empson's attitude to ambiguity does not extenuate defeat. Graham Greene once said, in reviewing a play of Gorki's, "Confusion is really the plot. A meat-merchant and a miller are introduced, whom one never succeeds in identifying even in the end." I myself, however, would rather be told too little than too much. The question then arises, How obscure may one be? And I suppose one should not be consciously obscure at all. In any case, a poem is a concentrate and has, as W. H. Auden says, "an immediate meaning and a possible meaning; as in the line,

a wedged hole ages in a bodkin's eye

where you have forever in microscopic space; and when George Herbert says,

I gave to Hope a watch of mine,
But he an anchor gave to me,

the watch suggests both the brevity of life and the longness of it; and an anchor makes you secure but holds you back."

I am prepossessed by the impassioned explicitness of the Federal Reserve Board of New York's letter regarding certain counterfeits, described by the Secret Service:

> $20 FEDERAL RESERVE NOTE . . . faint crayon marks have been used to simulate genuine fibre. . . . In the Treasury Seal, magnification reveals that a green dot immediately under the center of the arm of the balance scales blends with the arm whereas it should be distinctly separate. Also, the left end of the right-hand scale pan extends beyond the point where the left chain touches the pan. In the genuine, the pan ends where it touches the chain. The serial numbers are thicker than the genuine, and the prefix letter "G" is sufficiently defective to be mistaken for a "C" at first glance, . . . the letters "ry" in "Secretary" are joined together. In "Treasury" there is a tiny black dot just above the first downstroke in the letter "u." The back of the note, although of good workmanship, is printed in a green much darker than that used for genuine currency.
>
> December 13, 1948   Alfred M. Olsen, Cashier

I am tempted to dwell on the infectiousness of such matters, but shall return to verse. You remember, in Edward Lear's "The Owl and the Pussy-Cat," they said:

> "Dear Pig, are you willing to sell for a shilling
> Your ring?" Said the Piggy, "I will."

The word "Piggy" is altered from "Pig" to "Piggy" to fit the rhythm but is, even so, a virtue, as contributing gusto; and I never tire of Leigh Hunt's lines about the fighting lions: "A wind went with their paws." Continuing with cats, T. S. Eliot's account of "Mungojerrie and Rumpelteazer," "a very notorious couple of cats," is, like its companion pieces, a study in gusto throughout:

> If a tile or two came loose on the roof,
> Which presently ceased to be waterproof,
>
> .   .   .
>
> Or after supper one of the girls
> Suddenly missed her Woolworth pearls:

Then the family would say: "It's that horrible cat!
 It was Mungojerrie—or Rumpelteazer!"
—And most of the time they left it at that.

The words "By you" constitute a yet more persuasive instance of
gusto, in T. S. Eliot's tribute to Walter de la Mare upon Mr. de
la Mare's seventy-fifth birthday:

When the nocturnal traveller can arouse
No sleeper by his call; or when by chance
An empty face peers from an empty house,

By whom: and by what means, was this designed?
The whispered incantation which allows
Free passage to the phantoms of the mind?

By you; by those deceptive cadences
Wherewith the common measure is refined;
By conscious art practiced with natural ease;

By the delicate invisible web you wove—
An inexplicable mystery of sound.

Dr. Maurice Bowra, pausing upon the query, Can we have
poetry without emotion? seemed to think not; however, suggested
that it is not overperverse to regard Cowper's "The Snail" as a
thing of gusto although the poem has been dismissed as mere
description:

Give but his horns the slightest touch,
His self-collective power is such,
He shrinks into his house with much
            Displeasure.

Where'er he dwells, he dwells alone.
Except himself, has chattels none,
Well satisfied to be his own
            Whole treasure.

Thus hermit-like his life he leads,
Nor partner of his banquet needs,

And if he meets one, only feeds
The faster.

Who seeks him must be worse than blind,
He and his house are so combined,
If finding it, he fails to find
Its master.

Together with the helpless sincerity which precipitates a poem, there is that domination of phrase referred to by Christopher Smart as "impression." "Impression," he says, "is the gift of Almighty God, by which genius is empowered to throw an emphasis upon a word in such wise that it cannot escape any reader of good sense." Gusto, in Smart, authorized as oddities what in someone else might seem effrontery; the line in Psalm 147, for instance, about Jehovah: "He deals the beasts their food."

To everything that moves and lives,
Foot, fin, or feather, meat He gives,
He deals the beasts their food.

And in "A Song to David":

Strong is the lion—like a coal
His eyeball—like a bastion's mole,
His chest against the foes:
.   .   .
But stronger still, in earth and air
And in the sea, the man of pray'r,
And far beneath the tide;
And in the seat to faith assign'd
Where ask is have, where seek is find,
Where knock is open wide.

With regard to emphasis in Biblical speech, there is a curious unalterableness about the statement by the Apostle James: The flower "falleth and the grace of the fashion of it perisheth." Substitute, "the grace of its fashion perisheth," and overconscious correctness is weaker than the actual version, in which eloquence escapes grandiloquence by virtue of gusto.

Spenser is reprehended for coining words to suit the rhyme, but gusto in even the least felicitous of his defiances convicts the objecter of captiousness, I think, as in *The Shepheards Calender* (the "Chase After Love")—the part about "the swayne with spotted winges, like Peacocks trayne"—the impulsive intimacy of the word "pumies" substituted for a repetition of pumie stones brings the whole thing to life:

> I levelde againe
> And shott at him with might and maine,
>   As thicke as it had hayled.
> So long I shott, that al was spent;
> Tho pumie stones I hastly hent
>   And threwe; but nought availed:
> He was so wimble and so wight,
> From bough to bough he lepped light,
>   And oft the pumies latched.

In any matter pertaining to writing, we should remember that major value outweighs minor defects, and have considerable patience with modifications of form, such as the embodied climax and subsiding last line. Wallace Stevens is particularly scrupulous against injuring an effect to make it fit a stated mode, and has

> . . . iceberg settings satirize
>
>   .   .   .
>
> The demon that cannot be himself.

Beaumarchais, in saying, "A thing too silly to be said can be sung," was just being picturesque, but recordings of poetry convince one that naturalness is indispensable. One can, however, be careful that similar tones do not confuse the ear, such as "some" and "sun," and "injustice" with "and justice"; the natural wording of uninhibited urgency, at its best, seeming really to write the poem ' in pauses, as in Walter de la Mare's lines about the beautiful lady, the epitaph:

> Here lies a most beautiful lady,
> Light of step and heart was she;
> I think she was the most beautiful lady
> That ever was in the West Country.

All of which is to say that gusto thrives on freedom, and freedom in art, as in life, is the result of a discipline imposed by ourselves. Moreover, any writer overwhelmingly honest about pleasing himself is almost sure to please others. You recall Ezra Pound's remark? "The great writer is always the plodder; it's the ephemeral writer that has to get on with the job." In a certain account by Padraic Colum of Irish storytelling, "Hindered characters," he remarked parenthetically, "seldom have mothers in Irish stories, but they all have grandmothers"—a statement borrowed by me for something I was about to write. The words have to come in just that order or they aren't pithy. Indeed, in Mr. Colum's telling of the story of Earl Gerald, gusto as objectified made the unbelievable doings of an enchanter excitingly circumstantial.

To summarize: Humility is an indispensable ally, enabling concentration to heighten gusto. There are always objecters, but we must not be sensitive about not being liked or not being printed. David Low, the cartoonist, when carped at, said, "Ah, well—" But he has never compromised; he goes right on doing what idiosyncrasy tells him to do. The thing is to see the vision and not deny it; to care and admit that we do.

HENRY JAMES AS A CHARACTERISTIC AMERICAN

To say that "the superlative American" and the characteristic American are not the same thing perhaps defrauds anticipation, yet one must admit that it is not in the accepted sense that Henry James was "big" and did things in a big way. But he possessed the instinct to amass and reiterate, and is the rediscerned Small Boy who had from the first seen Europe as a verification of what in its native surroundings his "supersensitive nostril" fitfully detected and liked. Often he is those elements in American life—as locality and as character—which he recurrently studied and to which he never tired of assigning a meaning.

Underlying any variant of Americanism in Henry James's work is the doctrine, embodied as advice to Christopher Newman, "Don't try to be anyone else"; if you triumph, "let it then be all you." The native Madame de Mauves says to Euphemia, "You seem to me so all of a piece that I am afraid that if I advise you, I shall spoil you," and Hawthorne was dear to Henry James because he "proved to what a use American matter could be put by an American hand. . . . An American could be an artist, one of the finest, without 'going outside' about it . . . ; quite, in fact, as if Hawthorne had become one just by being American enough."

An air of rurality, as of Moses Primrose at the fair, struck Henry James in his compatriots, and a garment worn in his own childhood revealed "that we were somehow *queer*." Thackeray, he says, "though he laid on my shoulder the hand of benevolence, bent on my native costume the spectacles of wonder." On his return from Europe, James marveled at the hats men wore, but it is hard to be certain that the knowledge-seeking American in Europe is quite so unconsciously a bumpkin as Henry James depicts him. When Newman has said, "I began to earn my living when I was almost a baby," and Madame de Bellegarde says, "You began to earn your living in the cradle?" the retort, "Well, madam, I'm not absolutely convinced I *had* a cradle," savors of the connoisseur. Since, however, it is over-difficult for Henry James, in portrayals of us, not to be portraying himself, there is even in his rendering of the callow American a tightening of the consciousness that hampers his portrayal of immaturity.

"I am not a scoffer," the fellow countryman says to Theobald, the American painter, and if it were a question of being either evasive or ridiculous, James would prefer to seem ridiculous. His respectful humility toward emotion is brave, and in diffidence, reserve, and strong feeling, he reminds one of Whittier, another literary bachelor whom the most ardent sadist has not been able to soil. We remember his sense of responsibility for the United States during the World War, and his saying of the Civil War, in *Notes of a Son and Brother*, "the drama of the War . . . had become a habit for us without ceasing to be a strain. I am sure I thought more things under that head . . . than I thought in all other connections together." What is said in the same book of the death of Mary Temple, the cousin who so greatly "had a sense for verity of character and play of life in others," is an instance of reverent, and almost reverend, feeling that would defend him against the charge of casualness in anything, if ever one were inclined to make it. It is not the artist, but responsibility for living and for family, that wonders here about death and has about "those we have seen beaten, this sense that it was not for nothing they missed the ampler experience . . . since dire as their defeat may have been, we don't see them . . . at peace with victory." Things for Henry James glow, flush, glimmer, vibrate, shine, hum, bristle, reverberate. Joy, bliss, ecstasies, intoxication, a sense of trembling in every limb, a shattering first glimpse, a hanging on the prolonged silence of an editor; and as a child at Mr. Burton's small theater in Chambers Street, his wondering, not if the curtain would rise, but "if one could exist till then"; the bonfires of his imagination, his pleasure in the "tender sea-green" or "rustling rose-color" of a seriously best dress, are too live to countenance his fear that he was giving us "an inch of canvass and an acre of embroidery."

Idealism which was willing to make sacrifices for its self-preservation was always an element in the conjuring wand of Henry James. He felt about the later America "like one who has seen a ghost in his safe old house." Of "Independence Hall . . . and its dignity not to be uttered, . . . spreading staircase and long-drawn upper gallery, . . . one of those rare precincts of the past against which the present has kept beating in vain," he says, "nothing . . . would induce me to revisit . . . the object I so fondly evoke." He would not risk disturbing his recollections of *The Wonder-Book* and *Tanglewood Tales* by rereading them, and Dickens "always remained better than the taste of overhauling him." The aura is more than the thing. New Hampshire in September was "so *delicately* Arcadian, like . . . an old legend, an old love-story in fifteen volumes," and "Newport, . . . the dainty isle of Aquidneck," and "its perpetually embayed promontories of mossy rock," had "ingenuous old-time distinction . . . too latent and too modest for notation." Exasperated by the later superficiality of New York's determination "to blight the superstition of rest," he termed the public libraries "mast-heads on which spent birds sometimes alight in the expanses of ocean," and thought Washington Irving's Sunnyside, with its "deep, long lane, winding, embanked, overarched, such an old-world lane as one scarce ever meets in America, . . . easy for everything but rushing about and being rushed at." The "fatal and sacred" enjoyment of England "buried in the soil of our primary culture" leads him to regard London as "the great distributing heart of our traditional life"; to say of Oxford, "No other spot in Europe extorts from our barbarous hearts so passionate an admiration"; and for the two Americans in "hedgy Worcestershire" beneath an "English sky bursting into a storm of light or melting into a drizzle of silver, . . . nothing was wanting; the shaggy, mouse-colored donkey, nosing the turf, . . . the towering ploughman with his white smock-frock, puckered on chest and back." "We greeted these things," one says, "as children greet the loved pictures in a story-book, lost and mourned and found again . . . a gray, gray tower, a huge black yew, a cluster of village graves, with crooked headstones. . . . My companion was overcome. . . . How it makes a Sunday where it stands!"

Henry James's warmth is clearly of our doting native variety. "Europe had been romantic years before, because she was different from America," he said, "wherefore America would now be romantic because she was different from Europe." His imagination had always included Europe; he had not been estranged by travel nor changed by any "love-philtre or fear-philtre" intenser than those he had received in New York, Newport, or our American Cambridge. "Culture as I hold, is a matter of attitude quite as much as of opportunity," he said in *Notes of a Son and Brother*, and "one's supreme relation, as one had always put it, was one's relation to one's country." In alluding to "our barbarous hearts" he had, of course, no thought of being taken at his word—any more than Mrs. Cleve did when abusing America—and even in the disillusions attendant upon return to this country, he betrayed a parentally local satisfaction in the way American girls dressed.

Nationally and internationally "the sensitive citizen," he felt that patriotism was a matter of knowing a country by getting the clue. Our understanding of human relations has grown—more perhaps than we realize in the last twenty years; and when Henry James disappoints us by retaining the Northerner's feeling about the Confederate, we must not make him directly contemporary, any more than we dispute his spelling "peanut" with a hyphen. He had had no contact with the South, and all the bother-taking Henry James needed for doing justice to feeling was opportunity to feel.

"Great things . . . have been done by solitary workers," he said, "but with double the pains they would have cost if they had been produced in more genial circumstances." Education for him, in a large sense, was conversation. Speaking of Cambridge, he said, "When the Norton woods, nearby, massed themselves in scarlet and orange, and when to penetrate and mount a stair and knock at a door, and, enjoying response, then sink into a window-bench and inhale at once the vague golden November and the thick suggestion of the room where nascent 'thought' had again and again piped or wailed, was to taste as I had never done before, the poetry of the prime initiation and of associated growth."

We observe in the memoirs, treasured American types: "silent Vanderpool, . . . incorruptibly and exquisitely dumb," who looked so as if he came from 'good people,'. . . the very finest flower of shyness, . . . a true welter of modesty, not a grain of it anything stiffer—"; "the ardent and delicate and firm John May" —student at Harvard; and there was Robert Temple, a cousin, "with a mind almost elegantly impudent, . . . as if we had owed him to Thackeray"; and Mary Temple, " 'natural' to an effect of perfect felicity, . . . all straightness and charming tossed head, with long light and yet almost sliding steps and a large light post- poning laugh." There was "a widowed grandmother who dispensed an hospitality seemingly as joyless as it was certainly boundless," and Uncle Albert, a kinsman who was " 'Mr.' to his own wife . . . his hair bristling up almost in short-horn fashion at the sides," with "long, slightly equine countenance, his eyebrows ever elevated as in the curiosity of alarm."

A child is not a student of "history and custom, . . . manners and types"; but to say that Henry James as a child was "a-throb" with the instinct for meanings barely suggests the formidable paraphernalia which he was even then gathering. It is in "the waste of time, of passion, of curiosity, of contact—that true initiation resides," he said later; and no scene, strange accent, no adventure—experienced or vicarious—was irrelevant. When older, he alluded to "the maidenly letters" of Emerson; but in New York, Emerson had been strange and wonderful to the child he had invited "to draw near to him, off the hearth-rug." He was "an apparition sinuously and elegantly slim, . . . commanding a tone alien to any we heard round about"; and the schoolmate Louis De Coppet, in "his French treatment of certain of our native local names, Ohio and Iowa for instance, which he rendered . . . O-ee-oh and Ee-o-wah, . . . opened vistas." He said, "There hung about the Wards, to my sense, that atmosphere of apples and nuts . . . and jack-knives and 'squrruls,' of domestic Bible-reading and attendance at 'evening lecture,' of the fear of parental discipline and the cultivated art of dodging it, combined with great personal toughness and hardihood"; and there was " 'Stiffy' Norcom . . . whom we supposed gorgeous. . . . (Divided I was, I recall, between the dread and the glory of being so greeted, 'Well, Stiffy—!' as a penalty for the least attempt at personal adornment.)"

"You cannot make a man feel low," his Christopher Newman says, "unless you can make him feel base," and "a good conscience" is a pebble with which Henry James is extremely fond of arming his Davids. Longmore's "truth-telling eyes" are that in him which puzzled and tormented the Baron. "They judged him, they mocked him, they eluded him, they threatened him, they triumphed over him, they treated him as no pair of eyes had ever treated him." In every photograph of Henry James that we have, the thing that arrests one is a kind of terrible truthfulness. We feel also, in the letters and memoirs, that "almost indescribable naturalness" which seemed to him typical of his Albany relatives; a naturalness which disappears in the fancy writing of his imitators. If good-nature and reciprocity are American traits, Henry James was a characteristic American—too much one when he patiently suffered unsuitable persons to write to him, call on him, and give him their "work." Politeness in him was "more than a form of luxurious egotism" and was in keeping with the self-effacing determination to remain a devotee of devotees to George Eliot "for his own wanton joy," though unwittingly requested to "take away, please, away, away!" two books he had written. (Mrs. Greville had lent the books as introductory, previous to her calling with Henry James on the Leweses, but no connection was noticed between books and visitor.) The same ardor appears in the account of his meeting with Dickens. He speaks of "the extremely handsome face . . . which met my dumb homage with a straight inscrutability. . . . It hadn't been the least important that we should have shaken hands or exchanged platitudes. . . . It was as if I had carried off my strange treasure just exactly from under the merciless military eye—placed there on guard of the secret. All of which I recount for illustration of the force of action, unless I call it passion, that may reside in a single pulse of time."

Henry James belongs to "the race which has the credit of knowing best, at home and abroad, how to make itself comfortable," but there was in him an ascetic strain, which caused him to make Longmore think with disgust of the Baron's friend, who "filled the air with the odor of heliotrope"; and Eugene Pickering's American friend found "something painful in the spectacle of absolute inthralment, even to an excellent cause." Freedom, yes. The confidant, in comparing himself compassionately with the Eugene of their schooldays, says, "I could go out to play alone, I could button my jacket myself, and sit up till I was sleepy." Yet the I of the original had not "been exposed on breezy uplands under the she-wolf of competition," and there was not about him "the impertinent odor of trade." Some persons have grudged Henry James his freedom and have called it leisure; but as Theobald, the American painter, said of art, "If we work for her, we must often pause." Of *The Tragic Muse*, James said in a letter, "I took long and patient and careful trouble which no creature will recognize"; and we may declare of him as he did of John La Farge, "one was . . . never to have seen a subtler mind or a more generously wasteful passion, in other words a sincerer one." Reverting to the past of his own life, he was overpowered by "the personal image unextinct" and said, "It presents itself, I feel, beyond reason and yet if I turn from it the ease is less."

There was in him "the rapture of observation," but more unequivocally even than that, affection for family and country. "I was to live to go back with wonder and admiration," he says, "to the quantity of secreted thought in our daily medium, the quality of intellectual passion, the force of cogitation and aspiration, as to the explanation both of a thousand surface incoherences and a thousand felt felicities." Family was the setting for his country, and the town was all but synonymous with family; as would appear in what is said of "the family-party smallness of old New York, those happy limits that could make us all care . . . for the same thing at once." It "is always a matter of winter twilight, fire-light, lamplight." "We were surely all gentle and generous to-gether, floating in such a clean light social order, sweetly proof against ennui." "The social scheme, as we knew it, was, in its careless charity, worthy of the golden age . . . the fruits dropped right upon the board to which we flocked together, the least of us and the greatest"; "our parents . . . never caring much for things we couldn't care for and generally holding that what was good to them would be also good for their children." A father is a safe symbol of patriotism when one can remember him as "genially alert and expert"—when "human fellowship" is "the expression that was perhaps oftenest on his lips and his pen." "We need never fear not to be good enough," Henry James says, "if only we were social enough," and he recalls his mother as so participatingly unremote that he can say, "I think we almost contested her being separate enough to be proud of us—it was too like our being proud of ourselves." Love is the thing more written about than anything else, and in the mistaken sense of greed. Henry James seems to have been haunted by awareness that rapacity destroys what it is successful in acquiring. He feels a need "to see the other side as well as his own, to feel what his adversary feels"; to be an American is not for him "just to glow belligerently with one's country." Some complain of his transferred citizenship as a loss; but when we consider the trend of his fiction and his uncomplacent denouements, we have no scruple about insisting that he was American; not if the American is, as he thought, "intrinsically and actively ample, . . . reaching westward, southward, anywhere, everywhere," with a mind "incapable of the shut door in any direction."

T. S. ELIOT

1. *"It Is Not Forbidden to Think"* [1]

The *Collected Poems* of T. S. Eliot (1936), complete except for *Murder in the Cathedral*, are chronological through 1930, and two tendencies mark them all: the instinct for order and a "contempt for sham." "I am not sure," Mr. Eliot says in "The Uses of Poetry," "that we can judge and enjoy a man's poetry while leaving wholly out of account all the things for which he cared deeply, and on behalf of which he turned his poetry to account." He detests a conscience, a politics, a rhetoric, that is neither one thing nor the other. For him hell is hell in its awareness of heaven; good is good in its distinctness from evil; precision is precision as triumphing over vagueness. In *The Rock* he says, "Our age is an age of moderate virtue/And of moderate vice." Among Peter the Hermit's "hearers were a few good men,/Many who were evil,/And most who were neither."

Although, as a critic, Mr. Eliot manifests at times an almost combative sincerity, by doing his fighting in prose he is perhaps the more free to do his feeling in verse. But in his verse, judgment indeed remains awake. His inability to elude "the Demon of Thought" appears in Prufrock's decision:

> Oh, do not ask, "What is it?"
> Let us go and make our visit.

and in the self-satire of "Lines for Cuscuscaraway and Mirza Murad Ali Beg":

> How unpleasant to meet Mr. Eliot!
> With his features of clerical cut,
>
> . . .
>
> And his conversation, so nicely
> Restricted to What Precisely
> And If and Perhaps and But.

One sees in this collected work, conscience—directed toward "things that other people have desired," asking, "are these things right or wrong"—and an art which from the beginning has tended toward drama. We have in *The Waste Land* a stage for a fortune-teller, for a game of chess, for a sermon, for music of various kinds, for death by drowning and death from thirst; finally for a boat responding gaily "to the hand, expert with sail and oar," and for a premonition of Peace. "T. S. Eliot forged the first link between . . . psychological and historical discoveries of his period and his period's poetry," Louise Bogan says; "far from being a poem of despair," *The Waste Land* "projects a picture of mankind at its highest point of ascetic control—St. Augustine, Buddha—as well as mankind at its lowest point of spiritual stupor, ignorance, and squalor."

In *Ash Wednesday* and later, Mr. Eliot is not warily considering "matters that with myself I too much discuss/Too much explain"; he is *in* them, and *Ash Wednesday* is perhaps the poem of the book—a summit, both as content, in its unself-justifying humility, and technically, in the lengthened phrase and gathered force of enmeshed rhymes.

Mr. Eliot's aptitude for mythology and theology sometimes pays us the compliment of expecting our reading to be more intent than it is; but correspondences of allusion provide an unmistakable logic of preference: for stillness, intellectual beauty, spiritual exaltation, the white dress, "the glory of the humming-bird," childhood, and wholeness of personality—in contrast with noise, evasiveness, aimlessness, fog, scattered bones, broken pride, rats, draughts under the door, distortion, "the stye of content-ment." Horror, which is unbelief, is the opposite of ecstasy; and wholeness, which is the condition of ecstasy, is to be "accepted and accepting." That is to say, we are of a world in which light and darkness, "appearance and reality," "is and seem," are ineludable alternatives.

Words of special meaning recur with the force of a theme: "hidden," "the pattern," and "form." Fire, the devourer, is a purifier; and as God's light is for man, the sun is life for the natural world. Concepts and images are toothed together so that one poem rests on another and is part of what came earlier; the musical theme at times being separated by a stanza as the argument sometimes is continued from the preceding poem—"O hidden' in "Difficulties of a Statesman" completing the "O hidden" in "Triumphal March."

The period including *Ash Wednesday*, concerned with "The infirm glory of the positive hour," is succeeded by the affirmative one to which *Murder in the Cathedral* belongs, and "Burnt Norton" ("And do not call it fixity," "The detail of the pattern is movement."):

> We move above the moving tree
> In light upon the figured leaf
> And hear upon the sodden floor
> Below, the boarhound and the boar
> Pursue their pattern as before
> But reconciled among the stars.

In "Usk," Mr. Eliot depicts the *via media* of self-discipline:

> Where the roads dip and where the roads rise
> Seek only there

> Where the gray light meets the green air
> The hermit's chapel, the pilgrim's prayer.

One notices here the emphasis on visible, invisible, indoors, and outdoors; and that in these later poems statement becomes simpler, the rhythm more complex.

Mr. Eliot has tried "to write poetry which should be essentially poetry, with nothing poetic about it, poetry standing naked in its bare bones, or . . . so transparent that in reading it we are intent on what the poem *points at* and not on the poetry." He has not evaded "the deepest terrors and desires," depths of "degradation," and heights of "exaltation," or disguised the fact that he has "walked in hell" and "been rapt to heaven."

Those who have power to renounce life are those who have it; one who attains equilibrium in spite of opposition to himself from within, is stronger than if there had been no opposition to overcome; and in art, freedom evolving from a liberated constraint is more significant than if it had not by nature been cramped. Skepticism, also constraint, are part of Mr. Eliot's temperament. Art, however, if concealing the artist, exhibits his "angel"; like the unanticipated florescence of fireworks as they expand with the felicitous momentum of "unbroke horses"; and this effect of power we have in "Cape Ann"—denominated a minor poem:

> O quick quick quick, quick hear the song-sparrow,
> Swamp-sparrow, fox-sparrow, vesper-sparrow
> At dawn and dusk. . . .

Another unemphasized triumph of tempo and terseness, we have in "Lines for an Old Man":

> The tiger in the tiger-pit
> Is not more irritable than I.
> The whipping tail is not more still
> Than when I smell the enemy
> Writhing in the essential blood
> Or dangling from the friendly tree.
> When I lay bare the tooth of wit
> The hissing over the archèd tongue

Is more affectionate than hate,
More bitter than the love of youth,
And inaccessible by the young.
Reflected from my golden eye
The dullard knows that he is mad.
Tell me if I am not glad!

In the above lines we have an effect—have we not?—of order without pedantry, and of terseness that is synonymous with a hatred of sham.

II. *Reticent Candor* [2]

That T. S. Eliot and Wallace Stevens have certain qualities in common perhaps is obvious—in reticent candor and emphasis by understatement. Speaking as from ambush, they mistrust rhetoric—taking T. S. Eliot's definition of the word, in his "Rhetoric and Poetic Drama," as "any adornment or inflation of speech which is not used for a particular effect but for general impressiveness." Of "omnivorous perspicacity," [3] each has been concerned from the first with the art and use of poetry, and has continued to be a poet. And although too much importance should not be attached to this, the following passages are of interest, it seems to me, as revealing consanguinities of taste and rhythm; in T. S. Eliot's "La Figlia che Piange":

So I would have had him leave,
So I would have had her stand and grieve,

and Wallace Stevens' "Peter Quince at the Clavier":

So evenings die, in their green going,
A wave, interminably flowing.
. . .
So maidens die, to the auroral
Celebration of a maiden's choral.

Reviewing *The Waste Land*, Conrad Aiken said, "T. S. Eliot's net is wide and the meshes are small . . ."; [4] especially wide and small as prose bearing on poetry. In "The Music of Poetry," Mr. Eliot says, "Poetry must give pleasure";[5] "find the possibilities of your own idiom"; "poetry must not stray too far from the ordinary language we use and hear"—principles in keeping with the following statements quoted by Mr. Eliot from W. P. Ker: "the end of scholarship is understanding," and "the end of understanding is enjoyment," "enjoyment disciplined by taste."

T. S. Eliot's concern with language has been evident all along —as when he says in "A Talk on Dante," "The whole study and practice of Dante seems to me, to teach that the poet should be the servant of his language, rather than the master of it." And "To pass on to posterity one's own language, more highly developed, more refined, and more precise than it was before one wrote it, that is the highest achievement of the poet as poet. . . . Dante seems to me," he says, "to have a place in Italian literature which in this respect, only Shakespeare has in ours. They gave body to the soul of the language, conforming themselves to what they deemed its possibilities." Furthermore, "In developing the language, enriching the meaning of words and showing how much words can do," Mr. Eliot says, the poet "is making possible a much greater range of emotion and perception for other men because he gives them the speech in which more can be expressed." Then, "The kind of debt that I owe to Dante is the kind that goes on accumulating. . . . Of Jules Laforgue, for instance, I can say that he was the first . . . to teach me the poetic possibilities of my own idiom of speech. . . . I think that from Baudelaire I learned first, a precedent for the poetical possibilities, never developed by any poet writing in my own language, of the more sordid aspects of the modern metropolis, of the possibility of fusion between the sordidly realistic and the phantasmagoric, the possibility of the juxtaposition of the matter-of-fact and the fantastic . . . and that the source of new poetry might be found in what has been regarded [as] the intractably unpoetic. . . . One has other debts, innumerable debts," he says, "to poets of another kind. . . . There are those who remain in one's mind as having set the standard for a particular poetic virtue, as Villon for honesty, and Sappho for having fixed a particular emotion in the right and the minimum number of words" [6]—the words "poetic" and "minimum," explicit as if italicized.

To quote what is in print seems unnecessary, and manner is scarcely a subject for commentary; yet something is to be learned, I think, from a reticent candor in which openness tempts participation, and places experience at our service—as in the above-mentioned commentary, "A Talk on Dante"; as in "Poetry and Drama" (the Theodore Spencer Memorial Lecture); and in the retrospect of Ezra Pound that appeared in the September 1946 issue of *Poetry*.

In "Poetry and Drama," helpfully confidential again, Mr. Eliot asks if poetic drama has anything potentially to offer that prose can not. "No play should be written in verse," he says, "for which prose is dramatically adequate." "The audience should be too intent upon the play to be wholly conscious of the medium," and "the difference is not so great as we might think between prose and verse." "Prose on the stage," he says, "is as artificial as verse," the reason for using verse being that "even the pedestrian parts of a verse play have an effect upon the hearers without their being conscious of it." "If you were hearing *Hamlet* for the first time," Mr. Eliot says, "without knowing anything about the play, I do not think it would occur to you to ask whether the speakers were speaking in verse or prose." For example, the opening lines:

> Bernardo: Who's there?
> Francisco: Nay, answer me: stand and unfold yourself.
> Bernardo: Long live the king!
>
> .   .   .
>
> Francisco: Not a mouse stirring.
> Bernardo: Well, good night.[7]

Then of his own "intentions, failures and partial success," Mr. Eliot says that "*Murder in the Cathedral* was produced for an audience of those serious people who go to 'festivals' and expect to have to put up with poetry—though some were not quite prepared for what they got." "The style," he says, "had to be neutral, committed neither to the present nor to the past. As for the versification . . . what I kept in mind was the versification of *Everyman*"; despite its only "negative merit in my opinion," it "succeeded in avoiding what had to be avoided. . . . What I should hope might be achieved is that the audience should find . . . that it is saying to itself: 'I could talk in poetry too!' " "I was determined in my next play," he says, "to take the theme of contemporary life. *The Family Reunion* was the result. Here my first concern was . . . to find a rhythm in which the stresses could be made to come where we should naturally put them. . . . What I worked out is substantially what I have continued to employ: a line of varying length and varying number of syllables, with a caesura and three stresses. The caesura and the stresses may come at different places . . . the only rule being that there must be one stress on one side of the caesura and two on the other. . . . I soon saw that I had given my attention to versification at the expense of plot and character." Then the Furies. "We put them on the stage. They looked like uninvited guests from a fancy-dress ball. . . . We concealed them behind gauze. We made them dimmer, and they looked like shrubbery just outside the window"; diagnosis followed in the same vein of candor, by, "My hero now strikes me as an unsufferable prig." Next: "You will understand . . . some of the errors that I endeavored to avoid in designing *The Cocktail Party*. To begin with, no chorus, and no ghosts. . . . As for the verse, I laid down for myself the ascetic rule to avoid poetry which could not stand the test of dramatic utility: with such sucess, indeed, that it is perhaps an open question whether there is any poetry in the play at all." Then, as flatly objective, "I am aware that the last act of my play only just escapes, if indeed it does escape, the accusation of being not a last act but an epilogue." "I have, I believe," he says in conclusion, "been animated by a better motive than egoism. I have wished to put on record for what it may be worth to others, some account of the difficulties I have encountered and the weaknesses I have had to overcome, and the mistakes into which I have fallen." Now this kind of candor seems to me not short of sensational—as technical exposition to which carefully accurate informality lends persuasiveness.

The retrospect of Ezra Pound's London years shares the (to me, useful) tone of the Spencer lecture; I detect no difference between it and conversation. Mr. Eliot is speaking here of 1908 and of Ezra Pound as suggesting "a usable contemporary form of speech at a time of stagnation." He says, "Browning was more of a hindrance than a help for he had gone some way, but not far enough in discovering a contemporary idiom. . . . The question was still: where do we go from Swinburne? and the answer appeared to be, nowhere." One notes the adjectives, numerous without heaviness: "Pound was then living in a small dark flat in Kensington. In the largest room he cooked, by artificial light; in the lightest but smallest room, which was inconveniently triangular, he did his work and received his visitors. [He gave the impression of being transient,] due, not only to his restless energy—in which it was difficult to distinguish the energy from the restlessness and fidgits . . . but to a kind of resistance against growing into any environment. . . . For a time, he found London, and then Paris, the best center for his attempts to revitalize poetry. But though young English writers, and young writers of any nationality, could count on his support if they excited his interest, the future of American letters was what concerned him most."

"No poet, furthermore was, without self-depreciation, more unassuming about his own achievement in poetry," Mr. Eliot says. "The arrogance which some people have found in him is really something else. . . . [He] would go to any lengths of generosity and kindness; from inviting constantly to dinner, a struggling author whom he suspected of being under-fed, or giving away clothing (though his shoes and underwear were almost the only garments which resembled those of other men sufficiently to be worn by them), to trying to find jobs, collect subsidies, get work published and then get it criticized and praised."

Pound's critical writing, Mr. Eliot goes on to say, "forms a corpus of poetic doctrine. . . . The opinion has been voiced that Pound's reputation will rest upon his criticism and not upon his poetry. I disagree. It is on his total work for literature that he must be judged: on his poetry, *and* his criticism, *and* his influence at a turning point in literature. In any case, his criticism takes its significance from the fact that it is the writing of a poet about poetry; it must be read in the light of his own poetry, as well as of poetry by other men whom he championed. . . . You cannot wholly understand Aristotle's doctrine of tragedy without reference to the remains of the Attic drama upon which Aristotle's generalizations are founded." And, bearing upon this, Mr. Eliot quotes Ezra Pound as saying that "theoretically criticism tries to . . . serve as a gunsight, but that the man who formulates any forward reach of co-ordinating principle is the man who produces the demonstration. . . . They proceed as two feet of one biped."

"I know that one of the temptations against which I have to be on guard," Mr. Eliot says, "is trying to re-write somebody's poem in the way in which I should have written it myself. Pound never did that: he tried first to understand what one was attempting to do, and then tried to help one do it in one's own way." As part of the definiteness with openness which aids this commentary, we have the following aside: "In the Cantos there is an increasing defect of communication. . . . I am incidentally annoyed, myself, by occasional use of the peculiar orthography which characterizes Pound's correspondence and by lines written in what he supposes to be Yankee dialect. But the craftsman up to this moment . . . has never failed." (One notices "moment" as replacing the usual, less intent word "time.")

"Pound's 'erudition,'" Mr. Eliot says, "has been both exaggerated and . . . under-estimated: for it has been judged chiefly by scholars who did not understand poetry, and by poets who have had little scholarship." (Apropos here, Dr. Tenney Frank's statement to students at Bryn Mawr in connection with Ezra Pound's "Homage to Sextus Propertius": anyone might render a line impeccably; few can communicate appetite for the thing and present content with the brio with which Ezra Pound presents it.)

"Pound's great contribution to the work of other poets," Mr. Eliot says, "is his insistence upon the immensity of the amount of *conscious* labor to be performed by the poet; and his invaluable suggestions for the kind of training the poet should give himself— study of form, metric and vocabulary in the poetry of divers literature, and study of good prose. . . . He also provides an example of devotion to 'the art of poetry' which I can only parallel in our time by the example of Valéry, and to some extent that of Yeats: and to mention these names is to give some impression of Pound's importance as an exponent of the art of poetry" at a time when

> The "age demanded" chiefly a mould in plaster,
> Made with no loss of time,
> A prose kinema, not, not assuredly, alabaster
> Or the "sculpture" of rhyme.

As Ezra Pound, J. V. Healy says, followed T. E. Hulme's precept, that language "should endeavor to arrest you, and to make you continuously see a physical thing, and prevent your gliding through an abstract process," I would say that T. S. Eliot has not glided through an abstract process in formulating the three discourses just cited—exposition consonant in vividness with his best use of metaphor—"the seabell's perpetual angelus" and the lines about standing at the "stern of the drumming liner, watching the furrow that widens behind us."

Of poetry, current at Oxford, W. H. Auden says in the *Letter to Lord Byron*, "Eliot spoke the still unspoken word," and in the tribute by him "To T. S. Eliot on His Sixtieth Birthday," 1948, says:

> . . . it was you
> Who, not speechless from shock but finding the right
> Language for thirst and fear, did much to
> Prevent a panic.

The effect of Mr. Eliot's confidences, elucidations, and precepts, I would say, is to disgust us with affectation; to encourage respect for spiritual humility; and to encourage us to do our ardent undeviating best with the medium in which we work.

EZRA POUND

1. *The Cantos* [1]

These Cantos are the epic of the farings of a literary mind.

The ghost of Homer sings. His words have the sound of the sea and the cadence of actual speech. *And So-shu churned in the sea, So-shu also.*[2] In Canto III we have an ideograph for the Far East, consisting of two parts:

Green veins in the turquoise,
Or, the gray steps lead up under the cedars.

The Cantos are concerned with *books, arms,* and *men of unusual genius.* They imply that there is nothing like the word-melody of the Greek; we have that of Latin also—Vergil and Ovid. One's ear can learn from the Latin something of quantity. " 'Not by the eagles only was Rome measured./Wherever the Roman speech was, there was Rome.'/Wherever the speech crept, there was mastery." The Cantos imply that there is pleasure to be had from Propertius and Catullus, that Catullus is very winning; it is plain that in liking him, one has something of his attitude of mind. "Can we know Ovid," Mr. Pound asks in his "Notes on Elizabethan Classicists," "until we find him in Golding? . . . is not a new beauty created, an old beauty doubled when the over-change is well done?" On returning to Paris after seven years, *Knocking at empty rooms, seeking for buried beauty,*" Mr. Pound is told by A *strange concierge, in place of the gouty-footed,* that the friend he asks about is dead. For the attar of friendship of one long dead

Dry casques of departed locusts
        speaking a shell of speech. . .

are not a substitute. Golding afforded "reality and particularization"; whereas Paris is a thing of W*ords like the locust-shells, moved by no inner being;* and Mr. Pound thinks for a moment of the scarlet-curtain simile in the "Flight from Hippomenes" in Ovid's *Metamorphoses*, translated by Golding,[3] and murmurs, *The scarlet curtain throws a less scarlet shadow*. This Paris Canto—VII—is one of the best; the eleven last lines—memorable, stately.

It is apparent that the Latin line is quantitative. If poetics allure, the Cantos will also show that in Provençal minstrelsy we encounter a fascinating precision; the delicacy and exactness of Arnaut Daniel, whose invention, the sestina form, is "like a thin sheet of flame folding and infolding upon itself." In this tongue—you read it in manuscripts rather than in books—is to be found pattern. And the Cantos show how the troubadours not only sang poems but *were* poems. Usually they were in love, with My Lady Battle if with no other, and were often successful, for in singing of love one sometimes finds it—especially when the *canzos* are good ones. And there were jealous husbands. Miguel de la Tour is most pleasing to Mr. Pound in what he says of Piere de Maensac, who carried off the wife of Bernart de Tierci. "The husband, in the manner of the golden Menelaus, demanded her much," and there was *Troy* in *Auvergnat*. But it happened often that the minstrel was thrown into prison or put himself there, like Bernart of Ventadorn, who sang of the lark and who "ended his days in the monastery of Dalon." In this connection, disparity in station, under which people suffer and are patient, is regrettable; Madonna Biancha Visconti was married by her uncle to a peasant; and the troubadours oftener than not were frustrated in love; they were poor and were usually more gifted than the men whose appurtenance they were. But things are sometimes reversed, as when a man of title falls in love with a tirewoman. And not always are people to be balked, as we see in the case of this Pedro the persistent, who came to reign, murdered the murderers of the tirewoman, and married the dug-up corpse. Pedro's ghost sings in Canto III and again in XXX.

Mr. Pound brings to his reading, master-appreciation; and his gratitude takes two forms; he thanks the book and tells where you may see it. "Any man who would read Arnaut and the troubadours owes great thanks to Emil Lévy of Freiburg," he says in *Instigations*, "for his long work and his little dictionary (*Petit Dictionnaire Provençal-Français*, Karl Winter's Universitätsbuchhandlung, Heidelberg)." He sings of this in Canto XX—of the old man who at about 6:30/*in the evening, . . . trailed half way across Freiburg/before dinner, to see the two strips of copy.*

And as those who love books know, the place in which one read a book or talked of it partakes of its virtue in recollection; so for Mr. Pound the cedars and new-mown hay and far-off nightingale at Freiburg have the glamour of Provence. He says (Canto XX):

> You would be happy for the smell of that place
> And never tired of being there, either alone
> Or accompanied.

And he intimates that no lover of books will do himself the disservice of overlooking Lope de Vega, his "matchless buoyancy, freshness," "atmosphere of earliest morning," "like that hour before the summer dawn, when the bracing cool of the night still grips the air," his "sprightly spirit of impertinence," his tenderness. In Canto III is echoed the joke from the *Cid* about the gold—the two chests of sand "covered with vermilion leather" and pawned with the proviso that "they be not disturbed for a year"; and there are echoes of the slumber song that speaks of angels a-flying.

As for Dante, even the mind most unsparing of itself will not easily get all that is to be got from him. Books and arms. Either is not necessarily a part of the other any more than the books from the London Library that were taken to the late war by T. E. Hulme and were buried by a shell in a dugout. But we enjoy Homer, Vergil, Dante, and what they had to say about war. And arms are mentioned in the *Chanson de Roland* and in Shakespeare. And we enjoy the Cantos in which Mr. Pound sings of the wars between cities in an Italy of unsanitary dungeons and great painting, and what he says of diplomatic greed as disgusting and also comic; and like what he says of wigglings, split fees, tips, and self-interest:

Sigismundo, ally, come through an enemy force,
To patch up some sort of treaty, passes one gate
And they shut it before they open the next gate, and he says:
"Now you have me,
        Caught like a hen in a coop."

Speaking of Italy, we find in Canto XXVI a picture of Mr. Pound outside St. Mark's on one of his first visits to Venice, of which visit he says:

And
I came here in my youth
        and lay there under the crocodile
By the column . . .

To one looking up at it, it is small, like the silhouette of a lizard, this bronze crocodile, souvenir of Venetian acquisitiveness.

And at night they sang in the gondolas
And in the barche with lanthorns;
The prows rose silver on silver
        taking light in the darkness.

To return to fighting, "Dante fought at Campaldino, 'in the front rank,'" and "saw further military service," and other men of literary genius have survived war. Canto XVI alludes to Lord Byron, who once bore arms for Greece, though the canto alludes to him as wrapped in scarlet and resembling a funeral; not dead, merely drunk. But the drunkenness that is war! War such as this last:

And Henri Gaudier went to it,
        and they killed him.

Why cannot money and life go for beauty instead of for war and intellectual oppression? This question is asked more than once by the Cantos. Books and arms. Under the head of arms, as you will have noticed, come daggers—like Pedro's, and Giovanni Malatesta's sword that slew Paolo, the beautiful. Books, arms, men. To Dante antiquity was not a figment; nor is it to Mr.

Pound, any more than Mme. Curie is a figment, or the man he knew in Manhattan,

> 24 E. 47th, when I met him,
> Doing job printing.

Men of unusual genius, *Both of ancient times and our own.* Of our own (Canto VII), Henry James

> Moves before me, phantom with weighted motion,
> *Grave incessu*, drinking the tone of things,
> And the old voice lifts itself
> weaving an endless sentence.

And there was an exemplary American, favorable to music.

> "Could you," wrote Mr. Jefferson,
> "Find me a gardener
> Who can play the french horn?"

And the singer curses his country for being *Midas lacking a Pan!* To cite passages is to pull one quill from a porcupine. Mr. Pound took two thousand and more pages to say it in prose, and he sings it in a hundred-forty-two. The book is concerned with beauty. You must read it yourself; it has a power that is mind and is music; it comes with the impact of centuries and with the impact of yesterday. Amid the swarming madness of excellence, there is the chirping of "the young phoenix broods," the Chinese music, the slender bird-note that gives one no peace. "Great poets," Mr. Pound says, "seldom make bricks without straw. They pile up all the excellences they can beg, borrow, or steal from their predecessors and contemporaries, and then set their own inimitable light atop the mountain." Of the Cantos, then, what is the master-quality? Scholastically, it is "concentrating the past on the present," as T. S. Eliot says; rhetorically, it is certitude; musically, it is range with an unerring ear. Note Cantos XIII, XVII, XXI, and XXX. And in all this "wealth of motive," this *"largesse,"* this "intelligence," are there no flaws? Does every passage in this sym-

phony "relieve, refresh, revive the mind of the reader—at reason-
able intervals—with some form of ecstasy, by some splendour of
thought, some presentation of sheer beauty, some lightning turn
of phrase"? Not invariably. The "words affect modernity," says
William Carlos Williams, "with too much violence (at times)—a
straining after slang effects. . . . You cannot *easily* switch from
Orteum to Peoria without violence (to the language). These
images too greatly infest the Cantos."

Unprudery is overemphasized and secularity persists, refuted
though this charge is by the prose praise of Dante: "His work is
of that sort of art which is a key to the deeper understanding of
nature and the beauty of the world and of the spirit"; "for the
praise of that part of his worth which is fibre rather than surface,
my mind is not yet ripe, nor is my pen skilled." Most of us have
not the tongues of the spirit, but those who have, tell us that,
by comparison, knowledge of the spirit of tongues is as insignifi-
cant as are the clothes worn by one in infancy. We share Mr.
Pound's diffidence.

T. S. Eliot suspects Ezra Pound's philosophy of being anti-
quated. William Carlos Williams finds his "versification *still*
patterned after classic metres"; and, apropos of "feminolatry," is
not the view of woman expressed by the Cantos older-fashioned
than that of Siam and Abyssinia? knowledge of the femaleness of
chaos, of the *octopus*, of *Our mulberry leaf, woman,* appertaining
more to Turkey than to a Roger Ascham? Nevertheless Mr.
Pound likes the denouement of *Aucassin and Nicolette,* and in
comparing *Romeo and Juliet* with De Vega's *Castelvines y Mon-
teses,* sees "absolutely no necessity for the general slaughter at
the end of Shakespeare's play." He addresses the lutanists in their
own tongue (Canto VIII):

> "Ye spirits who of olde were in this land
> Each under Love, and shaken,
> Go with your lutes, awaken
> The summer within her mind,
> Who hath not Helen for peer,
>   Yseut nor Batsabe."

But, a practical man in these matters, he sees the need for anti-dotes to "inebriation from the *Vita Nuova*"; namely, Sir James Fraser and Rémy de Gourmont; one no longer mistakes the singer's habiliment for his heart any more than one acquainted with the prose of James Joyce would find the bloom on the poems in *Chamber Music* artless.

What about Cantos XIV and XV? Let us hope that "Disgust with the sordid is but another expression of a sensitiveness to the finer thing."

Petty annoyances are magnified; when one is a beginner, tribu-lation worketh impatience.

Stock oaths, and the result is ennui, as with the stock adjective.

An annoyance by no means petty is the lack of an index.

And since the Cantos are scrupulous against half-truth and against *what had been thought for too long*—ought they not to suggest to those who have accepted Calvin by hearsay—or heresy— that one must make a distinction between Calvin the theologian and Calvin the man of letters? Or is Mr. Pound indifferent to wit from that quarter—as sailors in the Baltic are said not to shave when the wind is favorable?

Those who object to the Cantos' obscurity—who prefer the earlier poems—are like the victims of Calvin who have not read him. It may be true that the author's revisions make it harder, not easier, for hurried readers; but flame kindles to the eye that contemplates it. Besides, these *are* the earlier poems. A critic that would have us "establish axes of reference by knowing the *best of each kind of written thing*" has persisted to success; is saying something "in such a way that one cannot re-say it more effec-tively." Note the affinity with material commonly called senti-mental, which in most writers becomes sickly and banal, and in the Cantos is kept keen and alive; and the tactility with which Mr. Pound enables us to relive antiquity: *Da Gama wore striped pants in Africa.* And he sets it "to paint" so that we may *see* what he says. The pale backgrounds are by Leonardo da Vinci; there are faces with the *eyes of Picasso*; the walls are by Mantegna. The yellow in Canto XVII, of the fawn and the broom, and the cerise grasshopper-wing, gain perhaps by contrast with a prevailing tendency, in the Cantos, to blue. *Malachite, green clear, and blue clear, blue-gray glass of the wave, Glare azure, Black snout of a porpoise.* The dramatist's eye that sees this and *Cosimo's red leather note book* and the *big green account book* and the lion whelps *vivos et piloses living and hairy, waves . . . holding their form/No light reaching through them,*

> And the waters richer than glass,
> Bronze gold, the blaze over the silver,
> Dye-pots in the torch-light,

finds the mechanistic world also "full of enchantments," "not only the light in the electric bulb, but the thought of the current hidden in the air," "and the rose that his magnet makes in the iron filings." And added to imagination is the idiosyncratic force of the words—the terseness in which some reflower and some are new. Of Mr. Pound and words, Dr. Williams says, "He has taken them up—if it may be risked—alertly, swiftly, but with feeling for the delicate living quality in them, not disinfecting, scraping them, but careful of the life." The skill that in the prose has been incomparably expert in epitomizing what others have bungled, shows us that "you can be wholly precise in representing a vagueness." This ambidextrous precision, born of integrity and intrepidity, is the poet's revenge upon those "who refuse to say what they think, if they do think," who are like those who see nothing the matter with bad surgery. And allied with veracity are translatorly qualities that nourish ingenuity in the possessor of them: a so unmixed zeal for essence that no assaying of merits in rendering is a trouble; an independence that will not subscribe to superstition—to the notion, for instance, that a text written in Greek is of necessity better than a text written in Latin. Even Homer can be put characteristically into Latin. *Andreas Divus* "plucked from a Paris stall" "gave him in Latin," *In officina Wecheli*, 1538,

> Caught up his cadence, word and syllable:
> "Down to the ships we went, set mast and sail,
> Black keel and beasts for bloody sacrifice,
> Weeping we went."

And the English of Golding's Ovid is as good as the Latin. "A master may be continually expanding his own tongue, rendering it fit to bear some charge hitherto borne only by some other alien tongue"; yet as Fontenelle said to Erasmus, "If before being vain of a thing" men "should try to assure themselves that it really belonged to them, there would be little vanity in the world."

The new in Mr. Pound, as in any author, hides itself from the dull and is accentuated for the quick. Certain implements in use by James Joyce are approved: the pun, the phonetic photography of dialect, propriety with vibrating edge of impropriety, the wry jest—'Hélion t' 'Hélion. "All artists who discover anything . . . must, in the course of things, . . . push certain experiments beyond the right curve of their art," Mr. Pound says, and some would say, the facing in many directions as of a quadriga drawn by centaurs, which we meet in the Cantos, puts strain on bipedal understanding; there is love of risk; but the experienced grafting of literature upon music is here very remarkable—the resonance of color, allusions, and tongues sounding one through the other as in symphonic instrumentation. Even if one understood nothing, one would enjoy the musicianship.

Thus the book of the mandates:

Feb. 1422.

We desire that you our factors give to Zohanne of Rimini our servant, six lire marchesini,
for the three prizes he has won racing our barbarisci,
at the rate we have agreed on. The races he has won
are the Modena, the San Petronio at Bologna
and the last race at San Zorzo.

(Signed) Parisina Marchesa

Mr. Pound says, "Everyone has been annoyed by the difficulty of indicating the *exact* tone and rhythm with which one's verse is to be read," but in the "capripedal" counterpoint of the above little fugue à la gigue he has put it beyond our power to stumble. And there is discovery in the staccato sound of the conclusion to Canto XXX, in the patterning of the "y" in "thirty" on the "i" in *mori*:

Il Papa mori.

Explicit canto
XXX

The master-quality throughout the Cantos is decision:

SIGISMUNDUS HIC EGO SUM
MALATESTA, FILIUS PANDULPHI, REX PRODITORUM

But however explicit the accents in the line, the fabric on which
the pattern is focused is indispensable to accuracy. There is the
effect sometimes, as in the medieval dance, of a wheel spun one
way and then the other; there is the sense of a horse rushing
toward one and turning, unexpectedly rampant; one has stepped
back but need not have moved. Note the luster of a subtle slowing
exactly calculated (Canto V):

> Fades the light from the sea, and many things
> "Are set abroad and brought to mind of thee."

"The music of rhymes depends upon their arrangement, not
on their multiplicity." We are aware in the Cantos of the skill of
an ear with a faculty for rhyme in its most developed arrange-
ments, but, like that of a Greek, against the vulgarity of rhyme; a
mind aware of instruments—aware of "the circular bars of the
Arabs, divided, like unjust mince pies, from centre to circum-
ference," and of "the beautiful irregularities of the human voice."
Whatever the training, however, "a man's rhythm" "will be, in
the end, his own, uncounterfeiting, uncounterfeitable"; and in
Canto XIII, in the symbolic discussion of the art of poetics, what
is said is illustrated by the manner of saying:

> And Tseu-lou said, "I would put the defences in order,"
> And Khieu said, "If I were lord of a province
> I would put it in better order than this is."
> And Tchi said, "I would prefer a small mountain temple,
> With order in the observances,
>   with a suitable performance of the ritual,"
>   · · ·

And Kung said, "They have all answered correctly,
That is to say, each in his nature."

. . .

And Kung said, and wrote on the bo leaves:
"If a man have not order within him
He can not spread order about him;

. . .

"Anyone can run to excesses,
It is easy to shoot past the mark,
It is hard to stand firm in the middle."

There is no easy way if you are to be a great artist; and the nature
of one, in achieving his art, is different from the nature of
another.

Mr. Pound, in the prose that he writes, has formulated his own
commentary upon the Cantos. They are an armorial coat of atti-
tudes to things that have happened in books and in life; they are
not a shield but a coat worn by a man, as in the days when
heraldry was beginning. He serves under Beauty, with the motto,
Τό Καλόν. "Ordinary people," he says in his turtle poem, "touch
me not." His art is his turtle-shell or snail house; it is all one
animal moving together, and

Who seeks him must be worse than blind,
He and his house are so combined,
If finding it he fails to find
its master.[4]

II. *"Teach, Stir the Mind, Afford Enjoyment"* [5]

Our debt to Ezra Pound is prodigious for the effort he has made
to share what he knows about writing and, in particular, about
rhythm and melody; most of all, for his insistence on liveness as
opposed to deadness. "Make it new," he says. "Art is a joyous
thing." He recalls "that sense of sudden growth we experience in
the presence of the greatest works of art." The ode to *Hugh Selwyn
Mauberley* applies of course to himself:

> For three years, out of key with his time,
> He strove to resuscitate the dead art
> Of poetry; to maintain "the sublime"
> In the old sense. . . .

And, above all, it is the art of letters in America that he has wished to resuscitate. He says in "Cantico del Sole":

> The thought of what America would be like
> If the classics had a wide circulation
> Troubles my sleep. . . .

America's imperviousness to culture irks him; but he is never as indignant as he is elated.

Instruction should be painless, he says, and his precept for writers is an epitome of himself: teach, stir the mind, afford enjoyment. (Cicero's *Ut doceat, ut moveat, ut delectet*.[6]) Dudley Fitts grants him his wish and says, "The Pound letters are weirdly written; they are nevertheless a treatise on creative writing, treasure-trove, *corpus aureum, mina de oro*. . . . The vivacity of these letters is enchanting." Hugh Kenner says, "The whole key to Pound, the basis of his Cantos, his music, his economics and everything else, is the concern for exact definition"—a passion shared by T. S. Eliot, Mr. Kenner adds—"a quality which neither has defined." What is it? a neatening or cleancutness, to begin with, as caesura is cutting at the end (*caedo*, cut off). For Dante, it was making you see the thing that he sees, Mr. Pound says; and, speaking of Rimbaud, says there is "such firmness of coloring and such certitude." Pound admires Chinese codifyings and for many a year has been ordering, epitomizing, and urging explicitness, as when he listed "A Few Don'ts" for Imagists:

> Direct treatment, economy of words; compose in the sequence of the musical phrase rather than that of the metronome.
> The true poet is most easily distinguished from the false when he trusts himself to the simplest expression and writes without adjectives.
> No dead words or phrases.
> A thought should be expressed in verse at least as well as it

could be expressed in prose. Great literature is language charged with meaning to the utmost possible degree. There is no easy way out.

Mr. Pound differentiates poetry as

logopoeia (music of words),
melopoeia (music of sound)—the music of rhymes, he says, depends upon their arrangement, not only on their multiplicity—and
phanopoeia (casting images on the imagination).

Under the last head, one recalls the statement by Dante that Beatrice walked above herself—*come una crana.* Confucius says the fish moves on winglike foot; and Prior, in his life of Edmund Burke, says Burke "had a peculiarity in his gait that made him look as if he had two left legs." Affirming Coleridge's statement that "Our admiration of a great poet is for a continuous under-current of feeling everywhere present, but seldom anywhere a separate excitement," Mr. Pound says Dante "has gone living through Hell and the words of his lament sob as branches beaten by the wind."

What is poetry? Dante said, "a song is a composition of words set to music." As for free verse, "it is *not* prose," Mr. Pound says. It is what we have "when the thing builds up a rhythm more beautiful than that of set metres"—as here:

> The birds flutter to rest in my tree,
> and I think I have heard them saying,
> "It is not that there are no other men—,
> But we like this fellow the best. . . ."

In Dante, "we have blending and lengthening of the sounds, heavy beats, running and light beats," Mr. Pound says. "Don't make each line stop dead at the end. Let the beginning of the next line catch the rise of the rhythm wave, unless you want a longish definite pause." For example, the lines from "Envoi" in *Mauberley*, when he speaks of "her graces":

I would bid them live
As roses might, in magic amber laid,
Red overwrought with orange and all made
One substance and one colour
Braving time.

This is the way in which to cement sound and thought. In
Mauberley, also note the identical rhymes in close sequence without conspicuousness, of "Medallion":

The face-oval beneath the glaze,
Bright in its suave bounding-line, as,
Beneath half-watt rays,
The eyes turn topaz.

"Words," T. S. Eliot says, "are perhaps the hardest medium of
all material of art. One must simultaneously express visual beauty,
beauty of sound, and communicate a grammatical statement." We
have in "her" a mundane word, but note the use of it in the
Portrait, from "La Mère Inconnue" (*Exultations*):

Nay! For I have seen the purplest shadows stand
Always with reverent chere that looked on her,
Silence himself is grown her worshipper
And ever doth attend her in that land
Wherein she reigneth, wherefore let there stir
Naught but the softest voices, praising her.

Again, from Ezra Pound's translation of Guido Cavalcanti: "A
Bernardo da Bologna,"

And in that Court where Love himself fableth
Telling of beauties he hath seen; he saith:
This pagan and lovely woman hath in her
All strange adornments that ever were.

William Carlos Williams is right. "Pound is not 'all poetry.'
. . . But he has an ear that is unsurpassable." "Some poems," Mr.
Pound himself says, "have form as a tree has form and some as
water poured into a vase." He also says, quoting Arnold Dolmetsch

and Mace, "Mark not the beat too much"—a precept essential to light rhyme and surprises within the line; but inapplicable to satire, as in W. S. Gilbert's *Pirates of Penzance*—the policemen:

> And yet when someone's near
> We manage to appear
> As unsusceptible to fear
> As anybody here.

"The churn, the loom, the spinning-wheel, the oars," Mr. Pound says, "are bases for distinctive rhythm which can never degenerate into the monotony of mere iambs and trochees"; and one notices in "Nel Biancheggiar" the accenting of "dies," in "but dies not quite":

> I feel the dusky softness whirr
> Of colour, as upon a dulcimer
> . . .
> As when the living music swoons
> But dies not quite. . . .

One notes in "Guido Invites You Thus" (*Exultations*) the placing of the pauses and quickened "flames of an altar fire":

> Lo, I have known thy heart and its desire;
> Life, all of it, my sea, and all men's streams
> Are fused in it as flames of an altar fire!

And "A Prologue" (*Canzoni*) has the same exactitude in variety:

> Shepherds and kings, with lambs and frankincense
> Go and atone for mankind's ignorance:
> Make ye soft savour from your ruddy myrrh.
> Lo, how God's son is turned God's almoner.

Unending emphasis is laid by Ezra Pound on honesty—on voicing one's own opinion. He is indignant that "trout should be submerged by eels." The function of literature, he says, is "to incite humanity to continue living; to ease the mind of strain; to feed it" (Canto XXV):

What we thought had been thought for too long;

. . .

We have gathered a sieve full of water.

. . .

The dead words, keeping form.

We suffer from

Noble forms lacking life,

. . .

The dead concepts, never the solid;

As for comprehension of what is set forth, the poet has a right to expect the reader, at least in a measure, to be able to complete poetic statement; and Ezra Pound never spoils his effects by over-exposition. He alludes as follows to the drowning of a Borgia:

The bust outlasts the shrine;
The coin, Tiberius.

. . .

John Borgia is bathed
at last. And the cloak floated.

"As for *Cathay*, it must be pointed out," T. S. Eliot says, "that Pound is the inventor of Chinese poetry of our time"; and seeing a connection between the following incident and "the upper-middlebrow press," Hugh Kenner recalls that when Charles Münch offered Bach to the regiment, the commandant said, "Here, none of that mathematical music." One ventures, commits one's self, and if readers are not pleased, one can perhaps please one's self and earn that slender right to persevere.

"A poet's work," Mr. Eliot says, "may proceed along two lines of an imaginary graph; one of the lines being his conscious and continuous effort in technical excellence," and the other "his normal human course of development. Now and then the two lines may converge at a high peak, so that we get a masterpiece. That is to say, an accumulation of experience has crystallized to form material of art, and years of work in technique have prepared an adequate medium; and something results in which medium and material, form and content, are indistinguishable."

In *The Great Digest and Unwobbling Pivot* of Confucius, as in his *Analects*, Ezra Pound has had a theme of major import. *The Great Digest* makes emphatic this lesson: He who can rule himself can govern others; he who can govern others can rule the kingdom and families of the Empire.

The men of old disciplined themselves.
Having attained self-discipline they set their houses in order.
Having order in their own homes, they brought good government
    to their own state.
When their states were well governed, the empire was brought into
    equilibrium.

We have in the *Digest*, content that is energetic, novel, and deep: "If there be a knife of resentment in the heart or enduring rancor, the mind will not attain precision; under suspicion and fear it will not form sound judgment, nor will it, dazzled by love's delight nor in sorrow and anxiety, come to precision." As for money, "Ill got, ill go." When others have ability, if a man "shoves them aside, he can be called a real pest." "The archer when he misses the bullseye, turns and seeks the cause of error in himself." There must be no rationalizing. "Abandon every clandestine egoism to realize the true root." Of the golden rule, there are many variants in the *Analects*: "Tze-kung asked if there was a single principle that you could practise through life to the end. He said sympathy; what you don't want, don't inflict on another" (Book Fifteen, xxiii). "Require the solid of yourself, the trifle of others" (Book Fifteen, xiv). "The proper man brings men's excellence to focus, not their evil qualities" (Book Twelve, xvi). "I am not worried that others do not know me; I am worried by my incapacity" (Book Fourteen, xxxii). Tze-chang asked Kung-tze about maturity. Kung-tze said: To be able to practise five things would humanize the whole empire—sobriety (*serenitas*), magnanimity, sticking by one's word, promptitude (in attention to detail), kindliness (*caritas*). As for "the problem of style. Effect your meaning. Then stop" (Book Fifteen, XL).

In "Salvationists," Mr. Pound says:

> Come, my songs, let us speak of perfection—
> We shall get ourselves rather disliked.

We shall get ourselves disliked and very much liked, because the zest for perfection communicates its excitement to others.

OTHER PROSE

IDIOSYNCRASY AND TECHNIQUE

1. *Technique*

In his inaugural lecture as Professor of Poetry at Oxford,[1] Mr. Auden said, "There is only one thing that all poetry must do; it must praise all it can for being as for happening." He also said, "Every poem is rooted in imaginative awe." These statements answer, or imply an answer, to the question: Why does one write?

I was startled, indeed horrified, when a writing class in which I have an interest was asked, "Is it for money or fame?" as though it must be one or the other—and writing were not for some a felicity, if not a species of intellectual self-preservation. Gorgeously remunerated as I am for being here, it would seem both hypocritical and inappropriate to feign that a love of letters renders money irrelevant. Still, may I say, and with emphasis, that I do not write for money *or* fame. To earn a living is needful, but it can be done in routine ways. One writes because one has a burning desire to objectify what it is indispensable to one's happiness to express; a statement which is not at variance with the fact that Sir Walter Scott, driven by a fanatically sensitive conscience, shortened his life writing to pay what was not a personal debt. And Anthony Trollope, while writing to earn a living, at the same time was writing what he very much loved to write.

Amplifying the impression which Bernard Shaw, as music critic, himself gives of his "veracity, catholicity, and pugnacity," [2] Hesketh Pearson says of him as stage manager of his plays, "No author could be more modest than Shaw. He did not regard his text as sacrosanct. He laughed over his own lines as if they were jokes by somebody else and never could repeat them accurately. Once, when an actor apologized for misquoting a passage, he remarked, 'What you said is better than what I wrote. If you can always misquote so well, keep on misquoting—but remember to give the right cues!' " [3] Writing was resilience. Resilience was an adventure. Is it part of the adventure to revise what one wrote?

Professor Ewing has suggested that something be said about this. My own revisions are usually the result of impatience with unkempt diction and lapses in logic; together with an awareness that for most defects, to delete is the instantaneous cure.

The rhythms of the King James Version of the Bible stand forever as writing, although certain emendations as to meaning seem obligatory. The King James Epistle of Paul to the Philippians, 3:20, reads: "For our conversation is in heaven"; the Revised Standard Version reads: "We are a heavenly body"; each a mistranslation, according to Dr. Alvin E. Magary, who feels that Dr. Moffat got it right: " 'We are a colony of heaven'—a Roman outpost as it were, in which people conformed their lives to the life of Rome—an interpretation which makes sense as applied to Christianity"; Dr. Magary also emphasizes that the beatitude, blessed are the meek, should have no connotation of subservience, since if rendered more strictly, the word would be, not the meek, but the "begging."

The revisions by Henry James of his novels, are evidently in part the result of an insistent desire to do justice to first intention. Reverting to pronouncements on Milton and Goethe made previously, T. S. Eliot seems to feel that after-judgment can not merely be taken for granted, and when accepting the Goethe Prize in 1954 he said, "As one's reading is extended [one begins] to develop that critical ability, that power of self-criticism without which the poet will do no more than repeat himself . . ."; then further on: "To understand what Wisdom is, is to be wise oneself: and I have only the degree of understanding that can be attained by a man who knows that he is not wise, yet has some faith that he is wiser than he was twenty years ago. I say twenty years ago, because I am under the distressing necessity of quoting a sentence I printed in 1933. It is this:

> Of Goethe perhaps it is truer to say that he dabbled in both philosophy and poetry and made no great success at either; his true role was that of a man of the world and sage, a La Rochefoucauld, a La Bruyère, a Vauvenargues."

Mr. Eliot says he ". . . never re-read the passage in which this sentence is buried [and had] discovered it not so very long ago in Mr. Michael Hamburger's introduction to his edition and translation of the text of Holderlin's poems." He then goes on to say of Goethe, "It may be that there are areas of wisdom that he did not penetrate: but I am more interested in trying to understand the wisdom he possessed than to define its limitations. When a man is a good deal wiser than oneself, one does not complain that he is no wiser than he is." [4]

Since writing is not only an art but a trade embodying principles attested by experience, we would do well not to forget that it is an expedient for making one's self understood and that what is said should at least have the air of having meant something to the person who wrote it—as is the case with Gertrude Stein and James Joyce. Stewart Sherman one time devised a piece of jargon which he offered as indistinguishable from work by Gertrude Stein, which gave itself away at once as lacking any private air of interest. If I may venture to say again what I have already said when obscurity was deplored, one should be as clear as one's natural reticence allows one to be. Laurence Binyon, reflecting on the state of letters after completing his Dante, said: "How indulgent we are to infirmity of structure . . ." [5] and structural infirmity truly has, under surrealism, become a kind of horticultural verbal blight threatening firmness at the core; a situation met long ago in *The Classic Anthology Defined by Confucius*:

> Enjoy the good yet sink not in excess.
> True scholar stands by his steadfastness. [6]
>
> . . . . . .
>
> Lamb-skin for suavity, trimmed and ornate,
> But a good soldier who will get things straight. [7]

In attaining this noble firmness, one must have clarity, and clarity depends on precision; not that intentional ambiguity cannot be an art. Reinhold Niebuhr is not famed as easy reading, but is at times a study in precision as when he says, "The self does not

realize itself most fully when self-realization is its conscious aim";
and of conscience, says, "We will define it provisionally at
least as capacity to view itself and judge obligation in contrast
with inclination." [8] It is not "the purpose [but] the function of
roots to absorb water," Dr. Edmund Sinnott notes in his book
The Biology of the Spirit, in which he discusses the self-regulating
properties of protoplasm—digressing, with a shade of outrage, to
deplore untidiness in the use of terms. One is corrected when
referring to certain African tribes for saying they worship the devil;
they propitiate the devil; and if precise, one weeds text of adjective, adverbs, and unnecessary punctuation. As an instance of such
concision, we have Mr. Francis Watson's account of Edwin
Arnold, "the traveller, linguist, and semi-mystic, with whom
Matthew Arnold did not like to be confused." [9] Informing us that
Edwin Arnold had been married three times and that two of his
wives had died—a lack-luster kind of statement which few of us
perhaps would avoid—Mr. Watson says, "after being twice
bereaved, he found a third wife from Japan, a land whose culture
he extolled in articles. . . ." Paramount as a rule for any kind
of writing—scientific, commercial, informal, prose or verse—we
dare not be dull. Finding Akira Durosawa's film *The Magnificent
Seven* too reiterative, Bosley Crowther says that "the director
shows so many shots of horses' feet tromping in the mud that we
wonder if those horses have heads." [10]

In his "Advice to a Young Critic" (Golding Bright),[11] Bernard
Shaw says, "Never strike an attitude, national, moral, or critical"—
an axiom he did not observe too fanatically if judged by the tele-
gram he is said to have sent to an actress with a leading part in
one of his plays: ". . . wonderful, marvelous, superb . . ." to
which the actress replied, "Undeserving such praise"; and he: "I
meant the play"; and she: "So did I."

I have a mania for straight writing—however circuitous I may
be in what I myself say of plants, animals, or places; and although
one may reverse the order of words for emphasis, it should not be
to rescue a rhyme. There are exceptions, of course, as when Mr.
Oliver Warner, speaking of Captain Cook, the explorer, in com-

mending the remarkable drawings made by members of the Captain's staff, says: "None of Cook's artists worked to preconceived notions. They drew what they saw and wonderful it was." [12] To say "and it was wonderful" would have been very flat. We have literature, William Archer said, when we impart distinctiveness to ordinary talk and make it still seem ordinary.

Like dullness, implausibility obscures the point; so, familiar though we are with "Fenimore Cooper's Literary Offenses," by Mark Twain,[13] allow me to quote a line or two. "It is a rule of literary art in the domain of fiction," Mark Twain says, "that always the reader shall be able to tell the corpses from the others. But this detail often has been overlooked in the *Deerslayer* tale. [Cooper] bends 'a sapling' to the form of an arch over [a] narrow passage, and conceals six Indians in its foliage." Then, ". . . one of his acute Indian experts, Chingachgook (pronounced Chicago, I think), has lost the trail of a person he is tracking . . . turned a running stream out of its course, and there, in the slush of its old bed, were that person's moccasin-tracks. . . ." Even the laws of nature take a vacation when Cooper is practicing "the delicate art of the forest."

What has been said pertains to technique (*teknikos* from the Greek, akin to *tekto*: to produce or bring forth—as art, especially the useful arts). And, indeed if technique is of no interest to a writer, I doubt that the writer is an artist.

What do I mean by straight writing, I have been asked. I mean, in part, writing that is not mannered, overconscious, or at war with common sense, as when a reviewer of *The Evolution of Cambridge Publishing*, by S. C. Roberts, refers to "a demure account of Cambridge's flirtation with the *Encyclopædia Britannica*." [14] At the risk of seeming to find every virtue in certain authors and these authors in a certain few books or critiques, let me contrast with the unreal manner, W. D. Howells' *My Mark Twain* and a similar uninfected retrospect by the Duke of Windsor. "Of all the literary men I have known," Howells says of Mark Twain, "he was the most unliterary in his make and manner. . . . His style was what we know, for good or for bad, but his manner, if I may difference the two, was as entirely his own as if no one had ever written before. [He] despised the avoidance of repetitions out of fear of tautology. If a word served his turn better than a substitute, he would use it as many times on a page as he chose. . . . [There] never was a more biddable man in things you could show him a reason for. . . . If you wanted a thing changed, very good, he changed it; if you suggested that a word or a sentence or a paragraph had better be struck out, very good, he struck it out. His proof sheets came back each a veritable 'mush of concession,' as Emerson says." "He was always reading some vital book . . . which gave him life at first hand," Howells continues. "It is in vain that I try to give a notion of the intensity with which he compassed the whole world. . . ."

The other instance of straight writing to which I referred is "My Garden," by the Duke of Windsor.[15] Prosperity and royalty are always under suspicion. "Of course they had help," people say. "Someone must have written it for them"; as they said of the shepherd made judge, in the fable of the shepherd and the King, ". . . *he* is given the credit; we did the work; he has amassed riches; we are poor." [16] So let me say, I have in the following narrative an impression of individuality, conviction, and verbal selectiveness.

"I think my deep enjoyment of gardening must be latent," the Duke begins. "At least it was not inherited. . . . The gardens at Sandringham and Windsor . . . made a fine show in summertime [a word with flavor, for me], but people did not really live with them. A garden is a mood, as Rousseau said, and my mood was one of intimacy, not splendor." Of his present gardening at The Mill, not far from Paris, he says, ". . . French gardens can be remarkably beautiful things. They look like continuations of the Savonnerie of Aubusson carpets in the great chateaus rolled outside the windows onto the lawns, perfectly patterned and mathematically precise. . . . I wanted an English type of garden, which means green grass and seemingly casual arrangement of flowers, and here I had the perfect framework." Commenting on one of the color photographs which supplement the account, he says, "The main entrance to the property has an old covered gateway with ancient oak doors and a cobbled drive which leads to the main building. There is a big sundial above the front door, put there when The Mill was restored about 1732. In the foreground is Trooper, one of our four pugs." Technically an oversight, perhaps—the f-o-r-e ground and f-o-u-r pugs in close proximity—this clash lends authenticity, has the charm of not too conscious writing. Unmistakably all along, the article embodies a zeal for the subject, a deep affection for flowers as seen in the complaint, "The mildest stone-mason turns scourge when it comes to plant life." The piece smiles, whereas saturninity is a bad omen. "We do not praise God by dispraising man." [17]

II. *Idiosyncrasy*

In considering technique, I tried to say that writing can be affirmative and that we must, as Dr. Nathan Scott says, "reject the attitude of philosophic distrust." The writer should have "a sense of upthrusting vitality and self-discovery" [18] without thinking about the impression made, except as one needs to make oneself understood.

We are suffering from too much sarcasm, I feel. Any touch of unfeigned gusto in our smart press is accompanied by an arch word implying, "Now to me, of course, this is a bit asinine." Denigration, indeed, is to me so disaffecting that when I was asked to write something for the Columbia Chapter of Phi Beta Kappa Class Day exercises, I felt that I should not let my sense of incapacity as an orator hinder me from saying what I feel about the mildew of disrespect and leave appreciation to Mr. Auden, to salute "literary marines landing in little magazines." I then realized that what I was so urgent to emphasize is reduced in the First Psalm to a sentence: Blessed is the man who does not sit in the seat of the scoffer.

Odd as it may seem that a few words of overwhelming urgency should be a mosaic of quotations, why paraphrase what for maximum impact should be quoted verbatim? I borrowed, at all events,

Ambassador Conant's title *The Citadel of Learning*, taken for his book from Stalin: "[Facing us] stands the citadel of learning. This citadel we must capture at any price. This citadel must be taken by our youth, if they wish to be the builders of a new life, if they wish, in fact, to take the place of the old guard." [19]

Blessed is the man

who does not sit in the seat of the scoffer—
    the man who does not denigrate, depreciate, denunciate;
      who is not "characteristically intemperate,"
who does not "excuse, retreat, equivocate; and will be heard."
(Ah, Giorgione! there are those who mongrelize
    and those who heighten anything they touch; although it
                        may well be
      that if Giorgione's self-portrait were not said to be he,
it might not take my fancy. Blessed the geniuses who know

that egomania is not a duty.)
    "Diversity, controversy; tolerance"—in that "citadel
      of learning" we have a fort that ought to armor us well.
Blessed is the man who "takes the risk of a decision"—asks

himself the question: "Would it solve the problem?
    Is it right as I see it? Is it in the best interests of all?"
      Alas. Ulysses' companions are now political—
living self-indulgently until the moral sense is drowned,

having lost all power of comparison,
    thinking license emancipates one, "slaves whom they
                  themselves have bound."
      Brazen authors, downright soiled and downright spoiled,
                  as if sound
and exceptional, are the old quasi-modish counterfeit,

mitin-proofing conscience against character.
    Affronted by "private lies and public shame," blessed is the
                      author
      who favors what the supercilious do not favor—
who will not comply. Blessed, the unaccommodating man.

Blessed the man whose faith is different
    from possessiveness—of a kind not framed by "things which
                        do appear"—
    who will not visualize defeat, too intent to cower;
whose illumined eye has seen the shaft that gilds the sultan's
                            tower.

I had written these lines about denigration as treason, and was assembling advice for some students of verse, when I found that Rolfe Humphries, in his little treatise entitled "Writing the Lyric," [20] has thrown light on the use of consonants. "Take the letter *s*," he says, "one of the most insidious sounds in the langauge, one which will creep in, in a sibilant reptilian fashion like the original serpent in the garden, and if you are not careful, not only drive you out of Paradise, but hiss you off the stage; . . . see if you cannot write a quatrain without using it at all." Pondering my "Blessed is the man who does not sit in the seat of the scoffer," I could only say that another's expertise might save one considerable awkwardness. Initiate John Barry came to my rescue by citing the *Aeneid* (II, 8):

           Et iam nox umida caelo
    praecipitat suadentque cadentia somnos.

Convinced that denigration is baneful, one readily sanctions the attack prompted by affection. In fact nothing is more entertaining than the fraternal accolade in reverse; as when *The London News Chronicle* of November 16, 1954, published a cartoon, and lines entitled "Winniehaha," [21] concerning Mr. Churchill—Prime Minister then—after a cousin of his, Captain Lionel Leslie, had referred to the drop of Indian blood inherited by Sir Winston through his grandmother, Clara Jerome. The complimentary cast of the sally—a parody of Longfellow's *Hiawatha*—which was written before Mr. Churchill had been knighted, when the date of his retirement was a subject of speculation, is apparent from even a line or two:

      In the center of the village
      In the wigwam of the wise ones,

Where the head men of the nation
Come to talk in solemn council,
Squats the old chief, Winniehaha,
Also known as Sitting Bulldog; . . .

Some there are with minds that wander
From the purpose of the powwow;
Minds that wonder will he give us
Just an inkling, to be candid,
Of the date of his retirement?
Not that we would wish to rush him,
Wish to rush old Winniehaha,
Rush our splendid Sitting Bulldog
From the headship of the head men
In the center of the village,
In the wigwam of the wise ones.
Still, it's just a bit unsettling
Not to know when Winniehaha
Will give place to handsome Pinstripe.
Will he tell us? Will he tell us?

In connection with personality, it is a curiosity of literature how often what one says of another seems descriptive of one's self. Would-be statesmen who spike their utterances with malice should bear this in mind and take fright as they drive home the moral of The Lion, The Wolf, and The Fox: "Slander flies home faster than rumor of good one has done." [22] In any case, Sir Winston Churchill's pronouncement on Alfred the Great does seem appropriate to himself—his own defeats, triumphs, and hardihood: "This sublime power to rise above the whole force of circumstances, to remain unbiased by the extremes of victory or defeat, to greet returning fortune with a cool eye, to have faith in men after repeated betrayals, raises Alfred far above the turmoil of barbaric wars to his pinnacle of deathless glory." [23]

Walter de la Mare found "prose worthy of the name of literature . . . tinged with that erratic and unique factor, the personal . . ." reminding one of the statement by Mr. F. O. Matthiessen, in his study of Sarah Orne Jewett, that "style means that the author has fused his material and his technique with the distinctive quality of his personality . . ." and of the word "idiolect" used by

Professor Harry Levin as meaning "the language of a speaker or writer who has an inflection of his own." In saying there is no substitute for content, one is partly saying there is no substitute for individuality—that which is peculiar to the person (the Greek: *idioma*). One also recalls the remark by Henry James: "a thing's being one's own will double the use of it." Discoveries in art, certainly, are personal before they are general.

Goya—in *The Taste of Our Time* series,[24] reviewed by Pierre Gassier somewhat as follows—should afford us creative impetus. After surviving a lethal threat, severe illness at Cádiz in 1792, Goya was left with his right side paralyzed, with dizzy spells, a buzzing in his head, and partial blindness. He recovered, only to find himself irremediably deaf. On returning to Madrid, he began work at once, painted eleven pictures for the Academy of San Fernando, and sent them with a letter to the director, Don Berbardo Iriarte. "In order to occupy an imagination mortified by the contemplation of my sufferings," he said, "and recover, partially at all events, the expenses incurred by illness, I fell to painting a set of pictures in which I have given observation a place usually denied it in works made to order, in which little scope is left for fancy and invention." Fancy and invention—not made to order—perfectly describe the work; the *Burial of the Sardine*, say: a careening throng in which one can identify a bear's mask and paws, a black monster wearing a horned hood, a huge turquoise quadracorne, a goblin mouth on a sepia fish-tailed banner, and twin dancers in filmy gowns with pink satin bows in their hair. Pieter Bruegel, the Elder, an observer as careful and as populous as Goya, "crossed the Alps and travelled the length of Italy, returning in 1555 to paint as though Michelangelo had never existed," so powerful was predilective intention.[25] In a television interview after receiving the National Book Award for *Ten North Frederick*, John O'Hara was asked if he might not have to find, as a background for fiction, something different from small-town life in Pennsylvania, to which he replied, "There is in one room in one day of one man's life, material for a lifetime." The artist does not —as we sometimes hear—"seek fresh sources of inspiration." A subject to which he is susceptible entices him to it; as we see in the epics of Marko Marulíc (1450–1524), the fifth centenary of whose birth Yugoslavia has celebrated, in honor largely of his Latin epic *Judita* (1501), enhanced by woodcuts such as *The Muster at Dubrovnic:* trumpeters, men at arms in an elephant-castle; dog; king, queen, and attendants. The New York Yugoslav Information Center says, "What is important is that in following the classics, Marulíc did not transplant . . . mechanically . . . but depended on his own poetic abilities," his novelty consisting in "comparisons taken from his own field of experience, in language abounding in speech forms of the people." An author, that is to say, is a fashioner of words, stamps them with his own personality, and wears the raiment he has made, in his own way.

Psychoanalysis can do some harm "taking things to pieces that it cannot put together again," as Mr. Whit Burnett said in a discourse entitled "Secrets of Creativeness." It has also been of true service, sharpening our faculties and combating complacence. Mr. Burnett drew attention to the biography of Dr. Freud by Ernest Jones, and to what is said there of genius as being not a quality but qualitative—a combination of attributes which differs with the person—three of which are honesty, a sense of the really significant, and the power of concentration.

Curiosity seems to me connected with this sense of significance. Thoreau, you may recall, demurred when commended for originality and said that it was curiosity: "I am curiosity from top to toe." I think I detect curiosity in the work of Sybille Bedford— in her novel *A Legacy*—in the statement, ". . . no one in the house was supposed to handle *used* notes [banknotes]. Everybody was paid straight off the press. The problem of change was not envisaged"; sententiousness in the writing, being offset by the unstereotyped juxtaposing of a word or two such as querulous and placid. Grandma Merz, for instance, "was a short bundle of a woman swaddled in stuffs and folds . . . stuck with brooches of rather gray diamonds. Her face was a round, large, indeterminate expanse . . . with features that escaped attention and an expression that was at once querulous and placid." [26]

In Marguerite Yourcenar's "Author's Note" to her *Memoirs of Hadrian* [27]—a study which does "border on the domain of fiction and sometimes of poetry," as has been said—one sees what concentration editorially can be. And Paul Delarue's "Sources and Commentary" appended to the *Borzoi Book of French Folk Tales* [28] are similarly impressive—besides affording an exciting knowledge of variants. In "The White Dove" (the story of Bluebeard, abridged by Perrault), the ninth victim's pretexts for delay become specific—in this early version—"to put on my petticoat, my wedding-gown, my cap, my bouquet." And we learn that "The Ass's Skin," enshrined for us by La Fontaine in "The Power of Fable," [29] is the "Story of Goldilocks," and of Madame d'Aulnoy's "Beauty and the Beast" (1698). The presentment here of obscure minutiae, demonstrating that tales of all nations have a common fabric, makes the most artful of detective stories seem tame.

Creative secrets, are they secrets? Impassioned interest in life, that burns its bridges behind it and will not contemplate defeat, is one, I would say. Discouragement is a form of temptation; but paranoia is not optimism. In an essay entitled "Solitude" (the theme chosen by the *Figaro* for an essay contest), Maxime Bennebon, a boy seventeen, visualizes "Michelangelo's *Moses*, head in hands, the attitude of the child who prays with eyes closed; of the pianist—his back to the audience; they must be alone that they may offer what is most treasurable, themselves."

The master secret may be steadfastness, that of Nehemiah, Artaxerxes' cupbearer, as it was of the three youths in the fiery furnace, who would not bow down to the image which the King had set up. "Why is thy countenance sad, seeing that thou art not sick?" the King asked. Nehemiah requested that he be allowed to rebuild the wall of Jerusalem and the King granted his request; gave him leave of absence and a letter to the keeper of the forest that he might have timber for the gates of the palace —subject to sarcasm while building, such as Sanballet's, "If a fox go up, he shall break down their wall." Summoned four times to a colloquy, Nehemiah sent word: "I am doing a great work and I cannot come down." Then when warned that he would be slain, he said, "Should such a man as I flee?" "So the wall was finished." [30] A result which is sensational is implemented by what to the craftsman was private and unsensational. Tyrone Guthrie, in connection with the theater, made a statement which sums up what I have been trying to say about idiosyncrasy and technique: "It is one of the paradoxes of art that a work can only be universal if it is rooted in a part of its creator which is most privately and particularly himself." [31]

Thomas Mann, fending off eulogy, rendered a service when he said, "Praise will never subdue skepticism." We fail in some degree—and know that we do, if we are competent; but can prevail; and the following attributes, applied by a London journal to Victor Gollancz, the author and publisher, I adopt as a prescription: we can in the end prevail, if our attachment to art is sufficiently deep; "unpriggish, subtle, perceptive, and consuming." [32]

BROOKLYN FROM CLINTON HILL

Decorum marked life on Clinton Hill in the autumn of 1929 when my mother and I came to Brooklyn to live. An atmosphere of privacy with a touch of diffidence prevailed, as when a neighbor in furred jacket, veil, and gloves would emerge from a four-story house to shop at grocer's or meat-market. Anonymity, without social or professional duties after a life of pressure in New York, we found congenial.

It was not unusual in those days, toward teatime, to catch a glimpse of a maid with starched cap and apron, adjusting accessories on a silver tray, in a certain particularly correct house of which the parlor-windows were screened by a Gauguin-green miscellany of glossy leaves—elephant-ear-sharp and rounder—amid ferns and tiny palms from the sill up, more than ever a grateful sight by contrast with starker windows.

"A city of churches," Brooklyn might also be called a city of trees. The wide leaves and violet blossoms of the catalpa lent an air of leisure to an occasional side- or back-yard. A linden at our corner diffused in spring just enough perfume, not too much; in autumn dropping its seeds, two on a stem from the center of each leaf, like the clustered bullet-tassels or fringe ornamenting Swedish wound wire silver buttons.

One year a scarlet tanager from a migrating flock chose as refuge to which it returned through several days, a nearby white magnolia in bloom—bouquet with removable jewel. Best of all there were the massive branches of elms with the anatomy of oaks, in Washington Park, emerging black after a shower through a mist of incipient emerald leaves.

One can scarcely refer to the Hill without mention of Dr. S. Parkes Cadman, who, late in his ministry, became pastor of the Clinton Avenue Presbyterian Church. Dr. Cadman's Counsel in the *New York Herald Tribune* was read by everyone and fascinatingly sane in its treatment of mighty topics—imaginatively inconclusive at need, as when suggesting that a chance of happiness is better if we want to do something than if we want to have something. A revolutionary force in the neighborhood also, is the Lafayette Avenue Presbyterian Church, its pastor since 1959, George Litch Knight, possessing momentum such that he and his congregation—compositely white, Negro, Puerto Rican, and Japanese (two uniqely rare sisters)—have renovated not only the building but in part its surroundings; mercury lights along South Oxford Street replacing the sinister shade cast by close-growing maples, enabling one to emerge from the subway without a police whistle, should stop-and-start patrons of some tavern inquire fictitiously for hospital or political headquarters.

Another landmark is the First Presbyterian Church on Henry Street—its pews having the original doors—a gallery, organ loft and air of simplicity with authority. In Dr. Phillips Packer Elliott, it has had a pastor for whom the term "a divine" is no archaism. His fraternal Presbyterial aid to other churches, sermons, and series of biographic studies—Great Preachers of the Past—make him one of the great preachers of the present. Following his sudden death on August 2, 1961, his "depth of compassion, humility, intellectual integrity, Christian commitment and ecclesiastical statesmanship are possessed by few religious leaders," the Reverend D. M. Potter, Executive Director of the Protestant Council, said in *The New York Times* of August 3. Students of "period," detained by Cuyler Gore—a tiny triangle of grass and elms between Fulton Street and Greene Avenue (named for Theodore Ledyard Cuyler, first pastor of the Lafayette Avenue church) —find meat in Dr. Elliott's conspectus of Dr. Cuyler—a Matthew Arnold with sideburns and Victorian gravity who, as a Princeton senior of twenty, about to embark on a kind of grand tour, wrote to Wordsworth, Carlyle, and Dickens, requesting appointments with them and as Dr. Elliott observes, "heard from them afterward." Of his published writings, *How to Write a Sermon* (best undertaken "before the sun has reached its meridian"), *Straight to the Point, Reminiscences of a Long Life,* and other work, so excited his interest that my grandfather added them to his library in Missouri and when urged by his congregation to take a vacation, said he needed none, merely wished to visit Brooklyn sometime and hear Dr. Cuyler preach in the Lafayette Avenue Church. Visitors on the Heights do not leave usually without seeing Henry Ward Beecher's Plymouth Church of the Pilgrims on Orange Street near Willow. The plantation aspect of the building with columns and portico at street level beside a parallelogram of shaven grass afford a parable in sculpture of Dr. Beecher "selling slaves out of slavery"—a result literally of disrupting service and directing ushers to "Pass the baskets." Dr. Beecher in bronze as in life—a slave at his feet with shoulder encircled by an angel of consolation at the rear of the green beside the church, stands out as on a stage.

Abraham Lincoln, upon first coming to Brooklyn, heard an impassioned abolitionist sermon by Dr. Beecher; and in 1865 "came once more to Orange Street." His "landau was seen to draw up at the corner of Columbia Heights and Pierpont Street," where "standing up and looking down at the Harbor" he is *said* to have said, "There may be more beautiful views in the world, but I have never seen them."

Brooklyn abounds in schools—Erasmus Hall, justifiably incorporating the name Erasmus, maintains an eminence in classics matching the severest college standards; and there is the Packer Collegiate Institute. Search the world over, you could not find a saner elegance, teaching more initiate, equipment more modern, together with a deep reverence for bequeathed value. Its rare book collection, oak-paneled chapel, shadowy organ, and gowned choir bring to life for me a linen-backed child's book I once had, *The Robin's Christmas Eve*. With beak parted to sing, scarlet breast lighted by a shaft of sun aslant the nave from painted windows, the robin shown resting on a church pillar wound with thick-berried holly.

Louis Zukofsky's anthology, *A Test for Poetry*, exhilarated me when it came out. It wears well and in his courses for engineers at the Polytechnic Institute on Livingstone Street not far from the Packer Institute, Mr. Zukofsky expertly presents poetry, composition, and American literature. The Brooklyn Technical High School for boys affords handsome confirmation that it is technical; its cast brass zodiac, sunk in the entrance floor, not yet having been worn away by the burnishing of countless feet. However, I was surprised to find that some who walk on it day by day have never noticed it. Their technical interests, however, do not seem to blind students to an interest in English, to Emil Gilels, "Cage and Cowell," or to Carlos Surinac's *Tientos* and Sylvia Marlowe—evaluated in neat clippings on a classroom bulletin board.

For its library school and prowess in design (engineering and aesthetic) Pratt Institute, renowned in the neighborhood and throughout the country, is an apex in performance, like its flag-pole—clean-cut from the angled circular stone bench at its base to the gilded pineapple at the top. Pratt Institute Free Library, no longer open to the public, was for me on coming to Brooklyn a veritable desert rescue. The row of new accessions near the circulation desk went to one's head, new books appearing almost simultaneously with the advertising. In the stacks, related items in a subject often became more important than the original quest. And sometimes one came on startling finds acquired from private library dispersals. Stairs of polished oak, wide and easy, to the Periodical Room on the second floor, admit one to a room aired and maintained with unlapsing vigilance; newspapers in the racks, *Litell's Weekly* (cinnamon-covered), *The Yale Review*—obdurate against my timidly persistent product—with, richly counteracting the thought of its cruelty, *The Illustrated London News* on stout glossy paper, and *Natural History*, in a copy of which I found Dr. Robert Hatt's pangolins with text and camera studies, vivid substitute for their reclusive behavior and scaly integument.

At the foot of Clinton Hill, the Brooklyn Institute of Arts and Sciences (Arts without an "s" originally) has a telescope on the roof, large enough to attract the initiate who confer with initiates, while gapers expecting high-powered lenses to make brightness brighter, stand dejected upon finding the blaze of Sirius a hesitant glow. In the structure of the building itself certain materials intrinsically seem to me a feature: the interlacing Italian-Irish designs of the ground-floor concourse—related in period to the ground-floor mosaics in the Plaza Hotel in Manhattan. Then, for some stonemason, a triumph: the unpieced aspect of the staircase— satin-smooth oyster-gray marble with massive hand-rail—a deeply-grooved extension of the wall, with which it is continuous.

One winter, I attended so many presentations in lecture room or auditorium that I was pitied at home for not being able to sleep in the building—on certain days absent morning, afternoon, and evening. If one takes time for a thing, one should get as much of it as possible, I felt, so I usually sat in a front row. One evening I was so near the lecturer's "material," selected from the Staten Island Zoo snake house by the Curator, Mr. Kauffield, to supplement his theme that snakes are an asset, as barely to be missed by a red racer which shot from the chromium tree which accommodated harmless snakes, into the lap of a boy in the first row, an incipient herpetologist evidently; or did the snake know him?

Daniel Gregory Mason, lecturing in that same room with piano to illustrate, converted me to Brahms, not a favorite with me, demonstrating the principle of restatement after contrast and the function of ornament, enlivening the series with such anecdotes as that of the woman who rushed up to Brahms with the impassioned inquiry, "Is this the great Brahms?" he replying, "His brother; you will find him over that hill." In the auditorium, Thornton Wilder in *one* evening characterized biography, poetry, fiction, and drama. George Russell, the Irish poet, AE—impressively unexaggerated in his attitude to dreams and extrasensory phenomena—told of visualizing from Dublin a certain house in New York, both street and number, associated with a man's death; the details verified by word received later.

In 1927, February 16, Stravinsky, in an all-Stravinsky program, no doubt exemplified the principle of restatement after contrast—primarily for me, I confess, rapt preoccupation with nicety of attack, fire, and tempo, projected concentratedly and unthreatened, in a manner so intent as to disable judgment. I can hear him still—a puzzle in the perfection of hoarded intentionalness.

For anyone with "a passion for actuality" there are times when the camera seems preferable to any other medium; or so I felt in 1896, enthralled by Lyman Howe Travelogues at the Opera House in Carlisle, Pennsylvania. As sequel to lantern-slides, cosmoscope, and stereopticon, Brooklyn Institute movies were Aladdin's magic. The documentary I should most like to see again is *Night Mail* with W. H. Auden's recitative dramatizing the mail-train's nonstop run from London to Scotland: the natural with the technical—steam from locomotive and fog on the meadow—a concentrate; the literal giving point to the figurative:

> "As it rushes past the farmhouse and no one wakes,
> a jug in a bedroom gently shakes."

The Brooklyn Museum, although representative, is not so vast as to justify the impression that gathered art can be the most lethal form of exhilaration. It has "the" Peruvian double-fish-motive textile, a closely woven parallelogram with widely spaced pairs of fish in pale thread on maroon; almost an entire floor devoted to finely jointed carapaces by Japanese armorers. There are costumes, including a French mull Empress Josephine long dress with high waist, embroidered in a tiny flower-cluster design, appropriate to a Leghorn hat with pale-blue streamers in a Turgenev picnic-scene by a waterfall. Not only is art primitive, early, and modern, exhibited by the Museum, it has a class in painting taught by William von Kienbusch, whose own work, naturalistic or abstract, has plenty of drive.

Beyond Prospect Park's knolls, elms, lake, and bridle paths is the Zoo, ideally compact yet varied. One summer day when I was there, a Brahma zebu with hump and pale velour ears which it allowed to be felt, stood out of doors near wide-meshed fencing which enclosed a yard with a tree, not far from the small cats. Among them an ocelot with matching stencil of horned-owl richness paraded coldly; next a typically inquisitive ring-tailed coatimundi. Launched from their shelter like stones from a sling, in twenty- or thirty-foot arcs, a herd of impala soared down a run bordering meadow grass where two young bears were playing, hugging and staggering till, forced to a stand-still, one climbed a slab of rock and lay down.

Opposite the Zoo, the Botanic Garden, with willows and birds by a brook, is yellow in spring with forsythia, Brooklyn's flower symbolizing "unity and brotherhood." The Garden has rock plants, a wild-flower garden, plots for children, pools of tropical and hardy water lilies, Japanese cherries, a rose-garden beautifully divided by narrow grass paths, and a fragrance-garden for the blind, built up so that it may be touched.

The Bridge—a word associated with fantasy, a sense of leisure, shade under willows or at sunset, a pair of Chinese herdmen "enjoying the breeze in a fishing-boat"—is in Brooklyn synonymous with endurance—sacrifice; first by John H. Roebling, whose death resulted from a foot crushed by an incoming ferry when he was surveying for the bridge; with death for his son, Washington A. Roebling, who suffered caisson bends; and with heroism on the part of Mrs. Washington Roebling, who mastered calculus and engineering with one objective, the completing of the bridge. It was opened May 24, 1883—a notable triumph—memorialized by the cables ("Roebling cable"), towers, and centrally fixed arcs of filament united by stress, refined till diaphanous when seen from the Manhattan Bridge, silhouetted either by sun or the moon.

Another memorial—stirring for humanitarian and personal reasons, the Quaker passion for rescue—is the plaque in Squibb Park at the end of Middagh Street, to Edward Robinson Squibb, fiery Quaker and idealist with a passion for art and a technical capacity with the drive of a Polaris missile. (*Doctor Squibb: The Life and Times of a Rugged Idealist* by Lawrence G. Blochman—an enthralling story. Simon and Schuster, 1958.)

The name Squibb a hundred years ago meant "ether" and the first reliable ether mask; becoming associated with toothpaste and vitamins twenty years and more after Dr. Squibb's death. As a Quaker, since he would not be killing people but making them well—logic adduced by an aunt—Dr. Squibb felt that he could serve as a doctor in the Navy.

Doctor Squibb was outraged that patients with smallpox had died by reason of inefficient vaccine, his indignation mounting upon finding drugs wormy, decayed, or adulterated with chalk, bark, some even with plaster of Paris, and he resolved to obtain an appropriation for a laboratory that would manufacture pure drugs of uniform strength. Impeded for years by legislators who hesitated, and closed the fist, restricting funds as they do today for use as folly dictates, he began the laboratory himself—unwilling to patent his discoveries, saying they were "for those who needed them." He probably would disapprove of the cerise neon "Squibb" in magnified capitals on the building at Furman Street and the River; yet would most certainly approve of George S. Squibb, his great-grandson—one of the firm's experts—present with Miss Margaret Squibb and city dignitaries at the dedicating of the plaque in Squibb Park on September 23, 1959. The Park, antiseptically airy, has a kind of seaside bleached look.

Seth Low—born in Brooklyn in 1859—was its mayor from 1882 to 1886, President of Columbia, 1890 to 1901, moved the College to Morningside Heights, then resigned to become Mayor of New York on the fusion ticket; improved City finances, made essential changes in City departments as he had made significant changes in education. An annoyed citizen of that day could scarcely have said as has been said by one today, concerning the city's chief financier, "His ingratitude cannot disguise his ineptitude." Professor W. E. Hocking lived on Grace Court "Street"; W. H. Auden on Monroe Place; Jennie Jerome, the mother of Sir Winston Churchill, on Henry Street; Grace Court—from Henry Street to the Esplanade—being one of our retreats for select persons, free from urban vexations, in autumn aglow with the artificial sunlight of falling leaves drying in tones of pale cadmium under Imperial trees of Japan.

In the Navy Yard, "westerly of the disbursing office (building 121), the Intelligent Whale may be seen"—said to be the first United States submarine, thirty feet long and about nine deep— to be propelled by hand at four knots—an evolution of Bushnell's Turtle, begun in New Jersey by Cornelius Bushnell, November 2, 1863, and completed in 1864 by a builder named Halstead. In a preliminary test of the Whale persevering Mr. Halstead nearly lost his life. The whale was condemned in 1872.

The *Monitor*—an iron-clad of wood like the *Merrimac*—was begun at Greenpoint, Brooklyn, in 1861 by John Ericsson and completed in 1862, defeating the *Merrimac* at Hampton Roads— changing the entire course of naval construction.

The Battle of Brooklyn is commemorated by the 1776–1951 heliotrope three-cent stamp: "Washington Saves His Army at Brooklyn," a figure on a white horse—arm raised—above the Bay dotted with sails. The designer of this stamp—now that a five-cent violet stamp is imminent—is commended to the Bureau of Printing and Engraving; also the behavior of the issue, which could not have given rise to Ogden Nash's recent complaint, rhyming with calf: "the perforations on sheets of stamps are optical delusions; if you believe that they are real you come up with either half a stamp or a stamp and a half." (Three sheets of *Washington Saves His Army* . . . —now gone—which matched a present of M. T. Bird violet, Crane single-sheet laid paper, accidentally but efficiently, I thought, emphasized history.)

Among Brooklyn streets,* the names Ocean, Surf, Mermaid, and Half Moon are self-explanatory. The origin of Willow Street is less obvious, although at No. 27 there is still one remaining willow, all curves and angles as though by Harunobu. (Willow became official, it is *said*, when a Miss Middagh, undetected, substituted for the name "Jones" shingles on which she had painstakingly inscribed "Willow.") Across the street from 27, its frame house of coldish lizard blue and side yard with the willow, the last house on the street is a stately one of red brick. The rectangular doorstep is reached by six steps, the first three rising in a curve prettily emphasized by the swirl of the railing. In Brooklyn a wreath, square knot, or part of a chaplet sometimes ornaments the keystone above a white door; but on Willow Street the doors are black or green, their brass knobs complementing the old-style italic numeral in gold leaf on glass above the door. The numeral is usually repeated, one above the left and one above the right double door with a gold dot between. Unlike any other, the upper third of one door is divisioned in small squares with glass above, the lace behind the glass being of the same design as that of the parlor curtains—a needlework tracery of flowers and vines on transparent net. Dr. Squibb lived on Columbia Heights, facing the end of Clark Street. After distilling pure ether, he "had turned his attention to chloroform, then to money." That is to say, he built two houses just alike, connected by a tunnel—one for himself, one for his two sons. His house has been demolished; the other stands

* Pierpont Street was named for Hezekiah Pierpont, grandson of a founder of Yale; and Montague Street is said to have been named by Henry Evelyn Montague (son of Hezekiah) for the family of Lady Mary Montague, a cousin, when the voyaging branch left to come to America. Clark Street commemorates James S. Clark, who joined Adrian Van Sinderen, Hezekiah Pierpont, and Adam Judall to found—in the basement of the Apprentice Library at Cranberry and Henry Streets—the Brooklyn Savings Bank, "a secure place of deposit for the savings of tradesmen, laborers, minors and servants." The managers, they said, "disclaim personal emolument in any form whatever"; and they did not accept deposits from the hyper-prosperous. The cornerstone of the Apprentice Library was laid by Lafayette, whom Lafayette Avenue commemorates, on which the Institute stands. Orange, Cranberry, and Pineapple Streets were named, *perhaps*, by the Hicks family—farmers and grocers—for their merchandise from Cape Cod and the West Indies. Remsen Street was named for Henry Remsen, President of the Bank of Manhattan.

—a kind of severe mansion of pale brick, now occupied by Jehovah's Witnesses.

Originally I knew Montague Street as housing a valuable branch of the Public Library; and as headquarters for the Dodgers at 115. There is an eminent stationer on the street, McDonough and Company, where, from concealment, a clerk invariably emerges with an eye for the fretful itinerant—swift to produce an Esterbrook numbered list, Norma pencil, non-curl carbon paper, or other product. Your dog may wait inside but not among the merchandise. Brooklyn has, in a Womrath's nearby, a really literary bookstore, the young saleswoman being a bookman who knows what the wanted thing is and where to find it—a paperbook, an art study or small expensive book of poetry among hardbacks, a greeting card (Swiss flowers or cats-in-costume) well apart from the books and of grown-up nature—like rice, wheat, or corn-checks from Checkerboard Square.

Of the several florists, all meriting a compliment, E. Frank, with many fresh flowers in small space, is willing to provide a gardenia not made offensive by silver sparkles, starched net, or cotton-backed ribbon.

Brooklyn is susceptible to the lure of steel—stainless, unfortunately—but one of its *objets d'art* with Herculean potentialities is in the vault of the Williamsburg Bank on Hanson Place: a Mosler safe, with the look of Cartier platinum and the burnish of a watch interior, its luster maintained year after year without a flaw.

Someone should delineate the Hill, the Heights, the center—doing justice to landmarks and losses. I like living here. Brooklyn has given me pleasure, has helped to educate me; has afforded me, in fact, the kind of tame excitement on which I thrive.

MY CROW, PLUTO—A FANTASY

It occurred to me one day to try a two-syllable-line, two-line-stanza piece about a crow—My crow/ Pluto// the true/ Plato// adagio

—but I am changing to prose as less restrictive than verse. I had always wanted a crow and received a mechanical one for Christmas. Then Pluto, whose rookery is in Fort Green Park about a block from me, adopted me—a dream come true. He may have been attracted to my favorite hat, a black satin-straw sailor with narrow moire ribbon tied at the side, overlapping the nibs of crow feathers laid in a fan around the brim. If a feather blew away or partly detached itself, I had been dependent on a friend or relative to send me one in a letter. Now, I could salvage one almost any day from assiduous preenings—blue-green of the most ineffable luster. The hat—which had been bought me by my mother—was by Tappé, whose "creations" fascinated me, sketched and with descriptions by him published serially. Nor was the crow's intuition amiss, since he liked a great many kinds of food I like— honey, Anheuser-Busch high-potency yeast, dehydrated alfalfa, watercress, buckwheat cakes; fruit of all kinds.

Crows have a bad reputation as robbing songbirds' nests, fruit to be marketed, corn newly planted; even outdoing magpies in carrying off rings, gold thimbles, and gems, loose or set; but since this crow lived with me most of the time, I acquired what he acquired; inconvenienced of course by having to restore what I could, with somewhat fraudulent explanations lest the culprit suffer. Although Chaucer has the phrase, "pull a finch," meaning filch, official investigation of crows' crops reveals comparatively innocent ravages of farm products. Is not the crow, furthermore, famed as an emblem of Providence, since ravens—certainly corvine—fed Elijah; and "of inspired birds, ravens were accounted the most prophetical," Macaulay says in his *History of St. Kilda*.

My crow was fanatically interested in detail—the pink-enameled heading on the stationery of *The Ladies' Home Journal* and the minuscule characters in *Harper's Bazaar* between the capital As of *Bazaar* on that magazine's black-embossed pale blue stationery. I liked to take him with me on errands, although he attracted attention in a drugstore or store like Key Food, where I was allowed to bring him if I kept an eye on him. He, however, had an eye for too much—cheese, grapes, nectarines, "party rolls,"

Fritos, and gadgets for the house. He was, happily, as literary as he was gastronomic—very fond of Doctor Zulli's 6:30 "Sunrise Semester" on Channel 2: "Landmarks in the Evolution of the Novel," and would perch on a brass knob at the foot of my bed as I took down the lecture, greatly convenienced by having a companion who could supply a word if I missed one. Also, because it was near the typewriter which interested him, he favored a bust as a perch—a bronze by Gaston Lachaise (cast and given me by Lincoln Kirstein)—but I could not induce him to say, "Nevermore." If I inquired, "What was the refrain in Poe's 'Raven,' Pluto?" he invariably would croak, "Evermore." He understood me, and I him from the first, even if our crow-Esperanto was not perfect; two squawks meant "no" and three "yes," a system a little like reading Braille raised dots, or guessing the word left out of a familiar text in Poetry Pilot contests, indicated by the number of letters omitted. Pluto—or Plato—as was inevitable from his habits and proficiencies, became alternates; choice depending on the vowel in the preceding word; after "eraser" it would be Pluto; after "cubic" it would be Plato. Pluto, from the perch on my head, could see and pick up anything I dropped, eraser or pencil. If I said, "Dictionary," he would fly to my case of miniature books in the front hall and bring me Webster's *Dictionary for the Vest Pocket*, 3¼ by 2½ (1911), thumb-indexed and half an inch thick, containing "Rules for Spelling and Punctuation; of Parliamentary Law, of National Bankruptcy Law, Postal Rates, Etc."—heresy though it would be to mention Webster's Pocket rather than *New World Dictionary*, recently endorsed by me—if the Pocket really were Webster's "Latest & Best."

We should exemplify what we require of others and, having badgered a neighbor into returning a raccoon to the woods where he got it, I asked one day, "Pluto, where were you born?" He said what sounded like "Correct account." I said, "Connecticut?" He cawed three times, so I took him to a Connecticut woods and liberated him—said, "Spread your wings. Fly," although "emancipated" is more accurate, since he was already free. "Fly?" Losing him was not simple but the spirit of adventure finally got the best of him. If what you have been reading savors of mythology, could I make it up? and if I could, would I impose on you? Remember, life is stranger than fiction.

IF I WERE SIXTEEN TODAY

When I was sixteen—in fact thirteen—I felt as old as at any time since; and what I wish I could have been when sixteen I am trying to be now—"hindered to succeed." If one cannot strike when the iron is hot, one can "strike till the iron is hot" (Lyman Abbott).

With every reason to feel confident—except that we were in straitened circumstances financially (my mother, brother, and I)—I felt insecure, and took a day at a time, not because I knew it was best but because I had to. I regarded myself as a wallflower; I did not like my face, and not many of my "best" clothes; was an introvert.

I experienced society vicariously; my brother was not introspective, or brooding, or too diffident, and abounded in invitations. He did not exalt "the power of life to renew itself"; he exemplified it. Cynicism was foreign to him; he would not have understood his own later warning to a boy who had completed preparatory-school work, whose mania was dancing. "Remember, every girl has one question: 'Is he going to marry me?' and every man: 'How safe am I?' "

I received the present of a bicycle—a maroon Reading Standard. Was I delighted? Not at all. I would have to learn to ride; riding itself was work. Little did I anticipate sweeping down smooth roads lined by tassels of waving locust blossoms, or pausing on a little bridge over a brook to drop leaves and see them whirled away as minnows veered or hung motionless.

If I could alter my attitude retroactively, I would say as my brother sometimes says, "Be confident; burn your bridges behind you. . . . You may have to get tough. A bear has paws and teeth and sometimes has to use them." And, taking the advice of James Stern in a *New York Times Book Review* section, beware of "the uncertain approach"; of objecting to what you object to "in no small degree"; of belonging to a school which the late George Orwell once described as "that of the not ungreen grass."

I would, if I could, let little things be little things—would be less susceptible to embarrassment. David Seabury says, "When you are saying, 'I can't be calm, I can't be calm,' you *can* be calm." Don't relive bad moments, or *revive them for others*, or be expecting more of them. To postponers, I would say, DO IT NOW; and to firebrands of impatience, ROME WAS NOT BUILT IN A DAY. "Superiority" is at the opposite pole from insight. Fashion can make you ridiculous; style, which is yours to control individually, can make you attractive—a near siren. What of chastity? It confers a particular strength. Until recently, I took it for granted as a universally regarded asset, like avoiding "all drugs."

Instead of hating an over-heavy curriculum and seeing the point of the hackneyed jest about the army: "the incompetent teaching the indifferent the irrelevant," I would give thought to the why rather than merely the what of a subject. Progressive forms in mathematics have "structure," and it means something. You may not like arithmetic; my aplomb suffers a trifle when a bank teller says, "Yes; it's all right; I just changed a six to a seven." Arithmetic demands of memory an exact kind of co-ordination; and in school I found geometry a relief; Smith's advanced algebra, easier than arithmetic; it exerted a certain fascination. Caesar's *Commentaries* are skillful, not traps for a drudge. Xenophon—on dogs and in his treatise on horsemanship—is an expert.

1. Whatever you do, put all you have into it.

2. Go to the trouble of asking, "What good does it do?" rather than "Why Portuguese? I may never use it."

3. Don't look on art as effeminate, and museums as "the most tiring form of recreation."

4. I would, like Sir Winston Churchill, refuse to let a betrayal rob me of trust in my fellow man.

5. One should above all, learn to be silent, to listen; to make

possible promptings from on high. Suppose you "don't believe in God." Talk to someone very wise, who believed in God, did not, and then found that he did. The cure for loneliness is solitude. Think about this saying by Martin Buber: "The free man believes in destiny and that it has need of him." Destiny, not fate.

And lastly, ponder Solomon's wish: when God appeared to him in a dream and asked, "What wouldst thou that I give unto thee?" Solomon did not say fame, power, riches, but an understanding mind, and the rest was added.

ABRAHAM LINCOLN AND THE ART OF THE WORD *

"I dislike an oath which requires a man to swear he *has* not done wrong. It rejects the Christian principle of forgiveness on terms of repentance. I think it is enough if the man does no wrong here-after." [1] It was Abraham Lincoln who said this—his controlled impetuosity exemplifying excellences both of the technician and of the poet.

The malcontent attacks greatness by disparaging it—by libels on efficiency, interpreting needful silence as lack of initiative, by distortion, by ridicule. "As a general rule," Lincoln said, "I abstain from reading attacks upon myself, wishing not to be pro-voked by that to which I cannot properly offer an answer." Expert in rebuttal, however, as in strategy, he often won juries and dis-interested observers alike, by anecdote or humorous implication that made argument unnecessary. His use of words became a per-fected instrument, acquired by an education largely self-attained— " 'picked up,' " he said, "under pressure of necessity." That the books read became part of him is apparent in phrases influenced by the Bible, Shakespeare, *The Pilgrim's Progress*, *Robinson Crusoe*, Burns, Blackstone's *Commentaries*; and not least, by some books of Euclid—read and "nearly mastered," as he says, after he had become a member of Congress. The largeness of the life entered into the writing, as with a passion he strove to persuade his hearers of what he believed, his adroit, ingenious mentality framing an art which, if it is not to be designated poetry, we may call a "grasp of eternal grace"—in both senses, figurative and literal. Nor was he unaware of having effected what mattered, as we realize by his determined effort, when a first attempt failed, to obtain from the *Chicago Press and Tribune* "a set of the late debates (if they may be so called)" he wrote, "between Douglas and myself . . . two copies of each number . . . in order to lay one away in the raw and to put the other in a scrapbook." One notes that he did not neglect to say, "if any debate is on *both* sides of one sheet, it will take two sets to make one scrapbook."

Of persuasive expedients, those most constant with Lincoln are antithesis, reiteration, satire, metaphor; above all *the meaning,* clear and unadorned. A determination "to express his ideas in simple terms became his ruling passion," his every word natural, impelled by ardor. In his address at the Wisconsin Agricultural Fair, he said—regarding competitive awards about to be made—"exultations and mortifications . . . are but temporary; the victor shall soon be vanquished, if he relax in his exertion; and . . . the vanquished this year may be the victor next, in spite of all competition." At the Baltimore Sanitary Fair of 1864, in an address conspicuously combining antithesis with reiteration, he said, "The world has never had a good definition of liberty. . . . We all declare for liberty; but in using the same *word* we do not all mean the same *thing.* With some the word may mean for each man to do as he pleases with himself, and the product of his labor; while with others the same word may mean for some men to do as they please with other men, and the product of other men's labor. Here are two, not only different, but incompatible things, called by the same name—liberty. . . . The shepherd drives the wolf from the sheep's throat, for which the sheep thanks the shepherd as a *liberator,* while the wolf denounces him for the same act as the destroyer of liberty, especially as the sheep was a black one."

In Lincoln's use of italics, one perceives that he is not substituting emphasis for precision but is impersonating speech. In declining an invitation to the Jefferson birthday dinner of 1859, he wrote, "The principles of Jefferson are the axioms of a free society. One dashingly calls them 'glittering generalities'; another bluntly calls them 'self-evident lies.'" And in combating repeal of the Missouri Compromise (which would have extended slavery), he said, "Repeal the Missouri Compromise—repeal all compromises—repeal the Declaration of Independence—repeal all history—you cannot repeal human nature."

Crystalline logic indeed was to be his passion. He wrote to James Conkling, "You desire peace; and you blame me that we do not have it. But how can we attain it? There are but three conceivable ways. First, force of arms. . . . Are you for it? . . . A second way is to give up the Union. Are you for it? If you are, you should say so plainly. If not for force, not yet for dissolution, Compromise. I am against that. I do not believe any compromise is now possible." And to General Schurz he said, "You think I could do better; therefore you blame me. I think I could not do better, therefore I blame you for blaming me."

Unsurpassed in satire, Lincoln said that Judge Douglas, in his interpretation of the Declaration of Independence, offered "the arguments that kings have made for enslaving the people in all ages of the world. They always bestrode the necks of the people, not that they wanted to do it, but that the people were better off for being ridden." Of slavery as an institution he said, "Slavery is strikingly peculiar in this, that it is the only good thing which no man seeks the good of for *himself*."

Metaphor is a force, indeed magnet, among Lincoln's arts of the word. Urgent that the new government of Louisiana be affirmed, he said, "If we reject it, we in effect say, 'You are worthless. We will neither help nor be helped by you.' To the blacks we say, 'This cup of liberty which these, your old masters, hold to your lips, we will dash from you, . . . discouraging and paralysing both white and black. . . . If on the contrary, we recognize and sustain the new government, we are supporting its efforts to this end, to make it, to us, in your language, a Union of hearts and hands as well as of states.' " Passionate that the Union be saved, he uses a metaphor yet stronger than the cup of liberty. He says, "By general law, life *and* limb must be protected; yet often a limb must be amputated to save a life; but a life is never wisely given to save a limb. . . . I could not feel that, . . . to save slavery, . . . I should permit the wreck of government, country, and constitution altogether."

Diligence underlay these verbal expedients—one can scarcely call them devices—so rapt Lincoln was in what he cared about. He had a genius for words but it was through diligence that he became a master of them—affording hope to the most awkward of us. To Isham Reavis he wrote, "If you are resolutely determined to make a lawyer of yourself, the thing is half done already. It is a small matter whether you read *with* anybody or not. . . . It is of no consequence to be in a large town. . . . I read at New Salem, which never had three hundred people living in it. The *books* and your *capacity* for understanding them, are just the same in all places."

Diligence was basic. Upon hearing that George Latham, his son Robert's classmate at the Phillips Exeter Academy, had failed entrance examinations to Harvard, Lincoln wrote, "having made the attempt you *must* succeed in it. '*Must*' is the word . . . you *can* not fail if you resolutely determine that you *will* not." This intensity we see heightened in Lincoln's torment of anxiety, during the war, that the struggle be ended. "The subject is on my mind day and night," he said. During August, 1862, in a letter to Colonel Haupt on the 29th, he begged, "What news from the direction of Manassas?" On that same day to General McClellan he wrote, "What news from the direction of Manassas Junction?" On August 30th, to General Banks, "Please tell me what news?" and again "What news?" on August 30th to Colonel Haupt. The result was a man wearing down under continuous desperation when General Meade, unable to conclude the war at Gettysburg, allowed the Confederate forces to retreat south.

In speeches and in letters, Lincoln made articulate an indomitable ideal—that what the framers of the Constitution embodied in it be preserved—"and that something is the principle of 'Liberty for all,' that clears the *path* for all—gives *hope* to all—and by consequence *enterprise* and *industry* to all." Inflexible when sure he was right—as in his reply to Isaac Schermerhorn, who was dissatisfied with the management of the war, he said, "This is not a question of sentiment or taste but one of physical force which may be measured and estimated as horse-power and Steam-power are measured and estimated. . . . Throw it away and the Union goes with it."

There is much to learn from Lincoln's respect for words taken separately, as when he said, "It seems to me very important that the statute laws should be made as plain and intelligible as possible, and be reduced to as small compass as may consist with the fullness and precision of the will of the legislature and the perspicuity of its language." He was "determined to be so clear," he said, "that no honest man can misunderstand me, and no dishonest one can successfully misrepresent me." Exasperated to have been misquoted, he protested "a specious and fantastic arrangement of words, by which a man can prove a horse-chestnut to be a chestnut horse." Consulted regarding a more perfect edition of his Cooper Institute speech, he said, "Of course I would not object, but would be pleased rather . . . but I do not wish the sense changed or modified, to a hair's breadth. Striking out 'upon' leaves the sense too general and incomplete. . . . The words 'quite,' 'as,' and 'or,' on the same page, I wish retained." Of Stephen Douglas he said, "Cannot the Judge perceive the difference between a purpose and an expectation? I have often expressed an expectation to die but I have never expressed a *wish* to die." The Declaration of Independence he made stronger by saying, "I think the authors of that notable instrument intended to include *all* men but they did not intend to declare all men were equal *in all respects*." And to quibblers, after the surrender of the South, he replied, "whether the seceded states, so-called, are in the Union or out of it, the question is bad . . . a pernicious abstraction!" Indelible even upon a feeble memory—we recall the phrase, "With malice toward none and charity for all," and in the second inaugural address, "Let us strive on to finish the work we are in." We are *in*. Lincoln understood in the use of emphasis that one must be *natural*. Instead of using the word "confidential" in a letter to A. H. Stephens, he wrote in italics at the head of the page, *"For your eye only."* The result of this intensified particularity was such that in his so-called Lost Speech of 1856, which unified the Republican party, "newspaper men forgot paper and pad . . . to sit enraptured," and instead of taking down his eulogy of Henry Clay, "dropped their pens and sat as under enchantment from near the beginning, to quite the end."

Lincoln attained not force only, but cadence, the melodic propriety of poetry in fact, as in the Farewell Address from Springfield he refers to "the weight of reponsibility on George Washington"; then says of "that Divine being without which I cannot succeed, with that assistance, I cannot fail." Consider also the stateliness of the three cannots in the Gettysburg Address: "We cannot dedicate—we cannot consecrate—we cannot hallow—this ground. The brave men, living and dead, who struggled here, have consecrated it far above our poor power to add or detract. The world will little note nor long remember what we may say here, but it can never forget what they did here." Editors attempting to improve Lincoln's punctuation by replacing dashes with commas, should refrain—the dash, as well known, signifying prudence.

With consummate reverence for God, with insight that illumined his every procedure as a lawyer, that was alive in his every decision as a President with civilian command of an army at bay, Lincoln was notable in his manner of proffering consolation; studiously avoiding insult when relieving an officer of his command; instantaneous with praise. To General Grant—made commander of the Union army after his brilliant flanking maneuver at Vicksburg—he said, "As the country trusts you, so, under God, it will sustain you." To Grant "alone" he ascribed credit for terminating the war. Constrained almost to ferocity by the sense of fairness, he begs recognition for "black men who can remember that with silent tongues, and clenched teeth, and steady eye and well-poised bayonet, they have helped mankind to this consummation" (preserving the Union). He managed to take time to retrieve the property of a barber, a Negro, who had not recorded the deed to land he owned. Emphasizing by vivid addendum his request for promotion of a "brave drummer-boy" who "had accompanied his division under heavy fire," Lincoln said, "he should have his chance." For "a poor widow whose son was serving a long sentence without pay"—recommending the son for re-enlistment with pay—he wrote, "she says she cannot get it acted on. Please do it." In constant disfavor with officers in charge of penalties, he said, "Must I shoot a simple soldier boy who deserts while I must not touch a hair of the wily agitator who induces him to desert? To silence the agitator and save the boy is not only constitutional but withal a great mercy." Of Captain McKnabb, dismissed on the charge of being a disunionist, Lincoln wrote, "He wishes to show that the charge is false. Fair play is a jewel. Give him a chance if you can." Afflicted by self-obsessed factions in Missouri, where private grievances should have been settled locally, he summarized the matter: "I have exhausted my wits and nearly my patience in efforts to convince both [sides] that the evils they charged on the others are inherent. I am well satisfied that the preventing of the remedial raid into Missouri was the only safe way to avoid an indiscriminate massacre, including probably more innocent than guilty. Instead of condemning, I therefore approve what I understand General Schofield did in that respect. . . Few things have been so grateful to my anxious feeling as when . . . the local force in Missouri aided General Schofield to so promptly send a large force to the relief of General Grant then investing Vicksburg and menaced by General Johnston. . . . My feeling obliges nobody to follow me and I trust obliges me to follow nobody."

With regard to presidential appointments, it was in 1849, during Zachary Taylor's administration, that Lincoln said, "I take the responsibility. In that phrase were the 'Samson's locks' of General Jackson, and we dare not disregard the lessons of experience"— lessons underlying the principle which he put into practice when appointing Governor Chase Secretary of the Treasury. Pressed, in fact persecuted, to appoint General Cameron, he said, "It seems to me not only highly proper but a *necessity* that Governor Chase shall take that place. His ability, firmness, and purity of character produce the propriety." Purity of character—the phrase is an epitome of Lincoln. To a young man considering law as a career, he said, "There is a vague popular belief that lawyers are necessarily dishonest. If you cannot be an honest lawyer, resolve to be honest without being a lawyer." Deploring bombast, yet tactful, he opposed investigating the Bank of Illinois: "No, Sir, it is the *politician* who is first to sound the alarm (which, by the way, is a false one). It is he, who, by these unholy means, is endeavoring to blow up a storm that he may ride upon and direct it. . . . I say this with the greater freedom, because, being a politician, none can regard it as personal." Firm in resisting pressure, he was equally strong in exerting it, as when he wrote to "Secretary Seward & Secretary Chase" jointly, "You have respectively tendered me your resignations . . . but, after most anxious consideration, my deliberate judgment is, that the public interest does not admit of it. I therefore have to request that you will resume the duties of your departments respectively. Your Obt. Servt."

In faithfulness to a trust, in saving our constituted freedom and opportunity for all, declaring that "no grievance is a fit object of redress by mob violence," made disconsolate by what he termed "a conspiracy" to "nationalize slavery," Lincoln—dogged by chronic fatigue—was a monumental contradiction of that conspiracy. An architect of justice, determined and destined to win his "case," he did not cease until he had demonstrated the mightiness of his "proposition." It is a Euclid of the heart.

ROBERT ANDREW PARKER

Robert Andrew Parker is one of the most accurate and at the same time most unliteral of painters. He combines the mystical and the actual, working both in an abstract and in a realistic way. One or two of his paintings—a kind of private calligraphy—little upward-tending lines of actual writing like a school of fish—approximate a signature or family cipher.

His subjects include animals, persons—individually and en masse; trees, isolated and thickset; architecture, ships, troop movements, the sea; an ink drawing of an elm by a stone wall between meadows. His *Sleeping Dog* is the whole in essence: simplicity that is not the product of a simple mind but of the single eye—of rapt, genuine, undeprecatory love for the subject. The dog's pairs of legs curve out parallel, his solid cylinder of tail laid in the same direction, the eye seen as a diagonal slit in the nondescript pallor of whitish skin; they focus thought on treatment, not just on the dog. A cursive ease in the lines suggests a Rembrandt-like relish for the implement in hand; better yet, there is a look of emotion synonymous with susceptibility to happiness. Entwined in a Beethoven-like Lost Grochen of rhythms, the chalk-gray and dead-grass tones of *Celery and Eggs, No. 2,* have resulted in something elate. The rigidly similar forms, in dark blue, of the audience in *Mario and the Magician* perfectly enunciate the suspense in the story, that one has never known how to define.

His Holiness Pope Pius XI's cloak of flawless violet, lined with ermine, against a black ground, is a triumph of texture, with tinges of lemon defining the four conjoined ridges of the Papal cap. In his satiric tendency and feeling for tones, Robert Parker resembles Charles Demuth; goes further; his wide swaths of paint with a big brush, and washes of clear color touched by some speck or splinter of paint—magenta or indigo—spreading just far enough, are surely in the same category with the Demuth cerise cyclamen and illustrations for Henry James. Robert Parker is not afraid of sweet-pea pink for the face of a soldier in khaki or for the dress of a lady with orange-gold hair. He has plenty of aplomb in his juxtaposings of rust, blood red, shrimp pink and vermilion. He is a specialist in marine blues, blue that could be mistaken for black, faded denim, sapphire-green and—thinking of *Oarsmen*—a Giotto-background blue or telephone-pole-insulator aquamarine. The design of the men and boat (*Oarsmen*) is integrated with the sea as seeds are set in a melon—the men braced by resistance to the mounding weight of deep water; the crisscross of the oars, uninterferingly superimposed on the vastness of a sea without sky. Payne's gray is another specialty of Mr. Parker's, as in the etched-over *Head of a Lady,* and in the fainter gray scene but explicit turrets and rig of the cruiser, *Admiral Hipper.*

Robert Parker is a fantasist of great precision in his studies of troop movements, seen in the *Invasion of an Island,* from the "Gyoncho" series—and in the balanced color pattern, dominated by white, of *East Yorkshire Yeomanry Disembarking from H.M.S. Cressy*—its caraway-seed multitudes pouring down the ship's sides in streams like sand in an hourglass, the sea choked with landing boats repeated to infinity. For this science of tea-leaf-like multitudes, there is an antecedent, if not counterpart, the swarming, seed-compact, arc- or circle-designed battle scenes in central Greece painted by Panaghiotes Zographos (1836–1840) for General Makryannis (reproductions in *Eikones,* April 1956). As multitudinous, although unaware of the Greek scenes, Mr. Parker manages to be epic without being archaic. His *October, 1917* is intensely his own. A platoon—sabers up—seen from the side, reduplicates identical-identical-identical boots that are as black as the men's tunics are flaming vermilion—with an effect resembling the leaves of a partly open book standing upright.

We have here masterpieces of construction plus texture, together with a passion for accuracies of behavior, as where, in the semi-frowning fixity of the eyes, in his portrait of Mrs. Parker, the artist has happily caught her unselfconscious naturalness. Warren Hennrich, moreover, has for his "Field Exercises" (*Wake* magazine, June 1945) the perfect illustration, in Robert Parker's *The Retreat from Caporetto*—a deadly uniformity of faces smothered by their own helmets:

> Harmonious men
> In harmonious masses
>
> Suspend at attention
> Bright, gleaming cuirasses,
>
> And then march away
> In monotonous classes.
>
> They follow the outline
> Of bordering grasses,
>
> Anonymous men
> In anonymous masses.

Mr. Parker has an eye: typified by the waiting horse, down on one haunch; by the flick-back of the hoof of a horse in motion, or rearing. *Hussar, 1900, South Africa*, charging with raised saber, down-darting tapered boot, and counterpoint of galloping hoofs, rivals *The Attack, No. 1*'s diversified unity. The excitement here is not all in sabers and furious action. Humor lurks in the beach scenes of distorted perspective; in the slightly over-curled-in claws and rumpled topknot of the *Fairy Shrimp* trundling along like a feather duster; in *Ugly Animal*, and *Another Dog*.

On no account should Mr. Parker's capacity for grandeur be underestimated—as embodied in the reverie at dusk aspect of *An Imaginary Monument to a Lancer, No. 1*, and in two rather similar equestrian statues, grand without being accidentally ironic— the rider in one, silhouetted against a glare of magenta fire; the other, massive above an ascending burst of yellowish fire.

Robert Parker is thirty—tall, slender, and meditative—born in Norfolk, Virginia. He is unmistakably American, reliable—in the sense pleasing to Henry James. That his likings and proficiencies should range wide and that, so young, he should have depth and stature unvitiated by egotism, seems remarkable. He is in a sense like Sir Thomas Browne, for whom small things could be great things—someone exceptional—*vir amplissimus*.

PAUL ROSENFELD

(1890–1946)

Paul Rosenfeld was an artist. In his performances one finds "a level of reality deeper than that upon which they were launched"; his experiences have not been "made by fear to conform with preconceived theories." Now to be thus "strong in oneself is to be strong in one's relationships. A give and take is effected, that feeds the powers"; powers that have afforded us "a great panorama of conclusions upon the contemporary scene." The mind which has harbored this greater than great Noah's ark of acknowledgments was characterized by an early compliment to it in the *Nation* as "courageous, clear, and biased."

Biased. Biased by imagination; a poet, as we see in Paul Rosenfeld's mechanics of verbal invention. Mass epithet would not do; sensibility exacted poetry; John Marin was "a timothy among the grasses"; *The Enormous Room* had a "brindled style"; "love and aversion" were "darts of light on a flowing stream; wave-caps cast up and annihilated again by a silently rolling ocean." The author of a first novel "tuned his fiddle like a tavern minstrel, and out of the little rocking or running design rises the protagonist solidifying from rhythm as heroes solidified from mist."

Matching the ardor of this method, there was in Paul Rosenfeld a republicanism of respect for that *ignis fatuus*, liberty; a vision of spiritual fitness without visa; of "inner healing" for white America's black victims, those "splintered souls" whose "elasticity of young rubber is weakened and threatened and torn." Although a bachelor, Paul Rosenfeld valued "woman," as Margaret Naumberg, Gertrude Stein, my timid self, and many another have testified. He understood children, their "infantine works and little houses"; their way of "cooking a meal without friction of personalities," since "the end irradiates the means."

He said, "The artist is no "lily-leaning wishful willowy waning sentimentalist," but "a man of stomach," producing "hard form which reveals itself the larger the more it is heard." "Heard" suggests music, and in this regard there is an Amazon to explore; an Amazon that was a river, "flowing and branching throughout a continent."

In objectifying what poets, novelists, educators, painters, photographers, sculptors had given him, Paul Rosenfeld poignantly exemplified his conviction that enrichment involves responsibility. He toiled to benefit his benefactors; or to put it exactly, to benefit benefaction; to justify justice. It is not merely D. H. Lawrence, E. E. Cummings, Gaston Lachaise, Nodier, El Greco, Marsden Hartley, Mozart, or Stravinsky, whom he craved to burnish, but painting, writing, music.

Nor was critical rectitude in Paul Rosenfeld something apart from more prosaic manifestations of conscience. "Michelangelo," he said, "does not stand entirely besmirched for having ceased work on the Medici tombs in order to fortify Florence against brutal Emperor and treacherous Pope." Paul Rosenfeld cared what becomes of us. "America," he said, "must learn to subordinate itself to a religious feeling, a sense of the whole life, or be dragged down into the slime."

Flamboyant generalities are the refuge of the lazy, things that sound well; but in this instance *are* well. Paul Rosenfeld in his impassioned and varied books was a poet. He was a scientist of music; a musician; the rescuer of Tristram and Iseult from the half-scholarship of judicious translating (Bédier); "contented," "refreshed," "rejoicing," "gladdened" by his multifariousness of gratitude—a figure best praised by his own myriad chivalries, drudgeries, and masteries. When everything has its price, and more than price, and anyone is venal, what a thing is the interested mind with the disinterested motive. Here it is. We have had it in Paul Rosenfeld, a son of consolation, a son of imagination, a man of deeds.

EDITH SITWELL, VIRTUOSO

Great in far greater ways, Dame Edith Sitwell is a virtuoso of rhythm and accent. She has given me immense pleasure, intensifying my interest in rhythm, and has also encouraged me in my rhythmic eccentricities. I can scarcely read the Bible without forsaking content for rhythm, as where the Apostle Paul speaks of the shipwreck on Malta and says, "when the ship could no longer bear up into the wind, we let her drive"—a better rhythm than "and were driven."

Façade, Dame Edith—or Miss Sitwell as she was then—insists, was but apprenticeship; of virtuoso quality with wit, one observes, as in "The Higher Sensualism" when Queen Circe said,

> "Young man, I will buy
> Your plumaged coat for my pig to try—
>
> Then with angels he'll go a'dancing hence
> From sensuality into sense!"

"I used to practice writing," Dame Edith says, "as a pianist practices music." She says that she would take a waltz or a polka or the music of the barrel organ beneath her window and translate it into words, as she has done in this phrase from "Country Dance":

> But Silenus
> Has seen us.

Dame Edith then considered the long line and its possibilities. William Carlos Williams has said in his book, *I Wanted to Write a Poem*, "I found I could not use the long line because of my nervous nature." An adagio, moreover, "is hard to sustain at concert pitch," as the *Times Literary Supplement* noted. We have it, however, when Edith Sitwell writes

> archipelagoes
> Of stars and young thin moons from great wings falling
> As ripples widen.

How pleasing, the dactyls: *porphyry, basilica, Babylon;* and *babioun* (*babioun* borrowed from Ben Jonson, as she says). How neat, the rhyme "Noctambulo" with "folio":

> The public scribe, Noctambulo
> Where moonlight, cold as blades of grass
> Echoes upon deserted walls,
> Turning his dusty folio;

and this: "old Bacchantes black with wine, / Whose very hair has changed into a vine." We have something of the self-impelled ease of Leslie Brooke's "Johnny Crow's Party":

> The snake
> Got entangled
> With the rake.
> The sheep
> Fell asleep
> And the armadillo
> Used him as a pillow.

Dame Edith's irregularities in set meter are hyper-skilful, as in creating a pause after *any* in "anybody": "Mary Stuart to James Bothwell" (Casket Letter No. 2):

> Leaving you, I was sundered like the sea!
> Departed from the place where I left my heart
> I was as small as any body may be.

That is to say, with the accent on *body.*

There is no melody in Pope, Dame Edith says, because there is no irregularity. "To have melody, there must be variations in the outward structure." An expert of the condensed phrase, she also says, "I try to make my images exact"; and does, in "sundered"; and by inventing "donkey's-hide grass" for the beast of the attorney:

> O'er donkey's-hide grass the attorney
> Still continues on his journey.

In the opening lines of "The Sleeping Beauty," the incantatory effect of the whole passage is a metaphor creating a sense of deep, mysterious, fairy-world remoteness:

> When we come to that dark house,
> Never sound of wave shall rouse
> The bird that sings within the blood
> Of those who sleep in that deep wood.

Katherine Anne Porter—reminded of Lully, Rameau, Monteverdi, and Purcell, "of old courtly music, weddings, christenings, great crystal-lighted banquets, in sweet-smelling gardens under the full moon"—is detained by the luster and admires the studiousness; says, "There is no finer sight than to see an artist growing great." Dame Edith's father, Sir George, said, "Edith will commit suicide when she finds she cannot write poetry." Need for this has not arisen.

One cannot be a virtuoso without being combated—an injustice prevalent in all the arts—noted by Mr. Henry McBride, art critic for *The Dial* and the *New York Sun.* He says, "One may judge the vitality of an artist by the extent to which he is resisted." Dame Edith recalls that lines of hers once received "a mingling of bouquets and brickbats—with a strong predominance of brickbats"; yet invariably, as the *New Statesman and Nation* said (June 23, 1954), "losing every battle, she won the campaign"; in fact, "emerged more majestic, more unaccountably modern than ever."

In *Façade* she said she found it necessary to find heightened expression for the heightened speed of our time. However, she added, "in spite of the fact that the rhythms which I practised in *Façade* were heightened, concentrated, and frequently more violent that those of the poets who had preceded us immediately, it was supposed by many that I had *discarded* rhythm. But we must not complain if the patterns in our mundane works are not perceived by the unobservant"—the allusion being to Bishop Burnet, who had found fault with the constellations and said, if only the stars had been composed "according to the rules of art and symmetry!"

Some may regard as arbitrary a word of Dame Edith's or find a statement too "oracular." In her choice of words, she is, to *herself*, always justified. "Neatness of execution is essential to sublimity," she says; improving De Quincey by considering language an "incarnation" of thought rather than "the *dress* of thought," and is instructively "neat" in revising her own work, as when substituting a general term for a specific in "Metamorphosis":

> When first the dew with golden foot
> Makes tremble every leaf and strawberry root.

This is made to read in the second version of 1946:

> Here once in Spring, the dew with golden foot
> Made tremble every leaf and hidden root.

When she presents other authors—Christopher Smart in her early three-volume anthology—and when in *The Book of the Winter* she selects examples from Herrick, Blake, and Donne, her wand is tipped with a diamond. Of compiling *The Book of the Winter* she said, "I was not concerned with producing a hodge-podge of everything . . . One of the greatest difficulties encountered in making an anthology of this kind is to resign oneself to omissions . . . many beauties because they pulled the pattern out of shape." From Donne, it is not verse that is quoted but this from a sermon preached by Donne in April 1629: "The root of all is God, but it is not the way to receive fruits to dig at the root but to reach to the boughs," and we have for Dylan Thomas a justly comprehensive apologia: "His love for those who have received no mercies from life is great." Fire and novelty mark *The Book of the Winter*—in Sir Thomas Browne's "Of Crystals and Icicles"; and in this apparition or vision from *I Live under a Black Sun*—Dame Edith's novel: "A figure would shine through the night, circling swiftly as if it were a swallow, or floating, a black swan on the wide water-black marble pavements. . . . Rag Castle after rag castle, the world of beggars was swept along, and night fell upon the two na-

tions, the rich and the poor, who alone inhabit the earth"—proto-
types of Lazarus and Dives made emphatic in later work. Tom
O'Bedlam (anonymous), quoted in part, perhaps epitomizes the
contagion of the whole anthology:

> While I do sing,
> "Any food, and feeding,
> Feeding, drink, or clothing,
> Come dame or maid
> Be not afraid
> Poor Tom will injure nothing,
>
> The meek, the wise, the gentle
> Me handle, touch, and spare not;
> But those that cross
> Tom Rhinoceros
> Do what the panther dare not.
>
> . . . . . .
>
> With an host of furious fancies,
> Whereof I am commander,
> With a burning Speare, and a horse of aire,
> To the wildernesse I wander.

In his introduction to Paul Valéry's *The Art of Poetry*, Mr.
Eliot includes a postscriptlike speculation: "How poetry is related
to life, Valéry does not say"—connected in my own mind with
Edith Sitwell's self-descriptive comment: "The behaviour of the
world affects our beliefs and incites the mind to tumult to speak as
a Cassandra or as an elegist." Reflecting current preoccupation,
Robert Frost answers the query, why write: "It is what every poem
is about—how the spirit is to surmount the pressure upon us of
the material world." In our battle, Dame Edith bears aid. As for
interest taken by the poet in his fellow human being, she says,
"He is a brother speaking to a brother . . . supporting his
brother's flagging footsteps"; and—overpowered by a sense of "the
Universal Cain, of brother as murderer of brother, of the chain-
gang sentenced to ninety-nine years"—says, "I come to testify."
Of this testimony W. B. Yeats said, "Something absent from all

literature was back again, passion ennobled by intensity, by endurance, by wisdom."

> "With what are these on fire?" she asks, "with passion, Hate,
> Infatuation, and old age, and death
> With sorrow, longing, and with laboring breath."

Summarizing her work in 1955, *Time* said, "she writes for the sake of sound, of color, and from an awareness of God and regard for man." For her "all great poetry is dipped in the dyes of the heart"; and, perhaps quoting Whitman, she says, "All things are in the clime of man's forgiveness"; saying of ideals she would reach, "How far I am from these no one could see more clearly than I. Technically, I would come to a vital language—each word possessing an infinite power of germination, spiritually give holiness to each common day." In her humility and compassion she cages conviction.

THE FORD CORRESPONDENCE

FORD MOTOR COMPANY
DEARBORN, MICHIGAN

October 19, 1955

Dear Miss Moore:

This is a morning we find ourselves with a problem which, strangely enough, is more in the field of words and the fragile meaning of words than in car-making. And we just wonder whether you might be intrigued with it sufficiently to lend us a hand.

Our dilemma is a name for a rather important new series of cars.

We should like this name to be more than a label. Specifically, we should like it to have a compelling quality in itself and by itself. To convey, through association or other conjuration, some visceral feeling of elegance, fleetness, and advanced features and design. A name, in short, that flashes a dramatically desirable picture in people's minds.

Over the past few weeks this office has confected a list of three hundred-odd candidates which, it pains me to relate, are characterized by an embarrassing pedestrianism. We are miles short of our ambition. And so we are seeking the help of one who knows more about this sort of magic than we.

As to how we might go about this matter, I have no idea. One possibility is that you might care to visit with us and muse with the new Wonder which now is in clay in our Advance Styling Studios. But, in any event, all would depend on whether you find this overture of some challenge and interest.

Should we be so fortunate as to have piqued your fancy, we will be pleased to write more fully. In summary, all we want is a colossal name (another "Thunderbird" would be fine). And, of course, it is expected that our relations will be on a fee basis of an impeccably dignified kind.

> Respectfully,
> Robert B. Young
> Marketing Research Department

Miss Marianne Moore
260 Cumberland Street
Brooklyn 5, New York

> October 21, 1955

Let me take it under advisement, Mr. Young. I am complimented to be recruited in this high matter.

I have seen and admired "Thunderbird" as a Ford designation. It would be hard to match; but let me, the coming week, talk with my brother who would bring ardor and imagination to bear on the quest.

> Sincerely yours
> and your wife's,*
> Marianne Moore

* Mr. Young's wife had met Miss Moore at luncheon at Mount Holyoke College. His first letter was reinforced by one from Mrs. Young, written on the same date, recalling the incident.

Mr. Robert B. Young
Marketing Research Division
Special Products Division
Ford Motor Company
P.O. Box 637
16400 Michigan Avenue
Dearborn, Michigan

October 27, 1955

Dear Mr. Young:

My brother thought most of the names I had considered suggesting to you for your new series, too learned or too labored, but thinks I might ask if any of the following approximate the requirements.

THE FORD SILVER SWORD

This plant, of which the flower is a silver sword, I believe grows only in Tibet, and on the Hawaiian Island, Maui on Mount Háleákalá (House of the Sun); found at an altitude of from 9,500 to 10,000 feet. (The leaves—silver-white—surrounding the individual blossoms have a pebbled texture that feels like Italian-twist back-stitch all-over embroidery.)

My first thought was of a bird series—the swallow species—Hirundo or phonetically, Aërundo. Malvina Hoffman is designing a device for the radiator of a made-to-order Cadillac, and said in her opinion the only term surpassing Thunder-bird would be hurricane; and I then thought Hurrican Hirundo might be the first of a series such as Hurricane aquila (eagle), Hurricane accipiter (hawk), and so on. "A species that takes its dinner on the wing" ("swifts").

If these suggestions are not in character with the car, perhaps you could give me a sketch of its general appearance, or hint as to some of its exciting possibilities—though my brother reminds me that such information is highly confidential.

Sincerely yours,
Marianne Moore

November 4, 1955

Dear Miss Moore:

I'm delighted that your note implies that you are interested in helping us in our naming problem.

This being so, in compliance with procedures in this rigorous business world, I think we should make some definite arrangement for payment of a suitable fee or honorarium before pursuing the problem further.

One way might be for you to suggest a figure which could be considered for mutual acceptance. Once this is squared away, we will look forward to having you join us in continuing our fascinating search.

Sincerely yours,
Robert B. Young
Marketing Research

November 7, 1955

Dear Mr. Young:

It is handsome of you to consider remuneration for service merely enlisted. My fancy would be inhibited, however, by acknowledgment in advance of performance. If I could be of specific assistance, we could no doubt agree on some kind of honorarium for the service rendered.

I seem to exact participation; but if you could tell me how the suggestions submitted strayed—if obviously—from the ideal, I could then perhaps proceed more nearly in keeping with the Company's objective.

Sincerely yours,
Marianne Moore

November 11, 1955

Dear Miss Moore:

The Youngs' philodendron has just benefited from an extra measure of water as, pacing about the room, I have sought words to respond to your generous note.

Let me state my quandary thus. It is unspeakably contrary to Procedures here to accept counsel—even needed counsel—without a firm prior agreement of conditions (and, indeed, without a Purchase Notice in quadruplicate and three competitive bids). But then, seldom has the auto business had occasion to indulge in so ethereal a matter as this.

So, if you will risk a mutually satisfactory outcome with us, we should like to honor your wish for a fancy unencumbered.

As to wherein your earlier suggestions may have "strayed," as you put it—they did not at all. We merely proposed a recess in production for orderly bookkeeping. Shipment 1 was fine and we would like to luxuriate in more of same. Even those your brother regarded as over-learned or labored.

For us to impose an ideal on your efforts would, I fear, merely defeat our purpose. We have sought your help to get an approach quite different from our own. In short, we should like suggestions that we ourselves would not have arrived at. And, in sober fact, have not arrived at.

Now we on this end must help you by sending some tangible representation of what we are talking about. Your brother was right; advance designs in Dearborn are something approaching the Sacred. But perhaps the enclosed sketches will serve the purpose. They are not IT, but they convey the feeling.

At very least, they may give you a sense of participation should your friend, Malvina Hoffman, break into brisk conversation on radiator caps.

Sincerely yours,
Robert B. Young
Marketing Research

November 13, 1955

Dear Mr. Young:

The sketches. They are indeed exciting; they have quality, and the toucan tones lend tremendous allure—confirmed by the wheels. Half the magic—sustaining effects of this kind. Looked at upside down, furthermore, there is a sense of fish buoyancy. Immediately your word impeccable sprang to mind. Might it be a possibility? The Impeccable. In any case, the baguette lapidary glamor you have achieved certainly spurs the imagination. Car-innovation is like launching a ship—"drama."

I am by no means sure that I can help you to the right thing, but performance with elegance casts a spell. Let me do some thinking in the direction of the impeccable, symmechromatic, thunderblender. . . . (The exotics if I can shape them a little.) Dearborn might come into one.

If the sketches should be returned at once, let me know. Otherwise, let me dwell on them for a time. I am, may I say, a trusty confident.

I thank you for realizing that under contract esprit could not flower. You owe me nothing, specific or moral.

Sincerely yours,
Marianne Moore

Some other suggestions, Mr. Young, for the phenomenon:
THE RESILIENT BULLET
or intelligent bullet
or bullet cloisonné   or bullet lavolta
   (I have always had a fancy for the THE INTELLIGENT WHALE—the little first Navy submarine, shaped like a sweet-potato; on view in our Brooklyn Yard).
   THE FORD FABERGÉ (that there is also a perfume FA-BERGÉ seems to me to do no harm here, allusion to the original silversmith).
   THE ARC-en-CIEL (the rainbow)
   ARCENCIEL?
Please do not feel that memoranda from me need acknowledgment. I am not working day and night for you; I feel that etymological hits are partially accidental.

Sincerely yours,
Marianne Moore

The bullet idea has possibilities, it seems to me, in connection with mercury (with Hermes and Hermes trismegistus) and magic (white magic).

I seem to admire variety in the sections of your address!

November 28, 1955

TO: Mr. Robert B. Young
From: Marianne Moore
  MONGOOSE CIVIQUE
  ANTICIPATOR
  REGNA RACER (couronne à couronne) sovereign to sovereign
  AEROTERRE
  fée rapide (aerofère, aero faire, fée aiglette, magifaire) comme
    il faire
  tonnere alifère (wingèd thunder)
  aliforme alifère (wing-slender a-wing)
  TURBOTORC (used as an adjective by Plymouth)
  THUNDERBIRD allié (Cousin Thunderbird)
  THUNDER CRESTER
  DEARBORN diamanté
  MAGIGRAVURE
  PASTELOGRAM
  I shall be returning the sketches very soon.
                                    M.M.

December 6, 1955

TO: Mr. Robert B. Young
From: Marianne Moore
  regina-rex
  taper racer   taper acer
  Varsity Stroke
  angelastro
  astranaut

chaparral

tir à l'arc (bull's eye)

cresta lark

triskelion (three legs running)

pluma piluma (hairfine, feather-foot)

andante con moto (description of a good motor?)

My findings thin, so I terminate them and am returning the sketches—two pastels, two photos: from Mr. M. H. Lieblich.

Two principles I have not been able to capture: 1. The topknot of the peacock and topnotcher of speed. 2. The swivel-axis (emphasized elsewhere)—like the Captain's bed on the whale-ship Charles Morgan—balanced so that it leveled, whatever the slant of the ship.

If I stumble on a hit, you shall have it. Anything so far has been pastime. Do not ponder appreciation, Mr. Young. That was embodied in the sketches.

M.M.

(over)

I can not resist the temptation to disobey my brother and submit

TURCOTINGO (turquoise cotinga—the cotinga being a solid indigo South American finch or sparrow)

I have a three-volume treatise on flowers that might produce something but the impression given should certainly be unlabored.

M.M.

December 8, 1955

Mr. Young:

May I submit UTOPIAN TURTLETOP?

Do not trouble to answer unless you like it.

Marianne Moore

The Ford Motor Company's response to this final suggestion was a floral tribute composed of twenty-four roses and white pine and spiral eucalyptus. The accompanying florist's Christmas card bore the greeting:

TO OUR FAVORITE TURTLETOPPER

December 26, 1955

Dear Mr. Young:

An aspiring turtle is certain to glory in spiral eucalyptus, white pine straight from the forest, and innumerable scarlet roses almost too tall for close inspection. Of a temperament susceptible to shock though one may be, to be treated like royalty could not but induce sensations unprecedently august.

Please know that a carfancyer's allegiance to the Ford automotive turtle—extending from the Model T Dynasty to the Young Utopian Dynasty—can never waver; impersonal gratitude surely becoming infinite when made personal. Gratitude to unmiserly Mr. Young and his idealistic associates.

Marianne Moore

January 17, 1956

Dear Miss Moore:

Please excuse my long delay in responding to your generous notes. Our label is still in a state of indecision. Contributions have been entered from many directions, and those from our "favorite turtletopper" rate among the most interesting of all.

We can scarcely begin to thank you for your interest and munificent help in our dilemma. The art of precise word picking is rarely joined with the mechanical genius of our automotive personnel. Your aid in this respect has been invaluable.

I hope you are entering another happy and healthy new year. Wishing you the best of everything. I remain your faithful utopian.

Robert B. Young
Marketing Research

November 8, 1956

Dear Miss Moore:

Because you were so kind to us in our early and hopeful days of looking for a suitable name, I feel a deep obligation to report on events that have ensued.

And I feel I must do so before the public announcement of same come Monday, November 19.

We have chosen a name out of the more than six-thousand-odd candidates that we gathered. It has a certain ring to it. An air of gaiety and zest. At least, that's what we keep saying. Our name, dear Miss Moore, is—Edsel.

I know you will share your sympathies with us.

Cordially,
David Wallace, Manager
Marketing Research

P.S. Our Mr. Robert Young, who corresponded with you earlier, is now and temporarily, we hope, in the service of our glorious U.S. Coast Guard.

I know he would send his best.

DW

November 11, 1956

Dear Mr. Wallace:

I thank you for the letter just received from you, of November 8th.

You have the certainly ideal thing—with the Ford identity indigenously symbolized. (I am a little piqued that I concentrated on physical phenomena.) At all events, thank you for informing me of the Company's choice—a matter to me of keen interest. Am quite partisan. I do wish the Company designs to "lead."

Sincerely yours,
Marianne Moore

Mr. Young is possessed of esprit and I hope is thriving.

TO "INFUSE BELIEF"

Review of Gate to the Sea, *by Bryher. (New York: Pantheon, 1958.)*

In *Gate to the Sea*, the gate is Paestum and the story—of the 4th century B.C.—parallels harrowing accounts in our own day: escape by plane, by sea, by plodding through enemy woods in snow almost waist-deep. Lykos, a Greek slave, and Harmonia, a priestess of Hera, attempt escape from foreign oppressors, Lucanian conquerors who have forbidden hereditary employment, observance of sacred rites, and the use by Greeks of even their own language.

As Lykos, Harmonia, and a few friends steal toward the sea at night they are detected before they can reach the small boat in which—all but overtaken—they row out to the ship which means freedom. Bryher's previous novels have, each, revived an incident in history symbolic of free spirits overpowered but unconquered: the Battle of Hastings, the execution of Raleigh, the fall of Rome, the London blitz. Of them all, *Gate to the Sea* seems the most vivid and expertly absorbing—a masterpiece.

The statement by Paul Valéry that "poetry is to prose as dancing is to walking," is one upon which T. S. Eliot pauses, since some prose is poetry. We certainly have the poetry of heightened prose in Bryher's work; as in *Gate to the Sea* the Greek coast is typified by brevity such as this: "The path ended suddenly in the middle of a dune"; and the sea is for me ideally personified in: "She clung to the seat [of the boat] as they soared up and forward . . . rode down into a hollow, rolled again, and rose upon a shieldlike surface of blue sea. . . ." The personalities are made to matter; the pulse of the predicament beats in the mind. Best of all, patriotism and ancient piety here "infuse belief." Bryher is an invigorator. Faith, virtue, and freedom are her Ulysses—her Odyssey— enhanced by Paestum's scarred columns and porches, her pines and their shadows, as photographed by Islay de Courcy Lyons.

"SENHORA HELENA"

Review of The Diary of "Helena Morley," translated and edited, with preface and introduction by Elizabeth Bishop. (New York: Farrar, Straus and Cudahy, 1957.)

My Life as a Little Girl was published in 1942—primarily to amuse family and friends and now a Brazilian classic. It continually rivals poetry; furthermore is "one of those rare stories that combines worldly success and a happy ending," its translator says; in its universal-personal insights is irresistible.

"Helena Morley" (a pseudonym) had, as ancestor, an English doctor who was for a time on the staff of a gold-mining affiliate of the São del Rey Mining Company and remained in Brazil for reasons of health, settled in Diamantina, and married a Brazilian lady. "Senhora Helena," now a favorite in Rio de Janeiro society, is the wife of Dr. Augusto Mario Caldeira Brant, President of the Bank of Brazil, at whose suggestion the Diary was published.

In Diamantina, a center for gold and diamond mining, the Diary depicts life as lived by the Morleys and their many relatives. That a translator should share the qualities of work translated, Miss Bishop exemplifies in her gift for fantasy, her use of words and hyper-precise eye. The attitude to life revealed by the Diary, Helena's apperceptiveness, and innate accuracy, seem a double portrait; the exactness of observation in the introduction being an extension, in manner, of Miss Bishop's verse and other writing, as when she differentiates between marbleized or painted window-frames to imitate stone, and stone ones painted to imitate grained wood; again, in the description of rain-pipe funnels "flaring like trumpets," sometimes with "tin petals or feathers down them and around the mouth . . . repeated in tiles set edgewise up the ridges of the roofs, dragonlike and very 'Chinese.'" And it would be hard to find a process more accurately described than this, of panning for diamonds in a stream by the road: "A small quantity of gravel in the wide round sieve is held just beneath the surface of the water, swirled around and around and lifted out" and, "with the gesture of a quick-fingered housewife turning out a cake," the panner "turned the whole thing upside down on the ground, intact. He put on his horn-rimmed glasses, lowered himself to his knees in the wet mud, and stared, passing a long wooden knife over the gravel from side to side"—"the simplest of all forms of diamond 'mining.' " "One sometimes gets the impression that the greater part of the town, black and white, 'rich' and poor, when it hasn't found a diamond lately, gets along by making sweets and pastries, brooms and cigarettes and selling to each other. . . ." "Black beans instead of the bread of other countries, seem to be equated with life itself."

The personality of Helena Morley would be hard to match. Besides an ardor synonymous with affection, she "steps in and out of superstition" as Miss Bishop says, "reason, belief, and disbelief, without much adolescent worrying. She would never for a moment doubt that the church is a good thing." "I admire good and holy people," she says, "but I can't possibly stop being the way I am." A main part of being the way she was, was compassion. On a night during the family's summer outing, when all were kept awake by a crying baby, Helena says, "To let her cry with pain, and then to beat her. I couldn't stand it. . . . I didn't even have to stay with her half an hour"—provoking a remonstrance from Mrs. Morley: "This girl, this mania of not being able to hear a baby cry without wanting to comfort it. She'll be the death of me." In recording the incident, Helena says, "I think if this little girl had been white, mama wouldn't have minded." On any page of the Diary we encounter similar "fire"; as here: "I don't have a corner to do my lessons in. So, with the help of God, I found something simply wonderful. I went to pick mulberries and climbed the tree to the very top. What a discovery. The mulberry was so overgrown with a vine that it looked like a mattress. I'd tell grandma that I was going to study under the mulberry-tree and then I'd climb up and stay on top looking at the view which is perfectly beautiful." Again, "José Rabela spends his time weighing vultures in the scales, in order to invent a flying-machine.

Wouldn't that be wonderful! . . . I feel envious when I see the vultures soaring up so high." Not everything was wonderful. Of visiting the dentist, Helena says, "It is more nauseating than finding a toad in one's bed. He can't say a thing without a diminutive. 'Will you do me the favor of opening your little mouth?' . . . 'little mouth, little ache, little tooth.' I almost fainted in the chair, I disliked him so much." The Diary has tone. With regard to having a post-office, Helena says, "Wouldn't it be better . . . if they put in street lamps for us so that on dark nights we wouldn't have to walk slowly for fear of falling over a cow. And water pipes . . . Nobody's going to die without a letter, but the water has killed lots of people who might have been living today." Then of submerged problems, "All year long, mama struggles with him [papa] to go to confession." "I suffered a great deal because of grandfather and don't want to suffer now too because of papa. My grandfather was not buried in the church because he was a Protestant. 'Any ground God made is holy ground,' he said. Alert to every pretext favorable to satire, Helena says, "Joas de Assis suffers from a strange complaint, he's so sorry for everyone, no matter who." and "Everybody says father is a good husband and yet nobody says mama is a good wife." She tells how, when a *calderao* is found (a pocket of diamonds), a slave falls on his knees, exclaiming, "My Lord and Heavenly Father, if this wealth endangers my soul, let it vanish." Charmed observation and reflexive ingenuity never pall. Helena's susceptibility to personality and commensurate candor constantly leave one with a sense of originality that nothing could impair. In an agony of diffidence because of having withheld at confession the sin of having thought a priest "homely," she is told that she should confess it, and to the same priest from whom she had withheld it; then admits, "But the priest is you, Father."

Being able to observe imagination in action here is like opening a watch and studying the continuous uninterfering operation of wheels amid wheels. We see, furthermore, as Miss Bishop says, "that happiness does not consist in worldly goods but in a peaceful home, in family affection,—things that fortune cannot bring and often takes away." And "it happened, that is the charm and the point of *Mina Vida de Menina.*"

SELECTED CRITICISM

Review *of* Selected Criticism: Prose, Poetry *by Louise Bogan.*
(*New York: Noonday Press, 1955.*)

This writing has fiber. The subject matter, reprinted from various sources, is arranged chronologically except as it has been regrouped for clarity. Miss Bogan's first book of poems was published in 1923; and in 1924 her first book review, in the *New Republic.* Her contributing of verse criticism to the *New Yorker* began in 1931, "at first as 'omnibus reviews' which covered the year's books at six-month intervals. From 1937 her *New Yorker* reviews have appeared as a regular subdepartment of 'Books' under the heading 'Verse.' "

An extensive survey, this; which includes besides Emerson, Emily Dickinson*—and her father "who stepped like Cromwell when he went to gather kindling"—Thoreau, "wholesome Thoreau-like Robert Frost," Henry James, Hardy, G. M. Hopkins, W. B. Yeats; also, as coloring their respective periods, Wyndham Lewis, Ezra Pound, T. S. Eliot, Wallace Stevens, E. E. Cummings, W. C. Williams and others; Edmund Wilson and R. P. Blackmur (as critics), Gide's Journals, Collette, Virginia Woolf, Robert Graves, and poets 1944–1955.

As precursors of modernism in literature, mingled sensibilities, tendencies, and inter-related experiments are accounted for by Miss Bogan and brought into sequence. "The population after the Cuban war," she says, "was infatuated with power . . . an era of gilt wicker furniture, hand-painted china, lace curtains, and

* As summarizing Emily Dickinson, Miss Bogan's review of the three-volume *Poems of Emily Dickinson,* edited by Thomas H. Johnson (*The New Yorker,* October 8, 1955), seems the natural apex of these studies—a masterly critique.

'sofa cushions,'" of "the pulp magazine" and "a taste for 'sordid elegance,'" "attacked by Thorstein Veblen and others from the left." "American realism finally broke through": we had Dreiser's novels, "'disguised autobiographies,'" and free verse. Wagner and Villiers de L'Isle-Adam, Debussy and Mallarmé, post-impressionist "anatomizing of nature" and the Armory show in 1913, are correlated. We have Gertrude Stein in Paris, Imagist poetry in England and America, and "the novel as a Luciferian universe in the hands of Joyce."

"With an eye to virtues rather than defects," Miss Bogan does not overbear. She has no literary nephews; her pronouncements are terse, rendered with laboratory detachment. Unmistakable emphasis is placed on two capacities as indispensable to achievement—instinctiveness and "coming to terms with one's self"—instinctiveness as contrasted with Henry James' Mona Brigstock, who was "all will." Goethe's central power is seen as "interpretive imagination," an interior compulsion linked with integrity. In *The Family Reunion*, "an integration," Miss Bogan sees T. S. Eliot "in complete control of himself." Was Joyce in *Finnegans Wake*, she asks, "the farceur" or have we here "immaturity transcending suffering"?—a query one connects with Henry James' observation in discussing Turgenev's fiction: "The great question as to a poet or novelist is, how does he feel about life? What in the last analysis is his philosophy? This is the most interesting thing their works offer us. Details are interesting in proportion as they contribute to make it clear."

These compact, unequivocal studies are set off by a kind of dry humor-incognito which is idiosyncratically eloquent. Henry James "really was a great poet and profound psychologist," Miss Bogan says. "He has been thought genteel when he had become the sharpest critic of gentility, a dull expatriate when his books flashed with incisive American wit." "He must be approached as one approaches music," she says. "He continuously shifts between development and theme, never stops, never errs." She affirms Rilke's conviction that "we must adhere to difficulty if we would make any claim to having a part in life" and feels that we have in Rilke "one of the strongest antidotes to the powers of darkness"; "often exhausted, often afraid, often in flight but capable of growth and solitude—he stands as an example of integrity held through and beyond change."

The combination of open writing, unstereotyped insights, and daring, is most attractive, as when Miss Bogan says, "Yeats and Pound achieved modernity. Eliot was modern from the start." We have Ezra Pound, "whom," Miss Bogan says, "time will in the end surely honor," delineated in his statement, "I am trying to use not an inch rule but a balance"; and perhaps with his tendency to diatribe in mind, she says, "Pound's ideal reader is a person who has experienced real discomfort in being shut up in a railway train, lecture hall, or concert room, with well-modulated voices expressing careful, well-bred opinions on the subject of the arts." Contradictions presented by W. B. Yeats are set forth: his august statement, "We are artists who are servants not of any cause but of mere nature" and his "lifelong struggle against the inertia of his nation"; "his variety of stress and subtlety of meaning"; his vehemence: "how hard is that purification from insincerity, vanity, malignance, arrogance, which is the discovery of style."

W. H. Auden is especially well observed. "He gives humanity a hard unprejudiced stare," Miss Bogan says—but is capable of gaiety which can even be "hilarity." "He points up and freshens the language," "describes with great originality the power drives of succeeding eras," and in *Poets of the English Language*, has participated, with Norman Pearson, in "a peculiarly modern achievement." His "lack of hatred, his fight against intellectual stupidity as well as outer horror" are noted; certain speeches in *The Sea and the Mirror: A Commentary on Shakespeare's The Tempest*, as constituting "a little museum of form: terza rima, followed by a sestina, a sonnet, and a ballade." We have in Mr. Auden, Miss Bogan feels, "a poet, one of whose urges always will be to transcend himself." Paul Valéry is portrayed at a stroke. While discerning his gifts—"that he continually denies them," Miss Bogan says, "lends to his work a faint continual tone of sophistry." And nothing said about Joyce seems to me sounder than this accounting for the effect on us of *Finnegans Wake*—its "miraculous virtuosity of language maintained through a thousand variations in its attack on every known patois—the whole resting on Bruno's theory of knowledge through opposites and Vico's theory of psychic recurrence." This "private language" of mixed meanings, "related to 'the puzlator' of Panurge," to the language of "Lear," "Carroll," and Mother Goose, is summed up by Miss Bogan in H. W. Fowler's definition of the pun as "a jocular or suggestive use of similarity between words or a word's different senses—'For a burning wood is come to dance insane.'" "The Letters of Rainer Maria Rilke and the study of Gide's Journals reveal the bristling amateur who fears to be soft"—show what philosophy that is equity can be; and typical of the whole temper of the book—Miss Bogan says of Yvor Winters, a writer "very nearly without listeners, let alone friends and admirers, his interest appears limited only because he has made choices, proof of probity and distilled power in unlikely times. These facts should delight us."

A fascinating book, abounding in important insights such as, "Loose form must have beneath, a groundswell of energy"; "If one hates anything too long . . . one forgets what it is one could love"; the advice of W. B. Yeats that we "write our thoughts as nearly as possible in the language we thought them in." And we are warned against "stubborn avant-gardism when no real need for a restless forward movement any longer exists; the moment comes," Miss Bogan says, "for a consolidation of resources, for interpretation rather than exploration."

One has here mastery of material and associative creative insight —a conspectus of the transition from fettered to new writing— "from minor to major art"; to precision and "a transcending of the self through difficulty." The book rises above literariness, moreover, and fortifies courage, in practicing a principle which is surely Confucian; implying that one need not demand fair treatment, but rather, see that one's treatment of others is fair.

A GRAMMARIAN OF MOTIVES

Review of Book of Moments: Poems 1915–1954 *by Kenneth Burke. (Los Altos, Calif.: Hermes Publications, 1955.)*

Kenneth Burke is a philosopher and a satirist—a humorist of the somatic kind, whose self-styled "flat tire of satire" has been indispensable to the lingual, political, moral, and poetic apparatus which has carried him to an enviable destination—the expert's. He feels that "eye, hand, and mental keenness" should be "busied for the good of the many" ("Plea of the People," page 58). "We would be men of good will," he says.

> To be strong in hate or to rot in wretchedness—
> Do not force us to this choice that is no choice.

In his "Neo-Hippocratic Oath," although he "cannot offer cures for stony hearts," he "swears that he will try not to belittle the work of those who would," and if he "comes upon unsavory private matters," he "will keep them to himself except insofar as he noises them abroad to everyone/ as observations about everyone" ("Moments," page 8). In his technique of persuasion, he is a philosopher of opposites. He is not "launching an attack; nor does he suffer a sense of defeat." "Each principle advocated is matched by an opposite principle." "The connoisseur will be will-less ("Counter-Statement"). The artist "must recognize the validity of contraries," he says. On the title page of his *Moments* he quotes Emerson's statement, "Our moods do not believe in each other." He is in agreement with Thomas Mann that "the problematical is the proper sphere of art." Concur and one "will find moral indignation impossible."

His "Moments" "treat of love, politics, and kindred conundrums," he says, and as if to match the philosophy of opposites he says they "are somewhat irresponsible in their way of cancelling out one another." Whatever else they do, they illustrate Plato's antithesis that if we think in universals, we feel in particulars. They are records of experience—"Delight, Promise, Victory, Regret, Apprehension, Arrival, Crossing, Departure, Loneliness, Sorrow, Despair, etc." and are reinforced at the back of the book by several pages of "Flowerishes"—dicta "which emerge these days somewhat dizzily," Mr. Burke says, and as print, flower in circles, serpentines, comet-tails, dotted lines, back to back and turning corners; some in light and some in dark-face. Here are two: "Must it always be wishful thinking? Can't it sometimes be thoughtful wishing?" "Draw out the time—and one part of an eddy going downstream might seem all your life to be going upstream."

In *Counter-Statement* (1931), discussing form "emotional and technical," "a work has form," Mr. Burke said, "insofar as one part leads a reader to anticipate another part and be gratified by the sequence." "Neglect organic progression and our emotions remain static." Alluding to virtues and diseases of form, he mentioned hypertrophy of information as a disease of form, said of Proust that whereas "a single page is astonishing, he becomes wearisome after extended reading"; noted also that "Shakespeare's style approaches mannerism insofar as it over-emphasizes metaphor." Eloquence, he said, consists in "matching the important with the important" and "by innovation is not meant something new but an emphasis to which the public is not accustomed." "A rhythm," he said, "is a promise which the poet makes the reader and in proportion as the reader comes to rely upon this promise, he falls into a state of general surrender which makes him more likely to accept, without resistance, the rest of the poet's material." His to me master-maxim is this: "Truth in art is not discovery of facts or addition to knowledge, it is the exercise of propriety."

With the foregoing aids to composition in mind, how does Mr. Burke come off poetically? He has in his "Problem of Moments"—if I am reliable—a masterpiece:

> I knew a man who would be wonder-wise,
> Having been born with both myopic eyes
> Scratched in again.
> —a symbol of "the motionless pursuit of us by pain," this man.

Note squirrel on log, how pert, now in, now out—
But classicists find either too much drought
Or too much rain.

(Wise, eyes, again
Absolute, pursuit, pain
Out drought, rain)

Here we have balance, compression, crescendo, and neatly articu-
lated, impeccably accelerated rhyme, with each stanza punctuated
by a rhymeword, the same words grouped in the same order, as
climax of the final stanza. "Star-Fire" is expert counterpoint:
"Fly-things sing-sit/ On grow-things. . . . Halló-la hélla-ló!"
There are many phases of Joyce inter-crossings: "As I lurk look
from Look-Out." Mr. Burke is a master of the mellow-sardonic
enforced by alliteration, as in his salute to alcohol: "ALKY, ME
LOVE . . . Always there was something or other/ Just couldn't
stand it"; not of the mellow-sardonic only but of the mellow: as
"Dozing" then "awaking to the cosmic roar"

Of the sea
(The onrushing, perpetual sea),

He never saw the sea so jammed with water.

Is not this "exposition," this picture of "Jack's Bandbox"?

The cover of this box is made secure
By a small catch of wire which, when released,
Permits the lid to open with a snap

And this an intrinsic pearl?

Beat the devil, beat the devil, beat the devil,
Beat the devil, beat the devil, beat the . . .

(Hear the train
Drive steadily on
Towards nowhere)

Alert to the practice of others, moreover, Mr. Burke reveals a strong liking for William Carlos Williams, ("The Wrens Are Back"); pleasure in E. E. Cummings ("Frigate Jones") "With hands like feet, and feet in turn like legs/ It was his job to lightly step on eggs"; in Wallace Stevens ("From Outside"):

> He could have called this place a bog; quaking
> With life, made cheap by multitude, . . .

and in the rhetoric of the Bible.

Complaints? With Rabelais and Joyce to brother him, Mr. Burke is sometimes coarse. Might he not recall that "the reader has certain categorical expectations that crave propriety?" that "self-expression of the artist is not distinguished by the uttering of emotion but by the evocation of emotion"? The theology in Mr. Burke's suggestions for a "Modernist Sermon," as in his "Lines in the Spirit of Negative Theology," is certainly negative. Led to expect some kind of counter-statement, we find "prayer" a mere figure of speech ("Invective and Prayer," "Dialectician's Prayer," "Industrialist's Prayer"). Looking elsewhere, we can say that solemnity and humility dominate "Night Piece," in which Mr. Burke says:

> I have stood on the edge of the jumping-off place
>
> Waiting
> Have looked down
>
> To see still stars at the bottom of a lake
> Looked out
> Upon a dark riddle within;

and in "Faustkunde," nowhere implies a somewhere—a constancy at least:

> In bed, one thinks of fearsome things.

"When up, one laughs and calls himself a devil." Here, one seems to have both shells of the clam, the seeker for truth, the self-misled—and something alive within. Eternity is made the focus of these reflections,

Während in dem Wogen, der Ewigkeit er wiegt.

Well; if it is not faith, it is poetry: "in dem wogen er wiegt."

"A capacity is a command to act in a certain way," Mr. Burke says; and, fortunately for us, he has been impelled to think and to teach. A philosopher, a grammarian of motives, a methodologist and precisionist, an authority on language who "uses logic not merely to convince but because he loves logic," he has "felt as opportunity what others feel as a menace" and "taken a professional interest in his difficulties"; is an artist. His "new precisions offer new possibilities of development" and his original theorems do not stale. A poet in what he says and in knowing how what is said has been said, he has—Coleridge-fashion—doubled roles and planted two harvests, so that in each we have the best strengths of both.

THE WAYS OUR POETS HAVE TAKEN SINCE THE WAR

Review of The New American Poetry, 1945–1960, *edited by Donald M. Allen. (New York: Grove Press, 1960.)*

"In the years since the war, American poetry has entered upon a singularly rich period," Mr. Allen says and specifies three main groups: older contemporaries—W. C. Williams, Ezra Pound, Wallace Stevens, for instance; a contemporary group—Robert Lowell, Elizabeth Bishop, and others; and a third group now emerging (1945–1960)—the contributors to this anthology—"allied to modern jazz and abstract expressionist painting," a new generation who "have already created their own tradition," the editor says, "their own press and their public." Of the new group, many have been students of Charles Olson at Black Mountain College, share his views, and have taken his verse as a model. He believes in a "loosened convention," "open form," and "composition by field," as he calls it. His Song 4, from "The Songs of Maximus," has a good climax:

> I know a house made of mud & wattles,
> I know a dress just sewed
> > (saw the wind
> blow its cotton
> against her body
> from the ankle
> > so!
> it was Nike

Robert Duncan, adopting Charles Olson's "open form," has imagination and is careful about cadence. In "Food for Fire, Food for Thought," he says,

> We trace faces in clouds: they drift apart.
> Palaces of air. The sun dying down sets them on fire. . . .
> You have carried a branch of tomorrow into the room.
> Its fragrance had awakend me. No.
> It was the sound of a fire on the hearth
> Leapd up where you bankd it
> . . . sparks of delight. . . .
> *If you look you will see the salamander—*
> to the very elements that attend us,
> fairies of the fire, the radiant crawling . . .

Denise Levertov has her own way of saying things in "Scenes from the Life of the Peppertrees"; and in "Pleasures" *is* a pleasure when she says,

> I like the juicy stem of grass that grows
> within the coarser leaf folded round . . .

With Robert Creeley's statement,

> . . . The unsure
> egoist is not
> good for himself

any would agree; and James Broughton also "thinks," has something to say about the self—about not mistaking "greed for need/
and your sentence of death as a book of love." Edward Dorn—
controlling the accent nicely—perfectly depicts a scene by "The
Rick of Green Wood":

> . . . in the november
> air, in the world, that was getting colder
> as we stood there in the woodyard talking
> pleasantly, of the green wood and the dry.

Lawrence Ferlinghetti knows how to expand a metaphor; says

> the poet like an acrobat
> climbs on rime
> to a high wire of his own making . . .
> performing entrechats
> and slight-of-foot tricks
> and other high theatrics
> and all without mistaking
> any thing
> for what it may not be

Jack Spicer is not indifferent to T. S. Eliot and is not hackneyed,
his specialty being the firefly flash of insight, lightening with dry
detachment, as here:

> Poetry, almost blind like a camera
> Is alive in sight only for a second. Click

the accents suiting the sense. Runovers, I think, might as well
end the line naturally; but Lew Welch in his "Chicago Poem"
has a runover of which the emphasis succeeds.

> I lived here nearly 5 years before I could
> meet the middle western day with anything like
> Dignity . . . .

Lew Welch is an observer, speaks of "The goggled men/doing strong things in/ Showers of steel-spark" and he saw a fish, a Blue Gill

> Lifted from its northern lake like a tropical. Jewel at its ear
> belly gold so bright you'd swear he had a
> Light in there . . . color fading with his life a small
>   green fish . . .

What he says about the "planet" on which we live, moreover, is applicable to poetry:

> . . . The trouble is
> always and only with what we build on top of it.
> There's nobody else to blame.

To insert an apostrophe could scarcely slow Richard Duerden's word "seas" too much in his apt lines about "the seas dark face./ Who'd call it lit, by the moon?" But in the way of discarded punctuation, "the seas dark face" is far outdone by Kirby Doyle's "Strange," a two-page sentence with *no* punctuation.

Jack Kerouac is not for prudish persons. His "146th Chorus" (I almost said Canto, and he does find it hard to get away from the manner of the Pound Analects and Cantos) has unity, a tune, and the feel of the mountains. Allen Ginsberg, quoting himself, has been "shopping for images in the poetic super-market" and can foul the nest in a way to marvel at, but it is an innocent enough picture of himself which he provides when he "sat down under the huge shade of a Southern Pacific locomotive." That he "found minds unable to receive love because not knowing the self as lovely" is a thoughtful statement. Gregory Corso has vehemence. His "Uccello" rings true:

> how I dream to join such battle!
> a silver man on a black horse with red standard and striped
>   lance   never to die but to be endless
>   a golden prince of pictorial war

He takes a resilient view of "Marriage" and has a pithy piece, "But I Do Not Need Kindness." James Schuyler in his "Salute" has set down what is evidently in his own special vein—treasure for us as well, about gathering

> . . . one
> of each kind of clover,
> daisy, paintbrush that
> grew in that field . . .

He says "February" was

> green and wet
> while the sky turns violet . . .
> I can't get over
> how it all works in together . . .

and in "Freely Espousing" he likes

> the tonic resonance of
> pill when used as in
> "she is a pill"

Frank O'Hara does not labor a simile: "It's as if I were carrying a horse on my shoulders/ and I couldn't see his face . . ."; and his "Why I Am Not a Painter"—about Mike's painting called SARDINES—is one of the book's rewards for authors out of context. John Ashbery's "Instruction Manual" also is a pleasure, a documentary with structure and content. There is for me a haunting allusiveness about Gilbert Sorrentino's "The Zoo": *Goliathus goliathus*, the one banana/ peeling beetle in the U S A, . . . is dead./ "Wrapped in his native grasses . . ."

In his "Statement on Poetics," Mr. Olson advocates open form or "composition by field," projective or field composition being offered as an improvement on inherited or "non-projective" form. Inherited non-projective form can be projective, I would say, and projective form may be weedy and colorless like suckers from an un-sunned tuber. Kenneth Burke's observation in *Counter-State-ment*, it seems to me, applies both to the "field" and the "library":

"a work may be said to have form in so far as one part leads a reader to anticipate another part and be gratified by the result." Elsewhere, "Great artists feel as opportunity what others feel as a menace. This ability does not, I believe, derive from exceptional strength; it probably arises purely from professional interest the artist may take in his difficulties." As a composer's directions influence the performer's interpretation, punctuation aids precision, and precision is the glory of the craftsman; syntax being equivalent to the staff in music, without which interpretation would surely overtax the performer. (Intentional ambiguity and inadvertent ambiguity, need it be said, are not the same, the perfect analogy for intentional ambiguity being Rousseau's "Rendezvous in the Forest," in which the illusion is the more precise by the fact that the adjoining horses—the dapple and the black—are so merged as to be almost indistinguishable.)

Willa Cather, as quoted by Malcolm Cowley, says, "The artist's real problem is not how to change his material but how to simplify it, 'finding what conventions of form and what detail one can do without and yet preserve the spirit of the whole—so that all that one has suppressed is there to the reader's consciousness as much as if it were in type on the page.'" It might be said here that the adjective "damn," the earmark of incompetence as an emphatic, operates in reverse, is equivalent to: "spare diagnosis; this is no writer." "Anaemia and incompetence," also, deplored by Mr. Olson, are not present when the writer is able to compel the reader to put the accent where the writer wishes it put.

With regard to content: Good content, as Samuel Butler said, is usually matched by good treatment, and poets specializing in "organs and feelings"—severed from culture and literature, dogged by redundance and stench—have a stiff task. By comparison with the vocabularies of science, which are creative, in fact enthralling, exhibitionist content—invaded by the diction of drug-vendors and victims, sex addicts and civic parasites—becomes poetically inoperative. "Imagination can be forced," as Alfred Kazin said, "but it cannot be simulated."

Niceties of composition perhaps are inapplicable; but from the title, *The New American Poetry*, the article should be omitted, since various new poets are not included—Daniel Hoffman, Robert Bagg, George Starbuck; also striking of late as a poet in prose, Jean Garrigue; and it seems literalistic not to include Mr. I. A. Richards, technically "new" and of great attraction.

A WRITER ON THE MOUND

Review of Out of My League, *by George Plimpton. Photographs by Garry Winogrand. (New York: Harper, 1961.)*

A defeated pitcher—"a rather proud figure . . . peering into the depths of his glove"—and a passion for sport had planted in George "Prufrock" Plimpton a craving to pitch from the mound in the Yankee Stadium in an exhibition game. Much time on the phone had resulted in no more than "a snort at the other end" or a "Whazzat? Let's go through that again, hey," and the dream of participating in a game at championship level might have come to nothing if Toots Shor, when consulted, had not proposed a thousand-dollar prize set up by *Sports Illustrated* to be divided by the team which got the most hits—Plimpton pitching. *How to Play Baseball* (John McGraw) or *Pitching in a Pinch* (Christy Mathewson) or *It's Great to Be Alive* (Roy Campanella)—allowing for disparity in the year—might be an appropriate title for what follows.

George Plimpton had played last in a French meadow, with "a brightly colored beach ball which didn't travel far in the thick grass." However—"a fanatic about pitching" from boyhood, so obsessed that he would even throw stones at tree trunks, he says—he had "change of pace," a curve, "a sneaky submarine ball," and "of course I had a fast ball." Knowing better than to brave the inveterate superstition of ballplayers against lending, he provided himself with suit, accessories, and a glove. On the day of the game, a Sunday, the glove was missing—stolen from the car, which had not been locked. The quest for a substitute was fruitless until almost time for the batting contest, as players "bent to their labors" of autographing balls in the locker room. The reprieve must be read at leisure, not paraphrased. In the theft of the mitt, the inopportune arrival of President Eisenhower's motorcade at the Triborough Bridge, and similar dilemmas, Plimpton's stamina has a tincture of Charlie Chaplin's smile of agonized gratitude in acknowledgment of rebuffs.

Before consulting Toots Shor, Plimpton had said to *Sports Illustrated* of his project, "If it works out . . . perhaps I could do some more sports" (modest fellow); and after his stint on the mound he looked carefully around the deserted locker room, he says, "so that I could remember it, not to write about it as much as to convince myself that I had been there."

Out of My League copes with the problem of the imaginary nightmare of walking every batter and the glittering triumph (the shutout) of striking them out, one after the other. Afterward, hungry and thirsty, impatient to see the National League play the American, unrecognized as the pitcher for *Sports Illustrated*, neither ballplayer nor spectator, Plimpton found an empty seat in the upper deck of the stadium, bought two hot dogs, and was paying the vendor for a beer when evicted for having no ticket stub. He "crouched briefly in the aisle— . . . as nomadic as the youngsters who scuttle in without paying and are flushed like shorebirds and flutter down two or three sections to settle" until ushered further.

George Plimpton, as is already apparent, shines in simile—his great device; also in characterization. He has an ear for vernacular, says Willie Mays "has a pleasant face to start with," sometimes explodes in mighty laughter, and "his eyebrows [can] arch up," making him look "as if his manager had just finished addressing him at length in Turkish." Bob Friend, as magnetic as he was unaware that he was, said, "I don't feel all that much at home either," in reply to Plimpton's "It's all a little new."

Verisimilitude? In *Out of My League* it is not so much easy to find as it is impossible to avoid. "Frank Thomas' size made him look dangerous. . . . I imagined I heard the bat sing in the air like a willow switch." Ernie Banks, who won a Most Valuable Player award for "his ability to lay off the bad pitches," was at the plate for such a long time that he "seemed to recede into the distance, along with [Elston] Howard [catching], until the two of them looked like figures viewed through the wrong end of a telescope." Elston Howard's detachment, in contempt of a stodgy task, had been painingly apparent to Plimpton. Then as Stan Lopata hit foul after foul, "lashing out like a cobra from his coil," Plimpton says, Howard "began to rise from his crouch after every pitch and fire the ball back . . . with an accuracy that mocked my control, harder than I was pitching it to him," inflicting "a deep bone bruise which discolored my left hand for over a week."

Christy Mathewson says, "a pitcher is not a ballplayer—he is a man in need of sympathy." Well . . . for a full-time man of letters, anonymity is a "role," and the reader's emotion is envy, envy of a man who retired his first two batters and later achieved the fine moment of his afternoon "when Mays hit that towering fly . . . forever available for recall." As Charles Poore says, "in a world where athletes are always signing ghost-written books this turnabout, with a writer ghosting an athlete, is fair play." If in *Out of My League* triumph does not dominate nightmare, something is wrong with the reader—if the performance by George Plimpton, his statistician, and photographer, Garry Winogrand, has not earned them the triple crown with "rim tucked under," for poetry, biography, and drama.

M. CAREY THOMAS OF BRYN MAWR

Review of Carey Thomas of Bryn Mawr *by Edith Finch*. (*New York: Harper, 1947.*)

Carey Thomas was a Quaker, with "an almost Renaissance imagination." She "gloried in combat and movement" and "never wasted energy in vain regrets," was "critical of praise," adept in reprimand. She had a passion for "joining in and setting things straight." "Slovenly enunciation irritated her." As a child she resented "having to listen in Bible class to a young woman preaching about simplicity, who must have spent an hour or two arranging 'the horrible little curls' that adorned her head." Longing to go to Vassar, she said, "There is one thing I can do and that is study"; and exhilarated by preparatory subjects, "I wish the air were pure oxygen, and then as it says in our chemistry, our life would sweep through its fevered burning course in a few hours and we would live in a perfect delirium of excitement and would die vibrating with passion, for anything would be better than this lazy sluggish life." She was undeterred by "the awful amount of drudgery a first-rate education" involves, remarking in later life, "I cannot remember a time when I did not read at every available moment." Each succeeding phase of study seemed more interesting than the last. Of Wordsworth's *The Prelude* she said, "He spoke right to me. I was almost frightened as I found thought after thought there that had come to me so often"; and on discovering *Jane Eyre*, "My throat was parched . . . and cheeks fairly scorched. Oh, though I dare say it isn't a good book, yet it seems to me as if it were something worth while to write something that should have the power to excite and intensely interest to such a degree." She was an irrepressible traveler, delighted in "horrid crags," "fir-clad ravines," "tall spires," and "dusky aisles touched with motes of color from stained windows." A rebel against ambiguous morality, she deplored over-concreteness in religion, yet could say of Leonardo da Vinci's sketch for the head of Christ and the *Last Supper* itself, "One bows before them as by magnetism and immediately one's past becomes a poor undeveloped thing because they have been wanting to it and one's future full of longing without them." Unself-protective if a cause required her to be, she was not afraid of failure; though so honest against herself as to say upon falling in love, "I never came to anything before, I could not partially at least manage."

This account of frustration upon frustration and crusade after crusade to free the mind from legal and other barriers, extends in significance far beyond Quakerism, family, and period. Sobered by obstruction, with forces knit by the injustices of convention, Carey Thomas avowed what in life she contradicted: "Secrecy and guile are the only refuge of a down-trodden sex." The victim of gossip because she had discussed a scholastic matter with a German student on what her landlady termed "the betrothal sofa," she thence behaved as she had in the Cornell "elegant garden of young men," "not only with decorum but marked decorum" and said years after, "Bryn Mawr need not be the less guarded because it is good."

The quest for a degree, from Leipzig to Göttingen to Zurich, seems a fantasy of anachronism. When raising the Women's Fund to establish the Johns Hopkins medical school, Carey Thomas and four of her friends—"The Ladies" as they were called —stipulated that women be admitted on an equality with men and that entrance requirements should not be less rigid than those prescribed by the committee. Miss Thomas, chairman, referring to herself and Miss Gwinn, said, "My father almost wept . . . that two young women should take such a position"; Doctor Welch remarking to Doctor Osler, "We are lucky to get in as professors, for I am sure that neither you nor I could ever get in as students."

Any who have thought of Carey Thomas as ipso facto Bryn Mawr, will find it difficult to realize what handicap "the shrine of womanhood" once constituted, and that a woman who was virtual administrator and dean of a college was made president officially by a majority of but one vote; then only after years of "wary foresight in holding back and driving forward at the right moments," was grudgingly elected to the board of trustees.

Mr. Blackmur says that writing nowadays lacks the positiveness which derives from conviction. Carey Thomas had it, conversationally and in her literature course—living in another world from that of "half happiness," "half love," and "the little little poems that were being written." By her "clarity," her "assurance of values, she impelled others toward . . . discriminations"; had the "power of gauging under what circumstances special capabilities might flower most fully," "spared no pains to push and prune," and in faculty selections was willing to give every chance to a candidate in whom she saw promise—"even though he saw little in himself," an insight confirmed by the continual loss of professors to larger colleges. Her name is—understandably—associated with education, the points she made in 1901 nearly coinciding with those made by the "Harvard Committee on the objectives of a general education in a free society" in 1945.

Again Miss Finch is, in her relentless justice, a Vermeer of circumstance and idiosyncrasy when she says of Carey Thomas, "the conflict between deliberate and natural behavior" made her "a little *farouche*." "She had no use for casual chitchat. Compelled to suffer it, the warmth of her manner chilled to bare civility, the heavy eyelids drooped . . . her face became a mask of controlled impatience and distaste." One perceives, moreover, that as a disdainer of casuistry, Miss Finch believes in Carey Thomas and means it when she attributes an appearance of "despotism and double-dealing" in her to "real open-mindedness" and "lapse of memory." Miss Gwinn is not less a personality than a type, in "the calculated impression" she made "of knowing all the answers had she chosen to give them," and of finding "struggling conversationalists a little dull."

This is portraiture, verisimilitude in personality matched by verity of setting. Student days in Germany come to life in the " 'regally cultivated' Grüneissen sisters, three maiden ladies of whom Fräulein Mathilde had 'read every one' of the five hundred books on art that comprised their father's library," and "knew almost every picture in existence painted by an Old Master"; she also painted, though "given no chance to train her talent or see the originals." At Leipzig, fellow students "often opened doors for the two expatriates from Baltimore—though sometimes hesitated, then passed through determinedly first, themselves"; yet as Carey Thomas said in her journal, "after a year they seemed to have developed 'a sort of contemptuous affection for us.' " Apparently subordinate descriptive statements have startling precision, as where at Cornell Carey Thomas's parents "plodded about the campus on its hill above the town, appraised the fine old trees and the still rather new-looking halls." Bryn Mawr, equally, is unmistakable in "the autumn smell of dry and burning leaves"; in the busts of the emperors on their golden oak pedestals in Taylor Hall, and in what is said of the Bible "on the square block of the speaker's desk at morning chapel, with Carey Thomas swiftly mounting the platform". . . then "reading some great passage."

We have here an instance of that difficult but, as Mr. Saintsbury considered, best method of exhibiting a personality—direct quoting; the whole thing so neatly compacted that even a summary of building expansion is not dull. The book is a performance, as biography and as the portrait of one who was for woman an impassioned emancipator.

INTERVIEW WITH DONALD HALL

INTERVIEW WITH DONALD HALL

Q.: Miss Moore, I understand that you were born in St. Louis only about ten months before T. S. Eliot. Did your families know each other?

A.: No, we did not know the Eliots. We lived in Kirkwood, Missouri, where my grandfather was pastor of the First Presbyterian Church. T. S. Eliot's grandfather—Dr. William Eliot—was a Unitarian. We left when I was about seven, my grandfather having died in 1894, February 20th. My grandfather like Dr. Eliot had attended ministerial meetings in St. Louis. Also, at stated intervals, various ministers met for luncheon. After one of these luncheons my grandfather said, "When Dr. William Eliot asks the blessing and says, 'and this we ask in the name of our Lord Jesus Christ,' he is Trinitarian enough for me." The Mary Institute, for girls, was endowed by him as a memorial to his daughter Mary, who had died.

Q.: How old were you when you started to write poems?

A.: Well, let me see, in Bryn Mawr. I think I was eighteen when I entered Bryn Mawr. I was born in 1887, I entered college in 1906. Now how old would I have been? Can you deduce my probable age?

Q.: Eighteen or nineteen.

A.: I had no literary plans, but I was interested in the undergraduate monthly magazine, and to my surprise (I wrote one or two little things for it) the editors elected me to the board. It was my sophomore year—I am sure it was—and I stayed on, I believe. And then when I had left college I offered contributions (we weren't paid) to the *Lantern*, the alumnae magazine. But I didn't feel that my product was anything to shake the world.

Q.: At what point did poetry become world-shaking for you?

A.: Never! I believe I was interested in painting then. At least I said so. I remember Mrs. Otis Skinner asking at Commencement time, the year I was graduated, "What would you like to be?" "A painter," I said.

"Well, I'm not surprised," Mrs. Skinner answered. I had something on that she liked, some kind of summer dress. She commended it—said, "I'm not at all surprised."

I like stories. I like fiction. And—this sounds rather pathetic, bizarre as well—I think verse perhaps was for me the next best thing to it. Didn't I write something one time, "Part of a Poem, Part of a Novel, Part of a Play"? I think I was all too truthful. I could visualize scenes, and deplored the fact that Henry James had to do it unchallenged.

Now, if I couldn't write fiction, I'd like to write plays. To me the theater is the most pleasant, in fact my favorite form of recreation.

Q.: Do you go often?

A.: No. Never. Unless someone invites me. Lillian Hellman invited me to *Toys in the Attic,* and I am very happy that she did. I would have had no notion of the vitality of the thing, have lost sight of her skill as a writer if I hadn't seen the play; would like to go again. The accuracy of the vernacular! That's the kind of thing I am interested in, am always taking down little local expressions and accents. I think I should be in some philological operation or enterprise, am really much interested in dialect and intonations. I scarcely think of any that comes into my so-called poems at all.

Q.: I wonder what Bryn Mawr meant for you as a poet. You write that most of your time there was spent in the biological laboratory. Did you like biology better than literature as a subject for study? Did the training possibly affect your poetry?

A.: I had hoped to make French and English my major studies, and took the required two-year English course—five hours a week —but was not able to elect a course until my junior year. I did not attain the requisite academic stand of eighty until that year. I then elected seventeenth-century imitative writing—Fuller, Hooker, Bacon, Bishop Andrewes, and others. Lectures in French were in French, and I had had no spoken French.

Did laboratory studies affect my poetry? I am sure they did. I found the biology courses—minor, major, and histology—exhilarating. I thought, in fact, of studying medicine. Precision, economy of statement, logic employed to ends that are disinterested, drawing and identifying, liberate—at least have some bearing on—the imagination, it seems to me.

Q.: Whom did you know in the literary world, before you came to New York? Did you know Bryher and H. D.?

A.: It's very hard to get these things seriatim. I met Bryher in 1921 in New York. H.D. was my classmate at Bryn Mawr. She was there, I think, only two years. She was a non-resident and I did not realize that she was interested in writing.

Q.: Did you know Ezra Pound and William Carlos Williams through her? Didn't she know them at the University of Pennsylvania?

A.: Yes. She did. I didn't meet them. I had met no writers until 1916 when I visited New York, when a friend in Carlisle wanted me to accompany her.

Q.: So you were isolated really from modern poetry until 1916?
A.: Yes.

Q.: Was that your first trip to New York, when you went there for six days and decided that you wanted to live there?

A.: Oh, no. Several times my mother had taken my brother and me sightseeing and to shop; on the way to Boston, or Maine, and to Washington and Florida. My senior year in college in 1909, I visited Dr. Charles Spraguesmith's daughter, Hilda, at Christmas time in New York. And Louis Anspacher lectured in a very ornamental way at Cooper Union. There was plenty of music at Carnegie Hall, and I got a sense of what was going on in New York.

Q.: And what was going on made you want to come back?

A.: It probably did, when Miss Cowdrey in Carlisle invited me to come with her for a week. It was the visit in 1916 that made me want to live there. I don't know what put it into her head to do it, or why she wasn't likely to have a better time without me. She was most skeptical of my venturing forth to bohemian parties. But I was fearless about that. In the first place, I didn't think anyone would try to harm me, but if they did I felt impervious. It never occurred to me that chaperones were important.

Q.: Do you suppose that moving to New York, and the stimulation of the writers whom you found there, led you to write more poems than you would otherwise have written?

A.: I'm sure it did—seeing what others wrote, liking this or that. With me it's always some fortuity that traps me. I certainly never intended to write poetry. That never came into my head. And now, too, I think each time I write that it may be the last time; then I'm charmed by something and seem to have to say something. Everything I have written is the result of reading or of interest in people, I'm sure of that. I had no ambition to be a writer.

Q.: Let me see. You taught at the Carlisle Indian School, after Bryn Mawr. Then after you moved to New York in 1918 you taught at a private school and worked in a library. Did these occupations have anything to do with you as a writer?

A.: I think they hardened my muscles considerably, my mental approach to things. Working as a librarian was a big help, a tremendous help. Miss Leonard of the Hudson Park branch of the New York Public Library opposite our house came to see me one day. I wasn't in, and she asked my mother did she think I would care to be on the staff, work in the library, because I was so fond of books and liked to talk about them to people. My mother said no, she thought not; the shoemaker's children never have shoes, I probably would feel if I joined the staff that I'd have no time to read. When I came home she told me, and I said, "Why, certainly. Ideal. I'll tell her. Only I couldn't work more than half a day." If I had worked all day and maybe evenings or overtime, like the mechanics, why, it would *not* have been ideal.

As a free service we were assigned books to review and I did like that. We didn't get paid but we had the chance to diagnose. I reveled in it. Somewhere I believe I have carbon copies of those "P-slip" summaries. They were the kind of things that brought the worst-best out. I was always wondering why they didn't honor me with an art book or medical book or even a history, or criticism. But no, it was fiction, silent-movie fiction.

Q.: Did you travel at this time? Did you go to Europe at all?

A.: In 1911. My mother and I went to England for about two

months, July and August probably. We went to Paris and we stayed on the left bank, in a pension in the rue Valette, where Calvin wrote his *Institutes*, I believe. Not far from the Panthéon and the Luxembourg Gardens. I have been much interested in Sylvia Beach's book—reading about Ezra Pound and his Paris days. Where was I and what was I doing? I think, with the objective, an evening stroll—it was one of the hottest summers the world has ever known, 1911—we walked along to 12, rue de L'Odéon, to see Sylvia Beach's shop. It wouldn't occur to me to say, "Here am I, I'm a writer, would you talk to me a while?" I had no feeling at all like that. I wanted to observe things. And we went to every museum in Paris, I think, except two.

Q.: Have you been back since?

A.: Not to Paris. Only to England in 1935 or 1936. I like England.

Q.: You have mostly stayed put in Brooklyn, then, since you moved here in 1929?

A.: Except for four trips to the West: Los Angeles, San Francisco, Puget Sound, and British Columbia. My mother and I went through the canal previously, to San Francisco, and by rail to Seattle.

Q.: Have you missed the Dodgers here, since *they* went West?

A.: Very much, and I am told that they miss us.

Q.: I am still interested in those early years in New York. William Carlos Williams, in his *Autobiography*, says that you were "a rafter holding up the superstructure of our uncompleted building," when he talks about the Greenwich Village group of writers. I guess these were people who contributed to *Others*.

A.: I never was a rafter holding up anyone! I have his *Autobiography* and took him to task for his misinformed statements about Robert McAlmon and Bryher. In my indignation I missed some things I ought to have seen.

Q.: To what extent did the *Others* contributors form a group?

A.: We did foregather a little. Alfred Kreymbourg was editor, and was married to Gertrude Lord at the time, one of the loveliest persons you could ever meet. And they had a little apartment somewhere in the village. There was considerable unanimity about the group.

Q.: Someone called Alfred Kreymbourg your American discoverer. Do you suppose this is true?

A.: It could be said, perhaps; he did all he could to promote me. Miss Monroe and the Aldingtons had asked me simultaneously to contribute to *Poetry* and the *Egoist* in 1917 at the same time.

Alfred Kreymbourg was not inhibited. I was a little different from the others. He thought I might pass as a novelty, I guess.

Q.: What was your reaction when H. D. and Bryher brought out your first collection, which they called *Poems,* in 1921 without your knowledge? Why had you delayed to do it yourself?

A.: To issue my slight product—conspicuously tentative—seemed to me premature. I disliked the term "poetry" for any but Chaucer's or Shakespeare's or Dante's. I do not now feel quite my original hostility to the word, since it is a convenient almost unavoidable term for the thing (although hardly for me—my observations, experiments in rhythm, or exercises in composition). What I write, as I have said before, could only be called poetry because there is no other category in which to put it.

For the chivalry of the undertaking—issuing my verse for me in 1921, certainly in format choicer than the content—I am intensely grateful. Again, in 1925, it seemed to me not very self-interested of Faber and Faber, and simultaneously of the Macmillan Company, to propose a *Selected Poems* for me. Desultory occasional magazine publications seemed to me sufficient, conspicuous enough.

Q.: Had you been sending poems to magazines before the *Egoist* printed your first poem?

A.: I must have. I have a little curio, a little wee book about two by three inches, or two and a half by three inches, in which I systematically entered everything sent out, when I got it back, if they took it, and how much I got for it. That lasted about a year, I think. I can't care as much as all that. I don't know that I submitted anything that wasn't extorted from me.

I have at present three onerous tasks, and each interferes with the others, and I don't know how I am going to write anything. If I get a promising idea I set it down, and it stays there. I don't make myself do anything with it. I've had several things in the *New Yorker*. And I said to them, "I might never write again," and not to expect me to. I never knew anyone who had a passion for words who had as much difficulty in saying things as I do and I very seldom say them in a manner I like. If I do it's because I don't know I'm trying. I've written several things for the *New Yorker*—and I did want to write *them*.

Q.: When did you last write a poem?

A.: It appeared in August. What was it about? Oh . . . Carnegie Hall. You see, anything that really rouses me . . .

Q.: How does a poem start for you?

A.: A felicitous phrase springs to mind—a word or two, say—simultaneous usually with some thought or object of equal attraction: "Its leaps should be *set*/to the flage*olet*"; "Katydid-wing subdivided by *sun*/till the nettings are *legion*." I like light rhymes, inconspicuous rhymes and un-pompous conspicuous rhymes: Gilbert and Sullivan:

> and yet when someone's near
> we manage to appear
> as impervious to fear
> as anybody here.

I have a passion for rhythm and accent, so blundered into versifying. Considering the stanza the unit, I came to hazard hyphens at the end of the line, but found that readers are distracted from the content by hyphens, so I try not to use them.

My interest in La Fontaine originated entirely independent of content. I then fell a prey to that surgical kind of courtesy of his.

> I fear that appearances are worshiped throughout France
> Whereas pre-eminence perchance
> Merely means a pushing person.

I like the unaccented syllable and accented near-rhyme:

> By love and his blindness
> Possibly a service was done,
> Let lovers say. A lonely man has no criterion.

Q.: What in your reading or your background led you to write the way you do write? Was imagism a help to you?

A.: No. I wondered why anyone would adopt the term.

Q.: The descriptiveness of your poems has nothing to do with them, you think?

A.: No; I really don't. I was rather sorry to be a pariah, or at least that I had no connection with anything. But I *did* feel gratitude to *Others*.

Q.: Where do you think your style of writing came from? Was it a gradual accumulation, out of your character? Or does it have literary antecedents?

A.: Not so far as I know. Ezra Pound said, "Someone has been reading Laforgue, and French authors." Well, sad to say, I had not read any of them until fairly recently. Retroactively I see that Francis Jammes' titles and treatment are a good deal like my own. I seem almost a plagiarist.

Q.: And the extensive use of quotations?

A.: I was just trying to be honorable and not to steal things. I've always felt that if a thing had been said in the *best* way, how can you say it better? If I wanted to say something and somebody had said it ideally, then I'd take it but give the person credit for it. That's all there is to it. If you are charmed by an author, I think it's a very strange and invalid imagination that doesn't long to share it. Somebody else should read it, don't you think?

Q.: Did any prose stylists help you in finding your poetic style? Elizabeth Bishop mentions Poe's prose, in connection with your writing, and you have always made people think of Henry James.

A.: Prose stylists, very much. Doctor Johnson on Richard Savage: "He was in two months illegitimated by the Parliament, and disowned by his mother, doomed to poverty and obscurity, and launched upon the ocean of life only that he might be swallowed by its quicksands, or dashed upon its rocks. . . . it was his peculiar happiness that he scarcely ever found a stranger whom he did not leave a friend; but it must likewise be added that, he had not often a friend long without obliging him to become a stranger." Or Edmund Burke on the colonies: "You can shear a wolf; but will he comply?" Or Sir Thomas Browne: "States are not governed by Ergotisms." He calls a bee "that industrious flie," and his home his "hive." His manner is a kind of erudition-proof sweetness. Or Sir Francis Bacon: "Civil War is like the heat of fever; a foreign war is like the heat of exercise." Or Cellini: "I had by me a dog black as a mulberry. . . . I swelled up in my rage like an asp." Or Caesar's *Commentaries*, and Xenophon's *Cynegeticus*: the gusto and interest in every detail! In Henry James it is the essays and letters especialy that affect me. In Ezra Pound, *The Spirit of Romance*: his definiteness, his indigenously unmistakable accent. Charles Norman says in his biography of Ezra Pound that he said to a poet, "Nothing, *nothing*, that you couldn't in some circumstance, under stress of some emotion, *actually say*." And Ezra said of Shakespeare and Dante, "Here we are with the masters; of neither can we say, 'He is the greater'; of each we must say, 'He is unexcelled.' "

Q.: Do you have in your own work any favorites and unfavorites?

A.: Indeed, I do. I think the most difficult thing for me is to be satisfactorily lucid, yet have enough implication in it to suit myself. That's a problem. And I don't approve of my "enigmas," or as somebody said, "the not ungreen grass."

I said to my mother one time, "How did you ever permit me to let this be printed?"

And she said, "You didn't ask my advice."

Q.: One time I heard you give a reading, and I think you said that you didn't like "In Distrust of Merits," which is one of your most popular poems.

A.: I do like it; it is sincere but I wouldn't call it a poem. It's truthful; it is testimony—to the fact that war is intolerable, and unjust.

Q.: How can you call it not a poem, on what basis?

A.: Haphazard; as form, what has it? It is just a protest—disjointed, exclamatory. Emotion overpowered me. First this thought and then that.

Q.: Your mother said that you hadn't asked her advice. Did you ever? Do you go for criticism to your family or friends?

A.: Well, not friends, but my brother if I get a chance. When my mother said "You didn't ask my advice" must have been years ago, because when I wrote "A Face," I had written something first about "the adder and the child with a bowl of porridge," and she said "It won't do."

"All right," I said, "but I have to produce something." Cyril Connolly had asked me for something for *Horizon*. So I wrote "A Face." That is one of the few things I ever set down that didn't give me any trouble. She said, "I like it." I remember that.

Then, much before that, I wrote "The Buffalo." I thought it would probably outrage a number of persons because it had to me a kind of pleasing jerky progress. I thought, "Well, if it seems bad my brother will tell me, and if it has a point he'll detect it."

And he said, with considerable gusto, "It takes my fancy." I was happy as could be.

Q.: Did you ever suppress anything because of family objections?

A.: Yes, "the adder and the child with a bowl of porridge." I never even wanted to improve it.

You know, Mr. Saintsbury said that Andrew Lang wanted him to contribute something on Poe, and he did, and Lang returned it. Mr. Saintsbury said, "Once a thing has been rejected, I would not offer it to the most different of editors." That shocked me. I have offered a thing, submitted it thirty-five times. Not simultaneously, of course.

Q.: A poem?

A.: Yes. I am very tenacious.

Q.: Do people ever ask you to write poems for them?

A.: Continually. Everything from on the death of a dog to a little item for an album.

Q.: Do you ever write them?

A.: Oh, perhaps; usually quote something. Once when I was in the library we gave a party for Miss Leonard, and I wrote a line or two of doggerel about a bouquet of violets we gave her. It has no life or point. It was meant well but didn't amount to anything. Then in college, I had a sonnet as an assignment. The epitome of weakness.

Q.: I'm interested in asking about the principles, and the methods, of your way of writing. What is the rationale behind syllabic verse? How does it differ from free verse in which the line length is controlled visually but not arithmetically?

A.: It never occurred to me that what I wrote was something to define. I am governed by the pull of the sentence as the pull of a fabric is governed by gravity. I like the end-stopped line and dislike the reversed order of words; like symmetry.

Q.: How do you plan the shape of your stanzas? I am thinking of the poems, usually syllabic, which employ a repeated stanza form. Do you ever experiment with shapes before you write, by drawing lines on a page?

A.: Never, I never "plan" a stanza. Words cluster like chromosomes, determining the procedure. I may influence an arrangement or thin it, then try to have successive stanzas identical with the first. Spontaneous initial originality—say, impetus—seems difficult to reproduce consciously later. As Stravinsky said about pitch, "If I transpose it for some reason, I am in danger of losing the freshness of first contact and will have difficulty in recapturing its attractiveness."

No, I never "draw lines." I make a rhyme conspicuous, to me at a glance, by underlining with red, blue, or other pencil—as many colors as I have rhymes to differentiate. However, if the phrases recur in too incoherent an architecture—as print—I notice that the words as a tune do not sound right.

I may start a piece, find it obstructive, lack a way out, and not complete the thing for a year, or years, am thrifty. I salvage anything promising and set it down in a small notebook.

Q.: I wonder if the act of translating La Fontaine's *Fables* helped you as a writer.

A.: Indeed it did. It was the best help I've ever had.

I suffered frustration. I'm so naïve, so docile, I *tend* to take anybody's word for anything the person says, even in matters of art. The publisher who had commissioned the *Fables* died. I had no publisher. Well, I struggled on for a time and it didn't go very well. I thought, I'd better ask if they don't want to terminate the contract; then I could offer it elsewhere. I thought Macmillan, who took an interest in me, might like it. *Might.* The editor in charge of translations said, "Well, I studied French at Cornell, took a degree in French, I love French, and . . . well, I think you'd better put it away for a while." "How long?" I said. "About ten years; besides, it will hurt your own work. You won't write so well afterward."

"Oh," I said, "that's one reason I was undertaking it; I thought it would train me and give me momentum." Much dejected, I asked, "What is wrong? Have I not a good ear? Are the meanings not sound?"

"Well, there are conflicts," the editor reiterated, as it seemed to me, countless times. I don't know yet what they are or were. (A little "editorial.")

I said, "Don't write me an extenuating letter, please. Just send back the material in the envelope I put with it." I had submitted it in January and this was May. I had had a kind of uneasy hope that all would be well; meanwhile had volumes, hours, and years of work yet to do and might as well go on and do it, I had thought. The ultimatum was devastating.

At the same time Monroe Engel of the Viking Press wrote to me and said that he had supposed I had a commitment for my *Fables*, but if I hadn't would I let the Viking Press see them? I feel an everlasting gratitude to him.

However, I said, "I can't offer you something which somebody else thinks isn't fit to print. I would have to have someone to stabilize it and guarantee that the meanings are sound."

Mr. Engel said, "Who do you think could do that? Whom would you like?"

I said, "Harry Levin," because he had written a cogent, very shrewd review of Edna St. Vincent Millay's and George Dillon's translation of Baudelaire. I admired its finesse.

Mr. Engel said, "I'll ask him. But you won't hear for a long time. He's very busy. And how much do you think we ought to offer him?"

"Well," I said, "not less than ten dollars a Book; there would be no incentive in undertaking the bother of it, if it weren't twenty."

He said, "that would reduce your royalties too much on an advance."

I said, "I don't want an advance, wouldn't even consider one."

"Well," he said, "that is like you."

And then Harry Levin said, quite soon, that he would be glad to do it as a "refreshment against the chores of the term." It was a very dubious refreshment, let me tell you. (He is precise, and not abusive, and did not "resign.")

Q.: I've been asking you about your poems, which is of course what interests me most. But you were editor of *The Dial*, too, and I want to ask you a few things about that. You were editor from 1925 until it ended in 1929, I think. How did you first come to be associated with it?

A.: Let me see. I think I took the initiative. I sent the editors a couple of things and they sent them back. And Lola Ridge had a party—she had a large apartment on a ground floor somewhere— and John Reed and Marsden Hartley, who was very confident with the brush, and Scofield Thayer, editor of *The Dial*, were there. And much to my disgust, we were induced each to read something we had written. And Scofield Thayer said of my piece, "Would you send that to us at *The Dial?*"

"I did send it," I said.

And he said, "Well, send it again." That is how it began, I think. Then he said, one time, "I'd like you to meet my partner, Sibley Watson," and invited me to tea at 152 W. 13th St. I was impressed. Doctor Watson is rare. He said nothing, but what he did say was striking and the significance would creep over you because unanticipated. And they asked me to join the staff, at *The Dial*.

Q.: I have just been looking at that magazine, the years when you edited it. It's an incredible magazine.

A.: *The Dial?* There *were* good things in it, weren't there?

Q.: Yes. It combined George Saintsbury and Ezra Pound in the same issue. How do you account for it? What made it so good?

A.: Lack of fear, for one thing. We didn't care what other people said. I never knew a magazine which was so self-propulsive. Everybody liked what he was doing, and when we made grievous mistakes we were sorry but we laughed over them.

Q.: Louise Bogan said that *The Dial* made clear "the obvious division between American *avant-garde* and American conventional writing." Do you think this kind of division continues or has continued? Was this in any way a deliberate policy?

A.: I think that individuality was the great thing. We were not conforming to anything. We certainly didn't have a policy, except I remember hearing the word "intensity" very often. A thing must have "intensity." That seemed to be the criterion.

The thing applied to it, I think, that should apply to your own writing. As George Grosz said, at that last meeting he attended at the National Institute, "How did I come to be an artist? Endless curiosity, observation, research—and a great amount of joy in the thing." It was a matter of taking a liking to things. Things that were in accordance with your taste. I think that was it. And we didn't care how unhomogeneous they might seem. Didn't Aristotle say that it is the mark of a poet to see resemblances between apparently incongruous things? There was any amount of attraction about it.

Q.: Do you think there is anything in the change of literary life in America that would make *The Dial* different if it existed today under the same editors? Were there any special conditions in the twenties that made the literary life of America different?

A.: I think it is always about the same.

Q.: I wonder if it had survived into the thirties if it might have made that rather dry literary decade a little better.

A.: I think so. Because we weren't in captivity to anything.

Q.: Was it just finances that made it stop?

A.: No, it wasn't the depression. Conditions changed. Scofield Thayer had a nervous breakdown, and he didn't come to meetings.

Doctor Watson was interested in photography—was studying medicine; is a doctor of medicine, and lived in Rochester. I was alone. I didn't know that Rochester was about a night's journey away, and I would say to Doctor Watson, "Couldn't you come in for a make-up meeting, or send us these manuscripts and say what you think of them?" I may, as usual, have exaggerated my enslavement and my preoccupation with tasks—writing letters and reading manuscripts. Originally I had said I would come if I didn't have to write letters and didn't have to see contributors. And presently I was doing both. I think it was largely chivalry —the decision to discontinue the magazine—because I didn't have time for work of my own.

Q.: I wonder how you worked as an editor. Hart Crane complains, in one of his letters, that you rearranged "The Wine Menagerie" and changed the title. Do you feel that you were justified? Did you ask for revisions from many poets?

A.: No. We had an inflexible rule: do not ask changes of so much as a comma. Accept it or reject it. But in that instance I felt that in compassion I should disregard the rule.

Hart Crane complains of me? Well, I complain of *him*. He liked *The Dial* and we liked him—friends, and with certain tastes in common. He was in dire need of money. It seemed careless not to so much as ask if he might like to make some changes ("like" in quotations). His gratitude was ardent and later his repudiation of it commensurate—he perhaps being in both instances under a disability with which I was not familiar. (Penalizing us for compassion?) I say "us," and should say "me." Really I am not used to having people in that bemused state. He was so *anxious* to have us take that thing, and so *delighted*. "Well, if you would modify it a little," I said, "we would like it better."I never attended "their" wild parties, as Lachaise once said. It was lawless of me to suggest changes; I disobeyed.

Q.: Have you had editors suggest changes to you? Changes in your own poems, I mean?

A.: No, but my ardor to be helped being sincere, I sometimes *induce* assistance:. the *Times*, the *Herald Tribune*, the *New*

Yorker, have a number of times had to patch and piece me out. If you have a genius of an editor, you are blessed: e.g., T. S. Eliot and Ezra Pound, Harry Levin, and others; Irita Van Doren and Miss Belle Rosenbaum.

Have I found "help" helpful? I certainly have; and in three instances when I was at *The Dial*, I hazarded suggestions the results of which were to me drama. Excoriated by George Haven Schauffler for offering to suggest a verbal change or two in his translation of Thomas Mann's *Disorder and Early Sorrow*, I must have posted the suggestions before I was able to withdraw them. In any case, his joyous subsequent retraction of abuse, and his pleasure in the narrative, were not unwelcome. Gilbert Seldes strongly commended me for excisions proposed by me in his "Jonathan Edwards" (for *The Dial*); and I have not ceased to marvel at the overrating by Mark Van Doren of editorial conscience on my reverting (after an interval) to keeping some final lines I had wished he would omit. (Verse! but not a sonnet.)

We should try to judge the work of others by the most that it is, and our own, if not by the least that it is, take the least into consideration. I feel that I would not be worth a button if not grateful to be preserved from myself, and informed if what I have written is not to the point. I think we should feel free, like La Fontaine's captious critic, to say, if asked, "Your phrases are too long, and the content is not good. Break up the type and put it in the font." As Kenneth Burke says in *Counter-Statement*: "[Great] artists feel as opportunity what others feel as a menace. This ability does not, I believe, derive from exceptional strength, it probably arises purely from professional interest the artist may take in his difficulties."

Lew Sarett says, in the *Poetry Society Bulletin*, we ask of a poet: Does this mean something? Does the poet say what he has to say and in his own manner? Does it stir the reader?

Shouldn't we replace vanity with honesty, as Robert Frost recommends? Annoyances abound. We should not find them lethal—a baffled printer's emendations for instance (my "elephant with frog-colored skin" instead of "fog-colored skin," and "the power of the invisible is the invisible," instead of "the power of the visible is the invisible") sounding like a parody on my meticulousness; a glasshopper instead of a grasshopper.

Q.: Editing *The Dial* must have acquainted you with the writers of the day whom you did not know already. Had you known Hart Crane earlier?

A.: Yes, I did. You remember *Broom?* Toward at the beginning of that magazine, in 1921, Lola Ridge was very hospitable, and she invited to a party—previous to my work on *The Dial*—Kay Boyle and her husband, a French soldier, and Hart Crane, Elinor Wylie, and some others. I took a great liking to Hart Crane. We talked about French bindings, and he was diffident and modest and seemed to have so much intuition, such a feel for things, for books —really a bibliophile—that I took special interest in him. And Doctor Watson and Scofield Thayer liked him—felt that he was one of our talents, that he couldn't fit himself into an IBM position to find a livelihood; that we ought to, whenever we could, take anything he sent us.

I know a cousin of his, Joe Nowak, who is rather proud of him. He lives here in Brooklyn, and is * at the Dry Dock Savings Bank and used to work in antiques. Joe was very convinced of Hart's sincerity and his innate love of all that I have specified. Anyhow, *The Bridge* is a grand theme. Here and there I think he could have firmed it up. A writer is unfair to himself when he is unable to be hard on himself.

Q.: Did Crane have anything to do with *Others?*

A.: *Others* antedated *Broom. Others* was Alfred Kreymbourg and Skipwith Cannéll, Wallace Stevens, William Carlos Williams. Wallace Stevens—odd; I nearly met him a dozen times before I did meet him in 1941 at Mount Holyoke, at the college's *Entretiens de Pontigny* of which Professor Gustav Cohen was chairman. Wallace Stevens was Henry Church's favorite American poet. Mr. Church had published him and some others, and me, in *Mésure*, in Paris. Raymond Queneau translated us.

During the French program at Mount Holyoke one afternoon

* *Was;* killed; his car run into by a reckless driver in April 1961.

Wallace Stevens had a discourse, the one about Goethe dancing, on a packet-boat in black wool stockings. My mother and I were there; and I gave a reading with commentary. Henry Church had an astoundingly beautiful Panama hat—a sort of pork-pie with a wide brim, a little like Bernard Berenson's hats. I have never seen as fine a weave, and he had a pepper-and-salt shawl which he draped about himself. This lecture was on the lawn.

Wallace Stevens was extremely friendly. We should have had a tape recorder on that occasion, for at lunch they seated us all at a kind of refectory table and a girl kept asking him questions such as, "Mr. Stevens have you read the—*Four—Quartets?*"

"Of course, but I can't read much of Eliot or I wouldn't have any individuality of my own."

Q.: Do you read new poetry now? Do you try to keep up?

A.: I am always seeing it—am sent some every day. Some, good. But it does interefere with my work. I can't get much done. Yet I would be a monster if I tossed everything away without looking at it; I write more notes, letters, cards in an hour than is sane.

Although everyone is penalized by being quoted inexactly, I wonder if there is anybody alive whose remarks are so often paraphrased as mine—printed as verbatim. It is really martyrdom.

In his book *Ezra Pound*, Charles Norman was very scrupulous. He got several things exactly right. The first time I met Ezra Pound, when he came here to see my mother and me, I said that Henry Eliot seemed to me more nearly the artist than anyone I had ever met. "Now, now," said Ezra. "Be careful." Maybe that isn't exact, but he quotes it just the way I said it.

Q.: Do you mean Henry Ware Eliot, T. S. Eliot's brother?

A.: Yes. After the Henry Eliots moved from Chicago to New York to—is it 68th Street? It's the street on which Hunter College is—to an apartment there, they invited me to dinner, I should think at T. S. Eliot's suggestion, and I took to them immediately. I felt as if I'd known them a great while. It was some time before I felt that way about T. S. Eliot.

About inaccuracies—when I went to see Ezra Pound at St. Elizabeth's, about the third time I went, the official who escorted me to the grounds said, "Good of you to come to see him," and I said, "Good? You have no idea how much he has done for me, and others." This pertains to an early rather than final visit.

I was not in the habit of asking experts or anybody else to help me with things that I was doing, unless it was a librarian or someone whose business it was to help applicants; or a teacher. But I was desperate when Macmillan declined my *Fables*. I had worked about four years on them and sent Ezra Pound several—although I hesitated. I didn't like to bother him. He had enough trouble without that; but finally I said, "Would you have time to tell me if the rhythms grate on you? Is my ear not good?"

Q.: He replied?

A.: Yes, said, "The least touch of merit upsets these blighters."

Q.: When you first read Pound in 1916, did you recognize him as one of the great ones?

A.: Surely did. *The Spirit of Romance*. I don't think anybody could read that book and feel that a flounderer was writing.

Q.: What about the early poems?

A.: Yes. They seemed a little didactic, but I liked them.

Q.: I wanted to ask you a few questions about poetry in general. Somewhere you have said that originality is a by-product of sincerity. You often use moral terms in your criticism. Is the necessary morality specifically literary, a moral use of words, or is it larger? In what way must a man be good if he is to write good poems?

A.: If emotion is strong enough, the words are unambiguous. Someone asked Robert Frost (is this right?) if he was selective. He said, "Call it passionate preference."

Must a man be good to write good poems? The villains in Shakespeare are not illiterate, are they? But rectitude *has* a ring that is implicative, I would say. And with *no* integrity, a man is not likely to write the kind of book I read.

Q.: Eliot, in his introduction to your *Selected Poems*, talks about your function as poet relative to the living language, as he calls it. Do you agree that this is a function of a poet? How does the poetry have the effect on the living language? What's the mechanics of it?

A.: You accept certain modes of saying a thing. Or strongly repudiate things. You do something of your own, you modify, invent a variant or revive a root meaning. Any doubt about that?

Q.: I want to ask you a question about your correspondence with the Ford Motor Company, those letters which were printed in the *New Yorker*. They were looking for a name for the car they eventually called the Edsel, and they asked you to think of a name that would make people admire the car—

A.: Elegance and grace, they said it would have—

Q.: ". . . some visceral feeling of elegance, fleetness, advanced features and design. A name, in short, which flashes a dramatically desirable picture in people's minds."

A.: Really?

Q.: That's what they said, in their first letter to you. I was thinking about this in connection with my question about language. Do you remember Pound's talk about expression and meaning? He says that when expression and meaning are far apart, the culture is in a bad way. I was wondering if this request doesn't ask you to remove expression a bit further from meaning.

A.: No, I don't think so. At least, to exposit the irresistibleness of the car. I got deep in motors and turbines and recessed wheels. No. That seemed to me a very worthy pursuit. I was more interested in the mechanics. I am interested in mechanisms, mechanics in general. And I enjoyed the assignment, for all that it was abortive.

Dr. Pick at Marquette University procured a young demonstrator of the Edsel to call for me in a black one, to convey me to the auditorium. Nothing was wrong with that Edsel! I thought it was a very handsome car. It came out the wrong year.

Q.: Another thing: in your criticism you make frequent analogies between the poet and the scientist. Do you think this analogy is helpful to the modern poet? Most people would consider the comparison a paradox, and assume that the poet and the scientist are opposed.

A.: Do the poet and scientist not work analogously? Both are willing to waste effort. To be hard on himself is one of the main strengths of each. Each is attentive to clues, each must narrow the choice, must strive for precision. As George Grosz says, "In art there is no place for gossip and but a small place for the satirist." The objective is fertile procedure. Is it not? Jacob Bronowski says in the *Saturday Evening Post* that science is not a mere collection of discoveries, but that science is the process of discovering. In any case it's not established once and for all; it's evolving.

Q.: One last question. I was intrigued when you wrote that "America has in Wallace Stevens at least one artist whom professionalism will not demolish." What sort of literary professionalism did you have in mind? And do you find this a feature of America still?

A.: Yes. I think that writers sometimes lose verve and pugnacity, and he never would say "frame of reference" or "I wouldn't know."

A question I am often asked is: "What work can I find that will enable me to spend my whole time writing?" Charles Ives, the composer, says, "You cannot set art off in a corner and hope for it to have vitality, reality, and substance. The fabric weaves itself whole. My work in music helped my business and my work in business helped my music." I am like Charles Ives. I guess Lawrence Durrell and Henry Miller would not agree with me.

Q.: But how does professionalism make a writer lose his verve and pugnacity?

A.: Money may have something to do with it and being regarded as a pundit; Wallace Stevens was really very much annoyed at being catalogued, categorized, and compelled to be scientific about what he was doing—to give satisfaction, to answer the teachers. He wouldn't do that.

I think the same of William Carlos Williams. I think he wouldn't make so much of the great American language if he were plausible; and tractable. That's the beauty of it; he is willing to be reckless; if you can't be that, what's the point of the whole thing?

NOTES

(A title becomes line 1 when part of the first sentence.)

From COLLECTED POEMS (1951)

Nine Nectarines and Other Porcelain (page 8)

"The Chinese believe the oval peaches which are very red on one side, to be a symbol of long life. . . . According to the word of Chin-noug-king, the peach *Yu* prevents death. If it is not eaten in time, it at least preserves the body from decay until the end of the world." Alphonse de Candolle, *Origin of Cultivated Plants* (1886).

"Brown beaks and cheeks." Anderson Catalogue 2301, to Karl Freund collection sale, 1928.

New York Sun, 2nd July 1932. *The World To-day*, by Edgar Snow, from Soochow, China: "An old gentleman of China, whom I met when I first came to this country, volunteered to name for me what he called the "six certainties." He said: "You may be sure that the clearest jade comes from Yarkand, the prettiest flowers from Szechuen, the most fragile porcelain from Kingtehchen, the finest tea from Fukien, the sheerest silk from Hangchow, and the most beautiful women from Soochow. . . ."

Line 41: *The kylin* (or Chinese unicorn). "It has the body of a stag, with a single horn, the tail of a cow, horses' hoofs, a yellow belly, and hair of five colors." Frank Davis, *Illustrated London News*, March 7, 1931.

New York (page 12)

Line 4: *Fur trade.* In 1921 New York succeeded St. Louis as the center of the wholesale fur trade.

Line 8: "About the middle of June 1916, a white fawn only a few days old was discovered in a thicket and brought to the hotel. Here, in the company of another fawn, it grew rapidly. During the earlier months this fawn had the usual row of white spots on back and sides, and although there was no difference between these and the body colour, they were conspicuous in the same way that satin needlework in a single colour may carry a varied pattern . . ." George Shiras III, *The Literary Digest*, March 30, 1918.

Line 20: "*If the fur is not finer* . . ." Frank Alvah Parsons quotes Isabella, Duchess of Gonzaga: "I wish black cloth even if it cost ten ducats a yard. If it is only as good as that which I see other people wear, I had rather be without it." *The Psychology of Dress* (New York: Doubleday, 1920).

Line 27: "*Accessibility to experience.*" Henry James.

Marriage (page 13)

Line 14: "*Of circular traditions . . .*" Francis Bacon.

Line 25: *Write simultaneously.* "Miss A—— will write simultaneously in three languages, English, German, and French, talking in the meantime. [She] takes advantage of her abilities in everyday life, writing her letters simultaneously with both hands; namely, the first, third, and fifth words with her left and the second, fourth, and sixth with her right hand. While generally writing outward, she is able as well to write inward with both hands." "Multiple Consciousness or Reflex Action of Unaccustomed Range." *Scientific American*, January 1922.

Line 42: "*See her, see her in this common world.*" "George Shock."

Line 49: "*Unlike flesh, stones . . .*" Richard Baxter, *The Saints' Everlasting Rest.*

Lines 65–66: "We were puzzled and we were fascinated, as if by something feline, by something colubrine." Philip Littell, reviewing Santayana's Poems, *New Republic*, March 21, 1923.

Line 83: "*Treading chasms.*" Hazlitt, "*Essay on Burke's Style.*"

Line 91: "*Past states . . .*" Richard Baxter.

Line 101: "He experiences a solemn joy . . ." "A Travers Champs," by Anatole France in *Filles et Garçons*: "le petit Jean comprend qu'il est beau et cette idée le pénètre d'un respect profond de lui-même. . . . Il goûte une joie pieuse à se sentir devenu une idole."

Line 108: "*It clothes me . . .*" Hagop Boghossian in a poem, "*The Nightingale.*"

Line 109: "*He dares not . . .*" Edward Thomas, *Feminine Influence on the Poets.*

Line 116: "*Illusion of a fire . . .*" Richard Baxter.

Line 121: "*As high as deep . . .*" Richard Baxter.

Line 125: "Marriage is a law, and the worst of all laws . . . a very trivial object indeed." Godwin.

Line 146: "*For love . . .*" Anthony Trollope, *Barchester Towers.*

Line 159: "*No truth . . .*" Robert of Sorbonne.

Line 167: "*Darkeneth her countenance . . .*" Ecclesiasticus.

Line 175: "Married people often look that way." C. Bertram Hartmann.

Line 176: "Seldom and cold." Richard Baxter.

Line 183: "*Ahasuerus' tête-à-tête banquet.* George Adam Smith, *Expositor's Bible.*

Line 185: "*Good monster, lead the way.*" The Tempest.

Line 189: "Four o'clock does not exist." The Comtesse de Noailles: *Femina*, December 1921. "Le Thé": "Dans leur impérieuse humilité elles jouent instinctivement leurs rôles sur le globe."

Line 196: "*What monarch . . .*" From *The Rape of the Lock*, a parody by Mary Frances Nearing, with suggestions by M. Moore.

Line 200: "*The sound of the flute.*" A. Mitram Rhibany: *The Syrian Christ.* Silence of women—"to an Oriental, this is as poetry set to music."

Line 202: "*Men are monopolists.*" Miss M. Carey Thomas, Founder's address, Mount Holyoke, 1921: "Men practically reserve for themselves stately funerals, splendid monuments, memorial statues, membership in academies, medals, titles, honorary degrees, stars, garters, ribbons, buttons and other shining baubles, so valueless in themselves and yet so infinitely desirable because they are symbols of recognition by their fellow-craftsmen of difficult work well done."

Line 209: *"The crumbs from a lion's meal."* Amos iii, 12. Translation by George Adam Smith, *Expositor's Bible.*

Line 213: *"A wife is a coffin."* Ezra Pound.

Line 225: *"Settle on my hand."* Charles Reade, *Christie Johnson.*

Lines 234–35: "Asiatics have rights; Europeans have obligations." Edmund Burke.

Line 254: *"Leaves her peaceful husband."* "Thus proceed pretty dolls when they leave their old home to renovate their frame, and dear others who may abandon their peaceful husband only because they have seen enough of him." Simone Puget, an advertisement entitled "Change of Fashion," *English Review,* June 1914.

Line 258: *"Everything to do with love . . ."* F. C. Tilney, *Fables of La Fontaine,* "Love and Folly," Book XII, No. 14 (Dutton).

Line 288: *"Liberty and Union . . ."* Daniel Webster (statue with inscription, Central Park, New York City).

Silence (page 22)

"My father used to say, 'Superior people never make long visits. When I am visiting, I like to go about by myself. I never had to be shown Longfellow's grave or the glass flowers at Harvard.' " Miss A. M. Homans.

Line 13: Edmund Burke, in *Burke's Life,* by Prior: " 'Throw yourself into a coach,' said he. 'Come down and make my house your inn.' "

Rigorists (page 23)

Line 26: Sheldon Jackson (1834–1909). Dr. Jackson felt that to feed the Eskimo at government expense was not advisable, that whales having been almost exterminated, the ocean could not be restocked as a river can be with fish, and having prevailed on the Government to authorize the importing of reindeer from Siberia, he made an expedition during the summer of 1891, procured sixteen reindeer—by barter—and later brought others. *Report on Introduction of Domestic Reindeer into Alaska,* 1895; 1896; 1897; 1899, by Sheldon Jackson, General Agent of Education in Alaska. U.S. Educ. Bureau, Washington.

He "Digesteth Harde Yron" (page 24)

"The estritch digesteth harde yron to preserve its health." Lyly's *Euphues.*

Line 5: *The large sparrow.* "Xenophon (Anabasis I, 5, 2) reports many ostriches in the desert on the left . . . side of the middle Euphrates, on the way from North Syria to Babylonia." George Jennison, *Animals for Show and Pleasure* (Manchester University Press, 1937).

Lines 7 ff.: *A symbol of justice, men in ostrich-skins, Leda's egg*, and other allusions: "*Ostrich Eggshell Cups from Mesopotamia*" by Berthold Laufer, *The Open Court*, May 1926. "An ostrich plume symbolized truth and justice, and was the emblem of the goddess Ma-at, the patron saint of judges. Her head is adorned with an ostrich feather, her eyes are closed, . . . as Justice is blind-folded."

Line 41: *Six hundred ostrich brains*. At a banquet given by Elagabalus. See above, *Animals for Show and Pleasure*.

Lines 44–45: *Egg-shell goblets*. E.g., the painted ostrich-egg cup mounted in silver-gilt by Elias Geier of Leipzig about 1589. Edward Wenham, "*Antiques in and About London*" *New York Sun*, May 22, 1937.

Line 45: *Eight pairs of ostriches*. See above, *Animals for Show and Pleasure*.

Line 61: *Sparrow-camel*. Στρουθιοκάμηλος.

Bird-Witted (page 26)

"If a boy be bird-witted." Sir Francis Bacon.

Virginia Britannia (page 28)

Cf. William Strachey, *Travaile into Virginia Britannia*.

Line 12: *A great sinner*. Inscription in Jamestown churchyard: "Here lyeth the body of Robert Sherwood who was born in the Parish of Whitechapel near London, a great sinner who waits for a joyful resurrection."

Lines 18–19: *Ostrich and horse-shoe*. As crest in Captain John Smith's coat of arms, the ostrich with a horse-shoe in its beak—i.e., invincible digestion—reiterates the motto, *Vincere est vivere*.

Lines 16-17: *Werewocomoco*. Powhatan's capitol. Of the Indians of a confederacy of about thirty tribes of Algonquins occupying Tidewater Virginia, Powhatan was war-chief or head werowance. He presented a deer-skin mantle—now in the Ashmolean—to Captain Newport when crowned by him and Captain John Smith.

Line 17: *Deer-fur crown*. "He [Arahatec] gave our Captaine his Crowne which was of Deare's hayre, Dyed redd." *Travels and Works of Captain John Smith, President of Virginia and Admiral of New England*, 1580–1631; with Introduction by A. G. Bradley (Arber's Reprints).

Line 63: "*Strong sweet prison*." Of Middle Plantation—now Williamsburg.

Lines 108–110: The one-brick-thick wall designed by Jefferson: in the grounds of the University of Virginia.

Lines 131–132: *Hedge-Sparrow*. The British Empire Naturalists' Association has found that the hedge-sparrow sings seven minutes earlier than the lark.

Spenser's Ireland (page 33)

Every name is a tune; it is torture; ancient jewellery; your trouble is their trouble. See Donn Byrne, "Ireland: The Rock Whence I Was Hewn," *National Geographic*, March 1927.

Lines 10–11: *Venus' mantle.* Footnote in Maria Edgeworth's *Castle Rackrent,* as edited by Professor Morley: "The cloak, or mantle, as described by Thady is of high antiquity. See Spenser, in his 'View of the State of Ireland.'"

Line 12: *The Sleeves* . . . In Castle Rackrent Thady Quirk says, "I wear a long great-coat . . . ; it holds on by a single button round my neck, cloak fashion."

Lines 39–43: "The sad-yellow-fly, made with the buzzard's wing"; and "the shell-fly, for the middle of July." Maria Edgeworth, *The Absentee.*

Line 53: *The guillemot.* The linnet. Denis O'Sullivan, *Happy Memories of Glengarry.*

Line 58: *Earl Gerald.* From a lecture by Padraic Colum.

Four Quartz Crystal Clocks (page 35)

Line 1: In the Bell Telephone Laboratories in New York, in a "time vault" whose temperature is maintained within 1/100 of a degree, at 41° centigrade, are the most accurate clocks in the world—the four quartz crystal clocks. . . . When properly cut and inserted in a suitable circuit, they will control the rate of electric vibration to an accuracy of one part in a million. . . . When you call MEridian 7–1212 for correct time you get it every 15 seconds." "The World's Most Accurate Clocks," Bell Telephone Company leaflet (1939).

Line 14: *Jean Giraudoux.* "Appeler à l'aide d'un camouflage ces instruments faits pour la vérité qui sont la radio, le cinéma, la presse?" "J'ai traversé voilà un an des pays arabes où l'on ignorait encore que Napoléon était mort." *Une allocation radiodiffusée de M. Giraudoux aux Françaises à propos de Sainte Catherine;* the *Figaro,* November 1939.

Line 45: *The cannibal Chronos.* Rhea, mother of Zeus, hid him from Chronos who "devoured all his children except Jupiter (air), Neptune (water), and Pluto (the grave). These, Time cannot consume." Brewer's *Dictionary of Phrase and Fable.*

The Pangolin (page 36)

"The closing ear-ridge," and certain other detail, from Dr. Robert T. Hatt, "Pangolins," *Natural History,* December 1935.

Lines 16–17: Stepping peculiarly. See Lyddeker's *Royal Natural History.*

Lines 23–24: Thomas of Leighton Buzzard's vine: a fragment of ironwork in Westminster Abbey.

Lines 66–67: "*A sailboat was the first machine.*" See F. L. Morse, *Power: Its Application from the 17th Dynasty to the 20th Century.*

Propriety (page 46)

Line 15: *Bach's Solfeggieto.* Karl Philipp Emanuel's (C minor).

Apparition of Splendor (page 51)

Lines 16–17: *"train . . . long."* Oliver Goldsmith in one of his essays refers to "a blue fairy with a train eleven yards long, supported by porcupines."

Line 21: *"with . . . nurse."* "All over spines, with the forest for nurse." "The Hedgehog, the Fox, and the Flies," Book Twelve, Fable XIII, *The Fables of La Fontaine* (New York: The Viking Press, 1954).

Then the Ermine (page 52)

Line 2: *". . . spotted."* Clitophon; "his device was the Ermion, with a speech that signified, Rather dead than spotted." Sidney's *Arcadia*, Book I, Chapter 17, paragraph 4. Cambridge Classics, Volume I, 1912; edited by Albert Feuillerat.

Line 12: *motto.* Motto of Henry, Duke of Beaufort: *Mutare vel timere sperno.*

Line 18: *Lavater.* John Kaspar Lavater (1741–1801), a student of physiography. His system includes morphological, anthropological, anatomical, histrionical, and graphical studies. Kurt Seligmann, *The Mirror of Magic* (New York: Pantheon Books, 1948, page 332).

Tom Fool at Jamaica (page 53)

Line 6: *mule and jockey.* A mule and jockey by "Giulio Gomez 6 años" from a collection of drawings by Spanish school children. Solicited on behalf of a fund-raising committee for Republican Spain, sold by Lord and Taylor; given to me by Miss Louise Crane.

Lines 8–9: *"There . . . said."* The Reverend David C. Shipley, July 20, 1952.

Line 9: *Sentir avec ardeur.* By Madame Boufflers—Marie-Françoise-Catherine de Beauveau, Marquise de Boufflers (1711–1786). See note by Dr. Achilles Fong, annotating Lu Chi's "Wên Fu" (A.D. 261–303)—his "Rhymeprose on Literature" ("rhymeprose" from "Reimprosa" of German medievalists): "As far as notes go, I am at one with a contemporary of Rousseau's: 'Il faut dire en deux mots / Ce qu'on veut dire'; . . . But I cannot claim 'J'ai réussi,' especially because I broke Mme. de Boufflers' injunction ('Il faut éviter l'emploi / Du moi, du moi.')" *Harvard Journal of Asiatic Studies*, Volume 14, Number 3, December 1951, page 529 (revised, *New Mexico Quarterly*, September 1952).

Air: *Sentir avec ardeur*

Il faut dire en deux mots
Ce qu'on veut dire;

Les longs propos
Sont sots.

Il faut savoir lire
Avant que d'écrire,
Et puis dire en deux mots
Ce qu'on veut dire.
Les longs propos
Sont sots.

Il ne faut pas toujours conter,
Citer,
Dater,
Mais écouter.
Il faut éviter l'emploi
Du moi, du moi,
Voici pourquoi:

Il est tyrannique,
Trop académique;
L'ennui, l'ennui
Marche avec lui.
Je me conduis toujours ainsi
Ici,
Aussi
J'ai réussi.

Il faut dire en deux mots
Ce qu'on veut dire;
Les longs propos
Sont sots.

Line 13: *Master Atkinson.* I opened *The New York Times* one morning
(March 3, 1952) and a column by Arthur Daley on Ted Atkinson and
Tom Fool took my fancy. Asked what he thought of Hill Gail, Ted
Atkinson said, "He's a real good horse, . . . real good," and paused a
moment. "But I think he ranks only second to Tom Fool. . . . I prefer
Tom Fool. . . . He makes a more sustained effort and makes it more
often." Reminded that Citation could make eight or ten spurts in a
race, "That's it," said Ted enthusiastically. "It's the mark of a champion to spurt 100 yards, settle back and spurt another 100 yards, giving
that extra burst whenever needed. From what I've seen of Tom
Fool, I'd call him a 'handy horse.'" He mentioned two others. "They
had only one way of running. But Tom Fool. . . ." Then I saw a picture
of Tom Fool (*New York Times*, April 1, 1952) with Ted Atkinson in

the saddle and felt I must pay him a slight tribute; got on with it a little way, then realized that I had just received an award from Youth United for a Better Tomorrow and was worried indeed. I deplore gambling and had never seen a race. Then in the *Times* for July 24, 1952, I saw a column by Joseph C. Nichols about Frederic Capossela, the announcer at Belmont Park, who said when interviewed, "Nervous? No, I'm never nervous. . . . I'll tell you where it's tough. The straight-away at Belmont Park, where as many as twenty-eight horses run at you from a point three quarters of a mile away. I get 'em though, and why shouldn't I? I'm relaxed, I'm confident and I don't bet."

In the way of a sequel, "Money Isn't Everything" by Arthur Daley (*New York Times*, March 1, 1955): " 'There's a constant fascination to thoroughbreds,' said Ted, '. . . they're so much like people. . . . My first love was Red Hay . . . a stout-hearted little fellow . . . he always tried, always gave his best.' [Mr. Daley: 'The same description fits Atkinson.'] 'There was Devil Diver, . . . the mare Snow Goose. One of my big favorites . . . crazy to get going. . . . But once she swung into stride . . . you could ride her with shoelaces for reins. . . . And there was Coaltown. . . . There were others of course, but I never met one who could compare with Tom Fool, my favorite of favorites. He had the most personality of all. . . . Just to look at him lit a spark. He had an intelligent head, an intelligent look and, best of all, was intelligent. He had soft eyes, a wide brow and—gee, I'm sounding like a lovesick boy. But I think he had the handsomest face of any horse I ever had anything to do with. He was a great horse but I was fond of him not so much for what he achieved as for what he was.' With that the sprightly Master Theodore fastened the number plate on his right shoulder and headed for the paddock."

Lines 14–15: "*Chance . . . impurity.*" The *I Ching* or *Book of Changes*, translated by Richard Wilhelm and Cary Baynes, Bollingen Series XIX (New York: Pantheon Books, 1950).

Line 29: *Fats Waller.* Thomas Waller, "a protean jazz figure," died in 1943. See *The New York Times*, article and Richard Tucker (Pix) photograph, March 16, 1952.

Line 31: *Ozzie Smith.* Osborne Smith, a Negro chanter and drummer who improvised the music for Ian Hugo's *Ai-Yé.*

Line 31: *Eubie Blake.* The Negro pianist in *Shuffle Along.*

The Web One Weaves of Italy (page 55)

Stanzas 1 and 2 mainly quotation from "Festivals and Fairs for the Tourist in Italy" by Mitchell Goodman, *New York Times*, April 18, 1954.

Line 12: "*fount . . . spilt.*" "The Monkey and the Leopard," Book Nine, Fable III, *The Fables of La Fontaine* (The Viking Press, 1954).

The Staff of Aesculapius (page 55)

Line 11: *Time*, March 29, 1954, article on the Salk vaccine.
Lines 17–20: *Selective . . . true.* Sloan-Kettering Institute for Cancer Research, *Progress Report VII*, June 1954; pp. 20–21.
Lines 22–25: *To . . . framework.* Abbott Laboratories, "Plastic Sponge Implants in Surgery," *What's New*, Number 186, Christmas 1954.

The Sycamore (page 56)

Lines 15–16: *nine . . . hairs.* Imami, the Iranian miniaturist, draws "with a brush made of nine hairs from a newborn she camel and a pencil sharpened to a needle point. . . . He was decorated twice by the late Riza Shah; once for his miniatures and once for his rugs." *New York Times*, March 5, 1954.

Rosemary (page 57)

Line 17: *"hath . . . language."* Sir Thomas More (see below).
According to a Spanish legend, rosemary flowers—originally white—turned blue when the Virgin threw her cloak over a rosemary bush, while resting on the flight into Egypt. There is in Trinity College Library, Cambridge, a manuscript sent to Queen Philippa of Hainault by her mother, written by "a clerk of the school of Salerno" and translated by "danyel bain." The manuscript is devoted entirely to the virtues of rosemary, which, we are told, never grows higher than the height of Christ; after thirty-three years the plant increases in breadth but not in height. See "Rosemary of Plesant Savour," by Eleanor Sinclair Rohde, *The Spectator*, July 7, 1930.

Style (page 58)

Line 8: *Dick Button.* See photograph, *New York Times*, January 2, 1956.
Line 10: *Etchebaster.* Pierre Etchebaster, a machine-gunner in the First World War; champion of France in chistera (jai alai), pala, and mainnues. He took up court tennis in 1922, won the American championship in 1928, and retired in 1954. (*New York Times*, February 13, 1954 and February 24, 1955.) *New York Times*, January 19, 1956: "Pierre Etchebaster, retired world champion, and Frederick S. Moseley won the pro-amateur handicap court tennis tournament at the Racquet and Tennis Club yesterday. . . . The score was 5–6, 6–5, 6–5. Moseley, president of the club, scored the last point of the match with a railroad ace. Johnson and McClintock had pulled up from 3–5 to 5–all in this final set."
Line 10: *Soledad.* Danced in America, 1950–1951.
Line 27: *Rosario's.* Rosario Escudero, one of the company of Vincente Escudero, but not related to him.

Logic and "The Magic Flute" (page 59)

The Magic Flute. Colorcast by NBC Opera Theater, January 15, 1956.
Line 11: *precious wentletrap. n.* [D. *wenteltrap* a winding staircase; cf. G.
  wendeltreppe.] The shell of *E. pretiosa*, of the genus *Epitonium.—*
  Webster's New International Dictionary.
Lines 23–24: " '*What is* . . . *it?* '" *Demon in Love* by Horatio Colony
  (Cambridge, Massachusetts: Hampshire Press, 1955).
Line 25: *Banish sloth.* "Banish sloth; you have defeated Cupid's bow,"
  Ovid, *Remedia Amoris.*

Blessed Is the Man (page 61)

Lines 1–2: *Blessed* . . . *scoffer.* Psalm 1:1.
Line 4: "*characteristically intemperate.*" Campaign manager's evaluation of
  an attack on the Eisenhower Administration.
Line 5: "*excuse* . . . *heard.*" Charles Poore reviewing James B. Conant's
  The Citadel of Learning (New Haven: Yale University Press)—quoting
  Lincoln. *New York Times*, April 7, 1956.
Line 8: *Giorgione's self-portrait.* Reproduced in *Life*, October 24, 1955.
Lines 11–12: "*Diversity* . . . *learning.*" James B. Conant, *The Citadel of
  Learning.*
Line 13: "*takes* . . . *decision.*" Louis Dudek: "poetry . . . must . . . take
  the risk of a decision"; "to say what we know, loud and clear—and if
  necessary ugly—that would be better than to say nothing with great
  skill." "The New Laocöon," *Origin*, Winter–Spring 1956.
Lines 14–15: "*Would* . . .*.*" "President Eisenhower Vetoes Farm Com-
  promise [Agricultural Act of 1956]," *New York Times*, April 17, 1956:
  "We would produce more of certain crops at a time when we need less
  of them. . . . If natural resources are squandered on crops that we
  cannot eat or sell, all Americans lose."
Line 19: *Ulysses' companions.* "The Companions of Ulysses," Book Twelve,
  Fable I, *The Fables of La Fontaine* (The Viking Press, 1954).
Line 22: *Mitin* (From *la mite*, moth). Odorless, non-toxic product of Geigy
  Chemical Corporation research scientists (Swiss). *New York Times*,
  April 7, 1956.
Line 23: "*private* . . . *shame.*" See note for line 13.
Line 27: "*things which* . . . *appear.*" Hebrews 11:3.

O TO BE A DRAGON

O to Be a Dragon (page 65)

Dragon: see secondary symbols, Volume II of *The Tao of Painting*, translated
  and edited by Mai-mai Sze, Bollingen Series 49 (New York: Pantheon,
  1956; Modern Library edition, p. 57).
Solomon's wish: "an understanding heart." I Kings 3:9.

Values in Use (page 66)

Philip Rahv, July 30, 1956, at the Harvard Summer School Conference on the Little Magazine, Alston Burr Hall, Cambridge, Massachusetts, gave as the standard for stories accepted by the *Partisan Review* "maturity, plausibility, and the relevance of the point of view expressed." "A work of art must be appraised on its own ground; we produce values in the process of living, do not await their historic progress in history." See *Partisan Review*, Fall 1956.

Hometown Piece for Messrs. Alston and Reese (page 67)

Messrs. Alston and Reese: Walter Alston, manager of the Brooklyn Dodgers; Harold (Peewee) Reese, captain of the Dodgers.

Line 1: *millennium.* "The millennium and pandemonium arrived at approximately the same time in the Brooklyn Dodgers' clubhouse at the Yankee Stadium yesterday." Roscoe McGowen, *New York Times*, October 5, 1955.

Line 2: *Roy Campanella.* Photograph: "Moment of Victory," *New York Times*, October 5, 1955.

Line 4: *Buzzie Bavasi.* "The policemen understood they were to let the players in first, but Brooklyn officials—Walter O'Malley, Arthur (Red) Patterson, Buzzie Bavasi and Fresco Thompson—wanted the writers let in along with the players. This, they felt, was a different occasion and nobody should be barred." Roscoe McGowen, *New York Times*, October 5, 1955. E. J. Bavasi: Vice President of the Dodgers. William J. Briordy, "Campanella Gets Comeback Honors," *New York Times*, November 17, 1955.

Line 6: *when Sandy Amoros made the catch.* [Joe Collins to Johnny Podres]: "'The secret of your success was the way you learned to control your change-up. . . .' 'I didn't use the change-up much in the seventh game of the world series,' said Johnny. 'The background was bad for it. So I used a fast ball that really had a hop on it.' . . . 'Hey, Johnny,' said Joe, 'how did you feel when Amoros made that catch?' 'I walked back to the mound,' said Podres, 'and I kept saying to myself, "everything keeps getting better and better." '" Arthur Daley, "Sports of the Times: Just Listening," *New York Times*, January 17, 1956.

Line 10: *"Hope springs eternal."* Roscoe McGowen, "Brooklyn against Milwaukee," *New York Times*, July 31, 1956.

Line 11: *8, Row 1.* The Dodgers' Sym-Phoney Band sits in Section 8, Row 1, Seats 1 to 7, conducted by Lou Soriano (who rose by way of the snare-drum). "The Sym-Phoney is busy rehearsing a special tune for the Brooklyn income tax collector: It's "All of Me—Why Not Take All of Me?" William R. Conklin, "Maestro Soriano at Baton for 18th Brooklyn Season," *New York Times*, August 12, 1956.

Line 16: *"Four hundred feet . . ."* "Gilliam opened the game with a push bunt for a hit, and with one out Duke Snider belted the ball more than

400 feet to the base of the right-center-field wall. Gilliam came home but had to return to base when the ball bounced high into the stands for a ground-rule double." Roscoe McGowen, "Dodgers against Pittsburgh." Duke Snider "hit twenty-three homers in Ebbets Field for four successive years." John Drebinger, *New York Times*, October 1, 1956.

Line 19: *"stylish stout."* [A catcher]: "He crouches in his wearying squat a couple of hundred times a day, twice that for double-headers." Arthur Daley, "At Long Last," *New York Times Magazine*, July 9, 1956.

Line 29: *Preacher Roe's number.* 28. Venerated left-handed pitcher for Brooklyn who won 22 games in the season of 1951.

Line 42: *Jake* . . . "He's a Jake of All Trades—Jake Pitler, the Dodgers' first-base coach and cheer-leader." Joseph Sheehan, *New York Times*, September 16, 1956, "Dodgers Will Have a Night for Jake"—an honor accepted two years ago "with conditions": that contributions be for Beth-El Hospital Samuel Strausberg Wing. Keepsake for the "Night": a replica of the plaque in the Jake Pitler Pediatric Playroom (for underprivileged children).

Line 44: *Don Demeter.* Center fielder, a newcomer from Fort Worth, Texas. "Sandy Amoros whacked an inside-the-park homer—the third of that sort for the Brooks this year—and Don Demeter, . . . hit his first major league homer, also his first hit, in the eighth inning." Roscoe McGowen, *New York Times*, September 20, 1956.

Lines 45–46: *Shutting* . . . *do.* Carl Erskine's no-hitter against the Giants at Ebbets Field, May 12, 1956. *New York Times*, May 27, 1956.

Enough (page 69)

On May 13, 1957—the 350th anniversary of the landing at Jamestown of the first permanent English settlers in North America—three United States Air Force super sabre jets flew non-stop from London to Virginia. They were the Discovery, the Godspeed, and the Susan Constant—christened respectively by Lady Churchill, by Mrs. Whitney (wife of Ambassador John Hay Whitney), and by Mrs. W. S. Morrison (wife of the speaker of the House of Commons). *New York Times*, May 12 and 13, 1957.

The colonists entered Chesapeake Bay, having left England on New Year's Day, almost four months before, "fell upon the earth, embraced it, clutched it to them, kissed it, and, with streaming eyes, gave thanks unto God . . ." Paul Green, "The Epic of Old Jamestown," *New York Times Magazine*, March 31, 1957.

Line 54: *if present faith mend partial proof.* Dr. Charles Peabody, chaplain at Yale, 1896, author of *Mornings in College Chapel*, said past gains are not gains unless we in the present complete them.

Melchior Vulpius (page 71)

"And not only is the great artist mysterious to us but is that to himself. The nature of the power he feels is unknown to him, and yet he has acquired it and succeeds in directing it." Arsène Alexander, *Malvina Hoffman—Critique and Catalogue* (Paris: J. E. Pouterman, 1930).

Line 11: *Mouse-skin-bellows'-breath.* "Bird in a Bush . . . The bird flies from stem to stem while he warbles. His lungs, as in all automatons, consist of tiny bellows constructed from mouse-skin." Daniel Alain, *Réalités*, April 1957, page 58.

No better than "a withered daffodil" (page 72)

Line 2: "Slow, Slow, fresh Fount" by Ben Jonson, from *Cynthia's Revels.*
Line 11: *a work of art.* Sir Isaac Oliver's miniature on ivory of Sir Philip Sidney. (Collection at Windsor.)

In the Public Garden (page 73)

Originally entitled "A Festival." Read at the Boston Arts Festival, June 15, 1958.

Lines 11–15: *Faneuil Hall . . . glittered.* "Atop Faneuil Hall, . . . market-place hall off Dock Square, Boston, Laurie Young, Wakefield gold-leafer and steeple-jack, applies . . . finishing paint on the steeple rod after . . . gilding the dome and the renowned 204-year-old grasshopper. *Christian Science Monitor*, September 20, 1946.

Line 13: *grasshopper.* "Deacon Shem Drowne's metal grasshopper, placed atop old Faneuil Hall by its creator in 1749, . . . still looks as if it could jump with the best of its kind . . . thought to be an exact copy of the vane on top of the Royal Exchange in London." *Christian Science Monitor*, February 16, 1950, quoting *Crafts of New England*, by Allen H. Eaton (New York: Harper, 1949).

Line 27: "*My work be praise.*" Psalm 23—traditional Southern tune, arranged by Virgil Thomson. "President Eisenhower attributed to Clemenceau . . . the observation, 'Freedom is nothing . . . but the opportunity for self-discipline.'. . . 'And that means the work that you yourselves lay out for yourselves is worthwhile doing—doing without hope of reward.' " *New York Times*, May 6, 1958.

Saint Nicholas (page 77)

Line 3: *a chameleon.* See photograph in *Life*, September 15, 1958, with a letter from Dr. Doris M. Cochran, curator of reptiles and amphibians, National Museum, Washington, D. C.

For February 14th (page 79)

Line 2: "*some interested law . . .*" From a poem to M. Moore by Marguerite Harris.

Combat Cultural (page 80)

Line 29: *Nan-ai-ans.* The Nanaians inhabit the frigid North of the Soviet Union.

Line 32: *one person.* Lev Golovanov: "Two Boys in a Fight." Staged by Igor Moiseyev, Moiseyev Dance Company, presented in New York, 1958, by Sol Hurok.

Leonardo da Vinci's (page 81)

See *Time,* May 18, 1959, page 73: "Saint Jerome," an unfinished picture by Leonardo da Vinci, in the Vatican; and *The Belles Heures of Jean, Duke of Berry, Prince of France,* with an Introduction by James J. Rorimer (New York: Metropolitan Museum of Art, 1958).

OTHER POEMS

Tell me, tell me (page 85)

The New Yorker, April 30, 1960.

Line 9: *Lord Nelson's revolving diamond rosette.* In the museum at Whitehall.

Lines 21–22: "The literal played in our education as small a part as it perhaps ever played in any and we wholesomely breathed inconsistency and ate and drank contradictions." Henry James, *Autobiography* (*A Small Boy and Others, Notes of a Son and Brother, The Middle Years*) edited by F. W. Dupee (New York: Criterion, 1958).

Carnegie Hall: Rescued (page 86)

The New Yorker, August 13, 1960.

Lines 3–4: *"Saint Diogenes . . ."* "Talk of the Town," *The New Yorker,* April 9, 1960.

Lines 13–14: *palladian majesty.* Gilbert Millstein, *The New York Times Magazine,* May 22, 1960.

"Sun" (page 88)

The Mentor Book of Religious Verse, Horace Gregory and Marya Zaturenska, editors (New York: New American Library).

Rescue with Yul Brynner (page 89)

The New Yorker, May 20, 1961.
See *Bring Forth the Children* by Yul Brynner (McGraw-Hill, 1960).
Line 30: *Symphonia Hungarica.* By Zoltán Kodály.

To Victor Hugo of My Crow Pluto (page 90)
Harper's Bazaar, October 1961.

From THE FABLES OF LA FONTAINE
(*From* BOOK THREE)

1. *The Miller, His Son, and the Ass* (page 98)
Monsieur de Maucrois. A canon of Rheims.

(*From* BOOK FOUR)

1. *The Lion in Love* (page 102)
Mlle. de Sévigné. Later Mme. Grignan, daughter of Mme. de Sévigné. Many of Mme. de Sévigné's letters were addressed to her.

2. *The Shepherd and the Sea* (page 104)
Line 29: *One who gains from the sea.* Referring to the East India Company.

From PREDILECTIONS

Humility, Concentration, and Gusto (page 123)
Address, The Grolier Club, December 21, 1948.

Henry James as a Characteristic American (page 130)
Hound and Horn, April–June 1934.

T. S. Eliot (page 138)
1. Review of T. S. Eliot's *Collected Poems* (1936) in *The Nation*, May 27, 1936.
2. From a series of commentaries on selected contemporary poets. Bryn Mawr, 1952.
3. Hugh Kenner in another connection (*Hudson Review*, Autumn 1949).
4. *New Republic*, February 7, 1923.
5. During World War II, George Dillon was stationed in Paris and, writing to *Poetry* (issue of October 1945), said: "The other night I went to hear T. S. Eliot's lecture on the poet's role in society. . . . The little

Salle des Centraux in the rue Jean-Goujon (Champs-Elysées neighborhood) . . . was packed with the most miscellaneous gathering. . . .
Finally Paul Valéry stepped to the platform. . . . After Valéry's introduction, Eliot stood to acknowledge the applause, then sat down, in
French fashion, to give his talk. . . . He made a few remarks in English,
expressing his emotion at being once more, and at such a time, in
Paris. . . . Then . . . he read his lecture in French—I was interested
to note, with an almost perfect French *rhythm*. His lecture elaborated
the distinction between the apparent role and the true role of the poet,
stressing the idea that *a writer who is read by a small number* over a
long period may have a more important social function than one who
enjoys great popularity over a limited period; also, that the people who
do not even know the names of their great national poets are not the
less profoundly influenced by what they have written. . . . He emphasized his belief that poetry must give pleasure or it cannot do good.
Good poetry is that which is '*capable de donner du plaisir aux honnêtes
gens*.' The part of his lecture which the French seemed to enjoy most
was his definition of the two kinds of bad poet—the '*faux mauvais*,'
those who have a spurt of writing poetry in their youth, and the '*vrais
mauvais*,' those who keep on writing it."

6. *Kenyon Review*, Spring 1952.

7. Lindsay Anderson says of Marcel Pagnol's *Amlé*, performed in the court-
yard of the thirteenth-century Château of the Roi René at Anger: "The
outstanding virtue of Pagnol's translation (never played before) is its
directness, its lucidity, its consistent sense of the dramatic. . . . Warmer,
more vital than Gide, the author of *Marius* has given his version [of
Hamlet] the impact of contemporary theatrical speech. . . . In its new
language, the lyric drama seems to reveal its contours afresh" (*The
Observer*, July 4, 1954).

Ezra Pound (page 149)

1. Review of Ezra Pound's *A Draft of XXX Cantos*, in *Poetry*, October
1931.

2. Material quoted from the Cantos appears in italic or is set in small type;
from other work, in double quotation marks.

3. "As when a scarlet curtain streyned against a playstred wall
Doth cast like shadowe, making it seeme ruddye there-with all."

4. "The Snail" by Cowper.

5. From a series of commentaries on selected contemporary poets, Bryn
Mawr, 1952.

6. See Kenneth Burke's "The Language of Poetry, 'Dramatistically' Considered," paper written for a symbolism seminar conducted in 1952–53,
by the Institute for Religious and Social Studies, New York (*Chicago
Review*, Fall 1954): "We would spin this discussion from Cicero's
terms for the 'three offices of the orator.' (See *Orator*, *De Oratore*, and
St. Augustine's use of this analysis of Christian persuasion in his *De*

Doctrina Christiana.) First office: to teach or inform (*docere*). Second office: to please (*delectare*). Third office: to move or 'bend' (*movere, flectare*)."

Idiosyncrasy and Technique (page 169)

Inaugurating the Ewing Lectures at the University of California, October 3 and 5, 1956; published as a pamphlet by University of California Press, Berkeley and Los Angeles, in 1958.

1. *Making, Knowing and Judging: An Inaugural Lecture by W. H. Auden Delivered before the University of Oxford on 11 June 1956* (Oxford at the Clarendon Press).
2. Michael Tippett, "An Irish Basset-Horn," *The Listener*, July 26, 1956.
3. Hesketh Pearson, "Bernard Shaw as Producer," *The Listener*, August 16, 1956.
4. "Discourse in Praise of Wisdom," reëntitled "Goethe as the Sage."
5. *The Dalhousie Review*, January 1943.
6. Translated by Ezra Pound (Cambridge: Harvard University Press, 1954), p. 55.
7. *Ibid.*, p. 80.
8. *The Self and the Dramas of History* (New York: Scribner, 1955).
9. "Edwin Arnold and 'The Light of Asia,'" *The Listener*, June 14, 1956.
10. *The New York Times*, November 20, 1957.
11. *The Listener*, June 14, 1956.
12. "In Honour of James Cook," *The Listener*, June 14, 1956.
13. *The Shock of Recognition*, edited by Edmund Wilson (New York: Doubleday, 1943).
14. Unsigned review in *The Times Literary Supplement*, London, March 2, 1956.
15. *Life*, July 16, 1956.
16. *The Fables of La Fontaine*, translated by Marianne Moore (New York: Viking, 1954), Book Ten, IX.
17. Dr. Alvin E. Magary.
18. Maxwell Geismar, *The Nation*, April 14, 1956.
19. As "freely translated" by Charles Poore, reviewing James B. Conant, *The Citadel of Learning* (New Haven: Yale University Press, 1956), in the *New York Times*, April 7, 1956.
20. In *Writers on Writing*, edited by Herschel Brickell (New York: Doubleday, 1949).
21. Anonymous. Reprinted in the *New York Times*, November 17, 1954.
22. *The Fables of La Fontaine*, Book Eight, III.
23. *A History of the English-Speaking Peoples*, Vol. I: *The Birth of Britain* (New York: Dodd, Mead, 1956).
24. "Essay on Prose," *The National and English Review* (in three sections, concluded in March 1955), quoted by *Arts* (New York).
25. Fritz Grossmann, *The Paintings of Bruegel* (New York: Phaidon Press, 1955).

26. Sybille Bedford, *A Legacy* (New York: Simon and Schuster, 1957).
27. Translated from the French by Grace Frick (New York: Farrar, Strauss and Young, 1954).
28. Translated by Austin E. Fife (New York: Knopf, 1956).
29. *The Fables of La Fontaine*, Book Eight, IV: "The moment The Ass's Skin commences, Away with appearances; I am enraptured, really am."
30. Nehemiah 2, 4, and 6.
31. *The New York Times Magazine*, November 27, 1955.
32. *The Observer*, March 11, 1956.

Brooklyn from Clinton Hill (page 182)

Vogue, August 1, 1960.

My Crow, Pluto—A Fantasy (page 192)

Harper's Bazaar, October 1961.

If I Were Sixteen Today (page 195)

World Week, November 7, 1958.

Abraham Lincoln and the Art of the Word (page 197)

Reprinted, with emendations, from R. G. Newman, editor, *Lincoln for the Ages* (New York: Doubleday, 1960). By permission of Mr. Carl Haverlin, Broadcast Music, Incorporated. Revised for *Lincoln: A Contemporary Portrait*, edited by Allan Nevins and Irving Stone (New York: Doubleday).

1. Quotations from Lincoln are taken from Earl S. Miers and Paul M. Angle, editors, *The Living Lincoln* (New Brunswick, N.J.: Rutgers University Press, 1955); and from Roy P. Basler, editor, *Abraham Lincoln: His Speeches and Writings* (New York: World, 1946).

Robert Andrew Parker (page 205)

Arts, April 1958.

Paul Rosenfeld (page 208)

The Nation, August 17, 1946.

Edith Sitwell, Virtuoso (page 210)

Four Poets on Poetry, Don Cameron Allen, editor (Baltimore: Johns Hopkins Press, 1959).

The Ford Correspondence (page 215)

Originally printed in *The New Yorker*, April 13, 1957; reprinted as a booklet by the Pierpont Morgan Library, New York City, in 1958. The Ford letters were composed by Mr. David Wallace but, with one exception, were transmitted over the signature of his associate, Mr. Robert B. Young. Addresses have been omitted here after the first exchange of letters.

To "Infuse Belief" (page 225)

Poetry, 1959.
A. W. Bryher—Sir John Ellerman's daughter—has, as a writer and as a citizen, adopted the name Bryher. She lives in Switzerland.

"Senhora Helena" (page 226)

Poetry, July 1959.

Selected Criticism (page 229)

Poetry London–New York, Winter 1955.

A Grammarian of Motives (page 233)

Poetry: London–New York, Winter 1956.

The Ways Our Poets Have Taken Since the War (page 237)

New York Herald Tribune, June 26, 1960.

A Writer on the Mound (page 243)

New York Herald Tribune, April 23, 1961.

M. Carey Thomas of Byrn Mawr (page 245)

The Hudson Review, Autumn 1948.

Interview with Donald Hall (page 253)

The Paris Review, Winter 1961.

INDEX

Eliot, George, 136
Eliot, Henry Ware, 270
Eliot, T. S., xv, 126–27, 138–48, 153, 154, 160, 162, 164, 170–71, 214, 225, 229, 230, 231, 239, 253, 268, 270, 271, 289–90
Eliot, William, 253
Ellerman, Sir John, 293
Elliott, Phillips Packer, 183, 184
Emerson, Ralph Waldo, 135, 174, 229, 233
Empson, William, 125
Engel, Monroe, 264
Ericsson, John, 190
Erskine, Carl, 69, 286
Escudero, Rosario, 59, 283
Escudero, Vincente, 58, 59, 283
Etchebaster, Pierre, 58, 59, 283
Euclid, 198, 204

Ferlinghetti, Lawrence, 239
Feuillerat, Albert, 280
Fife, Austin E., 292
Finch, Edith, 245, 248
Fitts, Dudley, 160
Fong, Achilles, 280
Fontenelle, Bernard le Bovier de, 157
Fowler, H. W., 232
France, Anatole, 276
Frank, Tenney, 147
Fraser, Sir James, 155
Freud, Sigmund, 180
Freund, Karl, 275
Frick, Grace, 292
Friend, Bob, 244
Frost, Robert, 214, 229, 268, 271
Fuller, Thomas, 254
Furillo, Carl, 68

Garrigue, Jean, 243
Gassier, Pierre, 179
Geier, Elias, 278
Geismar, Maxwell, 291
Gide, André, 229, 232, 290
Gieseking, Walter, 42
Gilbert, W. S., 163
Gilels, Emil, 87, 185
Gilliam, Jim, 67, 285
Ginsberg, Allen, 240
Giorgione, 61, 176, 284
Giraudoux, Jean, 35, 279

Godwin, William, 276
Goethe, Johann Wolgang von, 170, 171, 230, 270, 291
Golding, Arthur, 149, 150, 157
Goldsmith, Oliver, 280
Gollancz, Victor, 182
Golovanov, Lev, 288
Gonzaga, Isabella, Duchess of, 275
Goodman, Mitchell, 55
Gorki, Maxim, 125
Gourmont, Rémy de, 155
Grant, General Ulysses S., 202, 203
Graves, Robert, 229
Greco, El, 59, 209
Green, Paul, 286
Greene, Graham, 125
Gregory, Horace, 288
Grossmann, Fritz, 291
Grosz, George, 266, 273
Guthrie, Tyrone, 182

Harris, Marguerite, 287
Haile Selassie, 82
Hall, Donald, 253–73, 293
Hamburger, Michael, 171
Hardy, Thomas, 229
Hartley, Marsden, 209, 265
Hartmann, C. Bertram, 276
Harunobu (Suzuki), 191
Hatt, Robert, 186, 279
Hawthorne, Nathaniel, 131, 132
Hazlitt, William, 276
H.D. (Hilda Doolittle), 255, 258
Healy, J. V., 148
Hellman, Lillian, 254
Hennrich, Warren, 206
Henry, Duke of Beaufort, 280
Herrick, Robert, 213
Hocking, W. E., 190
Hodges, Gil, 68
Hoffman, Daniel, 243
Hoffman, Malvina, 217, 219, 287
Hölderlin, Friedrich, 171
Homans, A. M., 277
Homer, 149, 151, 156
Hopkins, Gerard Manley, 229
Howard, Elston, 245
Howells, William Dean, 173–74
Hsieh Ho, xii
Hugo, Victor, 54, 90
Hulme, T. E., 149, 151
Humphries, Rolfe, 177